Other mysteries by Mignon G. Eberhart
available in Bison Books Editions

THE HOUSE
ON THE ROOF

MIGNON G. EBERHART

Introduction to the Bison Books Edition
by Carl D. Brandt

University of Nebraska Press
Lincoln and London

Introduction © 1996 by the University of Nebraska Press
Manufactured in the United States of America

⊛ The paper in this book meets the minimum requirements of
American National Standard for Information Sciences—Permanence
of Paper for Printed Library Materials, ANSI Z39.48-1984.

First Bison Books printing: 1996
Most recent printing indicated by the last digit below:
10   9   8   7   6   5   4   3   2   1

Library of Congress Cataloging-in-Publication Data
Eberhart, Mignon Good, 1899–
The house on the roof / Mignon G. Eberhart; introduction to the Bison
books edition by Carl D. Brandt.
p.   cm.
ISBN 0-8032-6734-7 (pbk.: alk. paper)
I. Title.
PS3509.B453H68   1997
813'.52—dc20
96-26362   CIP

Reprinted from the original 1935 edition by Doubleday, Doran &
Company, Garden City, NY.

INTRODUCTION
Carl D. Brandt

Brandt & Brandt has been fortunate in representing Mignon Eberhart since 1933 and since I was not born until 1935, this brief introduction will have more to do with her working life than her personality. I do know from family pictures that Mignon spent weekends at our house near Clinton, New Jersey, when I was very young, but my childhood memories of her are vague. The image that remains is of a smallish woman with a well-controlled head of red-blond hair who had a surprisingly deep voice and a truly infectious giggle. She and my father loved telling stories, the longer and shaggier the better, and while most of them were far over my head, the joy and good humor were wonderful to be near.

In 1945 we moved to New York and I saw less of Mignon. We no longer had those weekends, and in any case I was busy with school and jobs for the next dozen years. When I did come into the office in the beginning of 1957, shortly before my father's death, Mignon was working with my mother, who remained as her agent until she herself died in 1984. Now she works with my able colleague, Charles Schlessiger, and while there is no new prose with which to work, there is still a great deal of interest in reprints both in the United States and abroad. Besides, Mignon's wonderful characters are sure to appeal to the many producers who are competing to successfully fill the ever growing hours on the ever growing number of television channels. She'll keep us busy, which is the way she has always wanted it to be.

There is one facet to Mignon's professional life about which I have seen little written, and that has to do with the role of magazines. They were of great importance to her and of even greater importance to many other writers. I believe that the disappearance of so many of the great magazines that were published in the thirties and forties and early fifties has had a disastrous effect on writing in this country, particularly on the writing of fiction. I'll get back to that, but first want to briefly describe Mignon's magazine career.

In 1933 she sold a novelette to *Redbook* for $2500, three short stories to *Tower* for $225, and another short story to *Delineator* for $700. In 1934 the *Delineator* bought one story for $700, and then commissioned six more, four at that price and two at $800. That same year, the *Ladies Home Journal* bought first serial rights to *The House on the Roof* for $7500. Remember, these are Depression dollars.

After 1934 there was a lively competition for serial rights in the novels between the *Journal, Colliers*, and the *Saturday Evening Post*, then a weekly. Her price rose rapidly, and while not every novel went to the magazines, a high proportion did. By 1939 she was getting $15,000, and that rose to $22,500 at the end of World War II. During this period she continued to write short stories and novelettes and she could count on a minimum of $35,000 a year after 1935 from magazines alone.

The money was, of course, welcome. But there was also the training in her profession that she received from a series of highly skilled editors who worked closely with her to ensure that what appeared was the result of her best efforts. In addition, the magazines allowed her to experiment with different ideas and styles, and paid her for doing so. She could write a story in the present tense, or the first person, and find out whether that style was comfortable and workable for one of the novels. She didn't have to run the risk of losing a half year's work to learn that something was not going to work in longer form . . . and she was paid to learn it.

By the mid-fifties many of those magazines had folded, or had changed format or frequency. The *American, Woman's Home Companion*, and *Colliers* joined the *Delineator, Bluebook*, and many others in the magazine graveyard. The *Saturday Evening Post* was to become a monthly, and the surviving magazines have continued to cut or even eliminate the amount of fiction they run. By the sixties, Mignon's first serial sales were limited to the Chicago Tribune Syndicate, which eventually phased out its fiction in the seventies.

Mignon was gifted, and the magazines played an important role in her life. She would have been a successful writer of mysteries without them, but they provided her with public recognition, money, and a graduate classroom.

It is the last two of these elements that I miss the most in the current scene. Where are writers going to learn their trade? It is vitally important for young writers to be professional in their work, and that means being paid for what they do while having to satisfy skilled, hardheaded, and patient editors. Book publishing cannot do that at the learning stage, and I find it hard to believe that teaching creative writing at an early age is an educational or broadening experience.

All of this seems distant from *The House on the Roof*. But reading it is the whole point, and Mignon would be the first to say that it should speak for itself. She has always been the complete professional, demanding of herself, and generously concerned with the fate of her fellow writers.

FOREWORD

Chicago is a city of the unexpected.

It has, of course, its likenesses to other great and teeming and exciting cities. It is often beautiful; it is frequently terrifying; it is occasionally pompous in its pride and power.

But mostly it is unexpected.

All of this story—and countless other stories—might have happened. So far as I know this one didn't; still it might have happened.

There is only one way in which I have not been true to a city as I see it. And that is about the police, and not alone with this book and this book's setting. For I have long been troubled by a strong suspicion that, no matter how ingenious the fictional solution of a fictional crime might be, real and living police would make short work of it.

But in that case there would be no story.

So a certain slowness and deliberation on the part of the fictional police, altogether contrary to the action of real police, is, as you can readily perceive, a rather necessary invention on the part of the author. For the author, at least, there must be a story.

But aside from that, this story might have taken place. A woman in maroon velvet might have waited at a door—I'm not sure she didn't. A girl might have paused upon a slippery fire escape to listen for footsteps that stopped. A man might have hurried through fog-masked streets.

Oh, yes, it might have happened. Or it might begin to happen. Unexpectedly—some day—at a little florist's on Brahms Street with mimosa in the window.

THE HOUSE ON THE ROOF

CHAPTER I

THE woman's eyes slid toward the door again, and Deborah very much wished she hadn't come.

The door, of course, was closed and black, and there was not a sound beyond it except the wind around the chimneys and the tall incinerator and whispering around the corners of the house itself. The roof must be, by this time, quite dark.

Deborah glanced at the window beyond the heaped concert piano. Small black panes of glass winked and glittered and reflected scraps of lights and tea things and Mary Monroe's maroon velvet gown. It was altogether dark then with the swift early fall of a December twilight. Deborah wondered how soon she could leave.

Mary Monroe's eyes were looking at her again; they were dark and rather sharp between heavily mascaraed eyelashes and dry, powdered wrinkles.

"Cream?" said Mary Monroe. The deep and still thrilling resonance of her speaking voice was a little roughened. "Sugar?"

"Cream," said Deborah and leaned forward to take the cup. For an instant she was a slim, clear-cut silhouette, young and rather handsome. Then a flame leaped in the fireplace just beyond and touched her hair to gold and her curved mouth to scarlet and made her dark gray eyes look black and mysteriously shadowed. She leaned back into the chair and tasted the hot tea.

Miss Monroe—or was she called Madame? Deborah couldn't remember—took a lump of sugar, and Deborah, over the rim of her teacup, noted the scarcely perceptible instant when the woman's hand paused rigid over her cup. Then it relaxed and the sugar dropped. She was listening again, thought Deborah and drank some of her tea.

The small, crowded room was sickeningly hot and stuffy with the heavy scent of tuberose which floated outward in waves every time Mary Monroe's maroon velvet gown rippled. Deborah did not like the room and did not like the stuffiness and quite suddenly did not like her hostess.

And she definitely did not like the house on the roof.

"So you didn't know about my house up here?" said Mary Monroe.

"No," said Deborah.

"Odd," said Mary Monroe. "And you've lived here—oh, it must be four or five years, isn't it?"

"Four," replied Deborah definitely.

"Extraordinary," said Mary Monroe, watching her.

"It isn't visible from below, is it?"

"No. It's set back, as you probably noticed. And then there's that high parapet around the roof. Wedged in between other buildings as this one is, there's the most marvelous feeling of seclusion." Her eyes flickered, and Deborah thought: "Seclusion? Do you really like it so well?"

Aloud she said: "Yes, I suppose so. No one would know that your house existed. I can't tell you how astonished I was when you told me of it."

Mary Monroe's eyes met Deborah's again, and she smiled.

"But then you've been away at school, I suppose."

"Yes. And visiting relatives."

"Something I've never been troubled with," said

Mary Monroe; her tone, however, was not airy, and she added: "Don't mind the sounds the wind makes."

"I hadn't noticed," said Deborah truthfully and at once found that it was no longer true and that she was conscious of the uneasy sighing of the wind.

It was very lonely up there, cut off so completely from the rest of the spacious old apartment building. Below there were people or at least the knowledge of their presence. Up here on the flat dark roof with the mysteriously looming shapes of chimneys and incinerators there was no one.

She wondered if Mary Monroe lived, as she seemed to do, entirely alone. Certainly there had been no sign of a servant.

Mary Monroe set down her cup with a clatter on the table and pushed her untidy, very black hair upward with both hands.

"You must have thought it rather odd," she said.

"The only thing I minded was the fire escape. It was a little slippery. And after I had actually closed the door upon the fire-escape landing—the one you said had a spring lock——"

Mary Monroe nodded. "Yes, of course."

"Why, then I knew I had to go on up the fire escape because the door had locked itself behind me." Deborah realized that a small and trivial comment had inexplicably become weighted and full of meaning.

"I know," said Mary Monroe in a quick, rather harsh tone. "Irrevocability. Gives you a horrid feeling. Always. Bridges burned behind you, and you've got to go on, for you can't go back. I know. I've burned plenty of bridges. —I expect it was a little dark."

Her voice was smooth again, though her eyes remained wary.

Deborah said: "A little. I kept thinking what a long way down it was to the court—alley—whatever it is, there at the back."

"It's a paved court. I often come all the way up by the fire escape. It is not really a long climb, you know: three flights. Good for my hips. Or rather," said Mary Monroe, "it's supposed to be good for my hips; I can't say it's been a conspicuous success as a reducer. But then in my day people liked full-bodied women." She laughed and then stopped sharply and turned her head very slowly toward the door. Deborah said quickly:

"Did you lose your keys in the street somewhere? Perhaps they'll be returned."

"The wind is very bad tonight," said Mary Monroe abstractedly. "Oh, yes—keys. I don't know, I'm sure. They are somewhere about. I often forget to take them when I go out. And it doesn't matter if I have lost them, for I always bolt the door to the house at night and that's all. It is always"—she hesitated—"it has always been so safe. And Brocksley or the janitor will give me another key to the main door downstairs and to the door at the fire-escape landing of the third floor." She sighed. "I do have a way of mislaying things."

"Brocksley?" said Deborah vaguely. "Oh, yes, he's the man with the thin little blonde wife."

"Dolly. They live on the first floor," said Mary Monroe. "How do you like my house, by the way?"

Deborah looked around her and hesitated. And she wished that Mary Monroe would get to the purpose—whatever it was—that underlay her singularly urgent invitation to tea.

"This room, of course," said Mary Monroe hurriedly, "is rather small—but I use it a great deal."

"There must be plenty of space for you," said Deborah, thinking of all the darkened windows she had passed before she reached the door. It was a small room, confusedly full of furniture and ornaments—the accumulation of years, probably, and all of it so ornate and so confused that the whole actually achieved a certain harmony. There were overlapping rugs and heavily framed and very bad oil paintings and many great cushions. There were photographs and vases and trinkets. There were lamps and deeply upholstered chairs and stacks of music and books and magazines.

Besides the door leading out upon the roof, there were in the room two other doors—one of them closed and evidently leading toward the dark and silent back part of the house, and the other open upon a bedroom, quite as laden and quite as packed with ornaments as the room in which they sat.

"Yes," said Mary Monroe. "There—are other rooms. Larger. But I like to use these two rooms." Her eyes roved about the room, selecting this vase and that photograph. The lamp just beside her was a little cruel to her face; under its brave make-up were sagging muscles, and flabby lines where it wasn't too full. She was a large woman, full-bosomed and full-hipped and tall. She had been once, Deborah remembered, a rather commanding figure.

Even now she was rather imposing in her maroon velvet with real lace at her throat and a brooch set with diamonds upon it, and diamonds at her wrist. In the vestibule, in furs and white kid gloves, she had looked a bit theatrical; overdressed.

"I was looking at your bracelet," said Deborah as Mary Monroe's eyes returned questioningly to her. "It's an interesting piece, isn't it?"

Mary Monroe looked at the broad gold band on her

arm, turned it idly, then slipped it over her hand and passed it to Deborah for closer inspection.

Deborah turned the bracelet in her own fingers and put it back in Mary Monroe's hand, murmuring something polite as the woman slipped it back on her wrist.

"They say diamonds are investments. But I've never found them anything but a liability.—How's your aunt?" said Mary Monroe unexpectedly.

"Why—quite well," said Deborah. "She's south with my father. Caring for him. He's ill, you know. But I didn't know that you and my aunt knew each other."

Something closed back of Mary Monroe's pouched dark eyes. She lifted one large, faintly dirty hand and made a negligible gesture. "I know so many people," she said carelessly. She looked full at Deborah and smiled in a warm, friendly way that it was almost impossible to resist.

"Why," Deborah wanted to say, "did you ask me up here? Why did you make it so impossible for me to refuse?" She couldn't say it just that way, of course.

She put down her cup and invested the gesture with a suggestion of leave-taking.

But Mary Monroe would have none of her going.

"You've just got here," she said briskly. "And what have you got to do besides sit in your apartment and be lonely and worry about your father! Besides I—I don't want you to go yet. Sit down again, my dear. Sit down."

Almost as if physically impelled by that vigorous, roughly resonant voice, Deborah sank into her chair again and managed to glance at her watch. A quarter to six. She had been there, then, about twenty minutes. Quite long enough, Aunt Juliet would have said. But then Juliet would have been appalled at her coming at all. Accepting the invitation of a perfectly strange woman to a hidden house on the roof.

Hidden? Not at all; what an extraordinary word. She had merely not known of it. Certainly Mary Monroe had been frank enough about it. And besides, Mary Monroe was not a perfectly strange woman. Deborah had often heard her sing.

Of course, that was some time ago. When Deborah was taken in frilled blue silk to dangle her white-socked legs in the box that on Saturday afternoons and Monday nights was at the disposal of the Caverts. Mary Monroe couldn't have been exactly young then, thought Deborah, calculating.

And she was aware, and felt a sharp queer distaste at the knowledge, that Mary Monroe was looking guardedly under her lashes toward the window.

She must have made some motion, for Mary Monroe turned to her quickly.

"The mimosa you brought me," she said hurriedly, "is so nice. I love looking at it."

But she hadn't been looking at the mimosa. Deborah turned her head toward the glowing, delicate yellow plumes, there in Deborah's own green vase upon the piano.

"I like it, too," said Deborah. "I got it at the little florist's on Brahms Street. It looked so—cheerful."

"I do love it," said Mary Monroe. "So you've heard me sing?"

She was all at once gracious, cordial, perfectly poised, her eyes looking straight at Deborah again instead of flickering in that odd way toward—well, toward what? asked Deborah of herself. Toward nothing, really.

Aloud she said:

"Many times."

Mary Monroe smiled and sighed.

"I did sing a lot," she said. "I was never a star, of course. But I was good in the rôles I did, and dependable." She laughed robustly. "Just a good old cart horse, I used to say. But I always had rôles, which is something the stars can't say."

A kind of shadow fell over her face, and she stopped smiling. "Never a star," she said. "Though I sang Elsa once,—see, there's my blonde wig in there. I bought it for that rôle and have kept it ever since." Her long hand motioned toward the bedroom. "Every once in a while I put it on and comb it out as I did today and imagine myself Elsa again. Ho-hum. Much water's gone under the bridge since then. But I was never a bad business woman. Always sensible. In a business and professional way. Otherwise——" She paused again, her eyes became clouded, and she smiled reminiscently. "Emotionally, my dear—I have been a magnet for drama. A lodestone for adventure." She put out her arms in a sweeping gesture that was more than a little theatrical, but there was a throb of something real under her voice. "Things have always happened to me. Odd, isn't it? Yet it's what I've always wanted of life. Drama is my breath. I could not live without it. Excitement, things happening——" She paused suddenly and frowned at the rug, and her arms dropped. "Of course, there's danger sometimes—too." Her attitude was weary, thoughtful—Deborah watched it gradually grow tense. "*What was that?*" said Mary Monroe in a sharp whisper.

There was a kind of heavy throb along her fleshy throat.

"I heard nothing," said Deborah.

"Oh," said Mary Monroe. "Well—I suppose there

was nothing. Will you have a cigarette?" She extended a cinnabar box.

"I should think it would be a bit lonely living up here," said Deborah, accepting a cigarette.

Mary Monroe looked at her queerly.

"I am not," she said after a moment, "lonely. Let me give you a light."

"There are matches here." Deborah reached for a little packet on the table beside her, struck a match, and held the tiny flame toward Miss Monroe, who leaned, puffing, to receive it. The cigarette between her heavily made-up lips was not too steady. The light fell strongly on her face again, and Deborah thought: "There's something wrong—she's not well—or is it something else——" Deborah put her own cigarette to her lips, discovered it was a perfumed Egyptian blend, and stifled her involuntary gasp of distaste. Mary Monroe saw it, however, and looked anxious.

"Don't you like it?" she said. "Don't smoke it. There are—oh, all kinds in the drawer of the table just behind you. Toss that one in the fire."

"It doesn't matter," said Deborah, but at Miss Monroe's impatient gesture she leaned over to throw her unlighted cigarette toward the fire and to pull open the drawer in the mahogany table near her. It stuck, however, and she was obliged to rise and stand beside the table in order to open it.

"Just give it a jerk," said Mary Monroe. "It always sticks. But look out for the lamp on the table."

The green glass lamp was rocking, and Deborah put one hand on it to steady it when, with the sheer genius for eccentricity which a drawer possesses, the thing came suddenly and wholly out, dumping a conglomeration of small articles onto the floor.

"Oh!" said Deborah, steadying the lamp and clinging with the other hand to the drawer. "I'm so sorry——"

"Never mind. It often does that. Just pick up the cigarettes you want and leave the rest. Come, I'm going to sing for you."

"But all this——" said Deborah helplessly. Such a lot of small things to be crammed into one small drawer. Cards, cigarettes, matches, newspaper clippings, letters, a paper weight—any number of other small, unrelated objects. She picked up a package of cigarettes and a silver lighter.

"I don't do this at all any more," Mary Monroe was saying, moving towards the piano. Her red skirt swished along the rug, and she put both hands to her untidy hair and pushed it upward. "But I will for you. Put down that drawer, child. You'll have to accompany me."

Deborah put down the drawer. It seemed rather silly just to leave it and the scattered small objects strewing the rug, yet she had no choice but to do so. She had suddenly had enough of the unexpected encounter. She would listen to the song and thank Mary Monroe and leave.

"Accompany you!" she said lightly. "I'll be glad to, of course, but I'm afraid it will have to be something I know."

Mary Monroe, sorting heaps of music from which dust rose in small wisps, said agreeably:

"Very well—choose your song. How about this? Or this?" She pulled the cord of a tall piano lamp, and there was suddenly a soft pool of light all round the polished dark piano and the tall woman in red. The window beyond them glittered and winked, and Mary Monroe approached it and pulled the heavy velvet curtains across it. "What a sense she has of the theater," thought Deborah, as Mary Monroe posed for a moment unconsciously against the green curtains. She said: "I think I can manage this."

"Just listen to the wind," said Mary Monroe, adjusting the curtains. "It's going to be a bad night. If there's any wind at all I get it up here. That's why I have all these heavy curtains." Her hands looked white against the green. "What is it you've chosen?"

"The Massenet 'Elégie,'" said Deborah, opening the sheet and looking at the key and feeling relieved to discover it was in flats, which had always seemed to her very much more comprehensible than sharps.

"*The*—'*Elégie*'!" said Mary Monroe sharply. Deborah looked up.

The singer's hands, still white against the curtain, were suddenly also rather stiff and quiet. Her dark, heavily made-up eyes were shining and strange, and she looked—which was absurd—frightened. The moment lengthened, and Deborah stared into the eyes of the older woman, and wind whistled eerily around a corner somewhere just outside the window. The small sound roused Deborah.

"Oh, I—I didn't mean——" she heard herself saying confusedly and stopped, bit her lip, and spoke more collectedly: "Perhaps that isn't one of your favorites. Let's do another one."

Mary Monroe's hands dropped, and she laughed. It was an uncertain laugh, and her dark eyes again swept the room swiftly and lingered on the door.

"Nonsense. I'll do 'Elégie.' Though I don't know how it will sound. The keys may be a bit dusty."

At her gesture Deborah sat down and put the sheet of music before her. The wind moaned again from the window just behind her, and Mary Monroe walked around to stand in the curve of the piano so that she faced Deborah. And also faced, said a queer chill little voice away inside Deborah, the window and the door. But that was an absurd implication—why shouldn't she be a bit watchful—living alone on the roof?—and besides it was nothing to Deborah Cavert; she would finish the song and leave immediately. She oughtn't to have come in the first place. She——

"It's a queer thing that you should have chosen that particular song," said Mary Monroe. Her voice was no longer loud and warmly resonant; it was, instead, rather strained and flat. "You see, the last time I sang that——" Her eyes became focused and conscious of Deborah, and she stopped abruptly and flung her head up. "Oh, well—I'll sing it," she said. "I'm not afraid. I have always been a child of fate.—Go on, my dear. Take it very *lentement*."

Deborah's fingers touched the keys. A child of fate; theatrical way of expressing herself. Yet perhaps she was just that; tossed by the winds, caught by the waves, yet somehow triumphant because, no matter where it carried her, at last she was in the very center of the whirlpool.

Deborah began the prelude—taking it *lentement*. Immediately the scene became unreal: the hot, crowded little room, the blackness outside, and the loneliness and the wind surging against the windows and the door, the bright mimosa, the tall woman in red with the untidy black hair and the sagging chins, the heavy scent of tuberose—herself, Deborah Cavert, in a plain tweed suit and a lemon yellow blouse was the only sane and sensible thing in the room, and she wasn't any too sure about that.

Then Mary Monroe began to sing with a full mellow sweep:

> "*O-oh, doux printemps d'autre fois,*
> *Vertes saisons,*
> *Vous avez fui pour toujours.*"

There was certainly a husky, unclear quality in the voice that filled the small room. But it still had color and temperament. "Oh, sweet spring of other times, green seasons, you have gone forever."
Deborah found herself unexpectedly sensitive to the accompaniment, as if it were new to her and very vivid.

> "*Je ne vois plus le ciel bleu;*
> *Je n'entends plus les chants joyeux des oiseaux!*"

But, Deborah realized suddenly, the woman was singing beautifully, with a depth and passion that transcended Deborah's slight knowledge of form. "I no longer see the blue sky, I no longer hear the happy songs of birds."
She felt herself carried into the song, lost in it, strangely swept by the tragedy of farewell. What an actress the woman must have been!

> "*En emportant mon bonheur,*
> *O bien-aimé tu t'en es allé!*
> *Et c'est en vain que revient le printemps.*"

The melody had never been so beautiful. The words had never been so true. "Carrying away my happiness, O loved one, thou hast gone! And it is in vain that spring returns." She had never experienced this poignant, mysterious feeling of participation. The woman wasn't acting. She was singing from a crowded tempestuous life. Deborah had a fleeting impression that she was singing *to* life. Her fingers went from the light delicacy of "*printemps*" to the louder, fuller:

> "*Oui, sans retour avec toi, le gai soleil*
> *Les jours riants——*"

Deborah was never sure why she looked up so quickly. Perhaps that full, husky voice shook and wavered. But she looked up, and Mary Monroe was staring at the door with great black eyes, and her face was a mask of terror. Her hands flung themselves upward, and she shrank back until she pressed into the piano, and there was a loud, awful crash of sound that filled the room as Mary Monroe's voice—as nothing ever could have filled it.

"*Les jours riants,*" mumbled Mary Monroe's purple lips vaguely. "*Sont—partis——*" And she gave a great strangling gasp and fell straight forward, heavily, through confusion and waves of receding sound and something that was faintly smoky.

There was no sound at all when Mary Monroe died. There was only that maroon velvet heap on the floor.

Then a door closed quietly.

And Deborah's hands slipped on the piano keys and made a confused eerie babble of sounds.

CHAPTER II

DEBORAH was standing, clutching at the piano. Deborah was screaming. Yet she couldn't have been screaming, for only a thin weak trickle of sound would come from her throat, in spite of an enormous effort. And she felt very dizzy and sick, and the room was terrifically hot, and that crimson heap on the floor was Mary Monroe. But it couldn't be, because Mary Monroe had been singing. Had been singing . . . "the gay sun, the laughing days have gone . . ."

The mimosa brought Deborah to her senses. For in averting her eyes in sheer panic from the thing that lay at her feet, she saw the yellow mimosa, and somehow her head cleared and she remembered herself and why she was here. And she knew that something must be done.

Somehow she moved from the piano.

The next thing she knew she was rising again, standing and looking down.

What did one do when there was death?

She must call—whom? Servants? But if anyone were in that house, surely he would have heard that sound. Doctors . . . telephone . . . help of some kind . . . there was a telephone on the table across the room.

Moving stiffly, as if not entirely conscious of her own actions, Deborah crossed the room and reached the telephone. And it was as she put out her hand toward it that she became conscious of the closed door that led out upon the roof as an object of dread.

Sharp and clear, cutting through the mists of shock and bewilderment, came the realization of exactly what had occurred.

Mary Monroe had been shot. And the shot had come from that door. It was closed now, and it had been open. She was sure of that, because Mary Monroe had looked at the door—she had seen what stood beyond it. And then Deborah had heard the door quietly close as the reverberations of the revolver shot were dying away. The person who had fired that shot had stood out there, just beyond the door. Might still be there.

And she, Deborah Cavert, was inexplicably in that house, had actually witnessed what had happened, and there was no one else there.

Yes, she must telephone. She must call the police first. Or a doctor. But Mary Monroe was dead. There was only emptiness where there had been all that surging vitality. There was no need to call a doctor, for he could do nothing. But it was murder. And when it was murder you must call the police.

She lifted the telephone and looked over it at the door and then fumbled confusedly at the dial, realized that she didn't know the number for the police and reached for the thick telephone book on the table beside her. Her fingers were shaking as she turned the brown cover aside; here it was on the very first page. Her eyes leaped upon it. Emergency Calls—Fire—Police. The little click of the dial was loud in the silent room: POL 1313. An easy number to remember! She'd never even looked for it before that. But why didn't someone answer? When you dialed a police number it was urgent. There was no sound at all from the telephone. She ought to hear the repeated buzz of the signal. Perhaps she'd dialed too hurriedly. She cut off the connection and

tried again, forcing herself to deliberation. P—O—L—
1—3—1—3. . . .

There was still no answer. There was nothing but
utter blank emptiness. Panic clutched her, and she
clicked the receiver frantically and dialed again, swiftly
this time and in unbelieving terror.

Emptiness . . . and an unstirring thing across the
room.

Her comprehension, when it came, was certain. The
wires had been cut. And they had been cut to prevent
this very thing.

She put down the telephone. She gripped her hands
together and tried to conquer a frenzy of terror that
threatened her. What could she do now? There was the
black roof outside. The black roof with the looming
shapes of chimneys and incinerators—any of which
might shelter the murderer. There was a long stretch
of fire escape and corridor, isolating the house on the
roof, cutting it off with terrifying completeness from
the rest of the apartment house. Her eyes circled the
room swiftly and returned again fixedly to the door.
How would she dare open it and venture out into that
darkness and——

The telephone rang sharply, insistently, cutting into
that silence. Deborah's hand went out toward it before
she realized that it couldn't be the telephone. The telephone was dead. But something was ringing, stabbing
with hideous shrillness in and through the house. It
rang again, terribly shrill, terribly imperative, loud
enough to rouse the dead.

To rouse the dead!

Deborah cast a frantic look toward that heap of
velvet and dark hair that did not move and put out her
hand confusedly toward the telephone again and knew

that it was not the telephone that was ringing but the annunciator telephone, connected from the vestibule. Her heart gave a great leap of relief. Someone was there, then; someone who would summon help—who would come to her own rescue.

It rang again demandingly, impatiently. Where was the thing?—ah, there, set into the wall beside the door, its flat little receiver hanging on a hook. She took the receiver. The door was just beside her now, and she hoped that there was nothing waiting there, listening, beyond the wooden panel.

And in that very instant recognized what she had not recognized sooner. And that was her own danger. Her own danger—not so much from any lurking thing upon that black roof. Not from the secret that house held. But from the police.

She had been alone with Mary Monroe when the woman was murdered. There was no way to prove that anyone else had been there. There was no way to prove that she herself had not murdered Mary Monroe.

Something was wrong with her breathing, and she felt ill and faint and cold. But she had not killed Mary Monroe. She was in no way responsible or even—save for her presence—connected with the crime.

A terrifying vista had opened before her in one sickening flash. She would not only be dragged through a murder trial as principal witness—which was in itself bad enough—but she would be in all probability their principal suspect. She—Deborah Cavert—accused of murder . . . She caught herself up shortly. It was fantastic; it was incredible; it was something out of nightmares; she must not give way to terror, she must think. Think as she had never done in her life before—stop gibbering—stop trembling . . . The bell rang again.

Confused, terrified, impelled by that insistent clamor, Deborah put the receiver to her ear and said: "H-hello."

Miraculously the sound of the bell stopped, and Deborah caught her breath.

"Oh, hello, Mary." It was a man's voice, vibrant with haste and loud and hollow from the resounding walls of the vestibule.

"Everything's O. K. I've got it for you. I'll be right up."

"No—no," cried Deborah in a strangled way. But he was gone.

After a long time Deborah found she was still holding the receiver, and she replaced it fumblingly on the little metal hook.

He was coming straight up, he had said.

He was even now opening the door that led from the vestibule into the inner hall. He was ringing for the elevator. Or coming up the two long flights of stairs that wound around it. In a very few moments he would be there. He would—— But wait; how could he enter the apartment house? The vestibule, of course; anyone could enter the vestibule. But between the vestibule and the apartment house itself there was a heavy locked door. And she hadn't pushed the small bell button below the annunciator telephone which would allow that door to be opened from the outside. Well, then, he would wait a moment and ring again.

But he didn't. And for Deborah, standing there as if frozen, time quite suddenly ceased to be, for terror had seized upon her again and held her as if helpless—terror of the police, terror of the silent house, terror of murder. She could not think, and the heat of the room seemed to submerge her in confused, dizzy waves. The man in the vestibule had not rung again, therefore he was coming up through the apartment house to the house on the roof. What could she tell him?—nothing certainly but the truth. But would he believe her?

A faint sound from somewhere jerked her eyes toward the door. Had the man below had time to reach the roof —or was it something else?

Her eyes were fixed upon the doorknob, and her heart was suddenly bursting in her throat. The doorknob was turning, and she was horribly certain of it, because there was a faint little rasp of the latch. It turned and turned, and there was something so slow and so stealthy about that turning that Deborah shrank back and tried to move and could not and tried to scream and could not do that, either. And then the bright brass knob clicked backward suddenly, as if it had been suddenly released, and no one entered.

No one entered, and the knob was still.

Who, then, had turned it? If it had been the man who telephoned from the vestibule he would have rung or knocked or, even, have boldly opened the door. She was sure of that.

A long ten seconds passed, with Deborah utterly oblivious of their passage. Then quite suddenly the door flung itself open and she stopped the scream on her lips with her hands.

A man stood in the doorway. A tall, youngish man in an ulster with the collar turned up and his hat pulled low over his eyes. There was something faintly familiar about his dark eyes and his straight eyebrows and straight nose and straight mouth.

"You," gasped Deborah and stopped as his eyes took in her attitude and flashed quickly around the room and found Mary Monroe. She did not follow his glance and yet knew the exact fractional second when he saw that *red heap. He made no motion of surprise or alarm, except that his eyes became fixed and his face rather white and guarded. She waited, and presently his arm went out behind him slowly and closed the door and he moved across the room and bent for a moment over Mary Monroe's body.

Deborah thought she did not move, but she must have made some motion, for he whirled toward her and said sharply:

"*Don't move!*"

She saw then that he held a small blue-black object in one hand and that it was a revolver, and she looked at it dully, because it was so entirely incredible that it should be pointed at her.

He rose, still holding her covered by the revolver.

"So you killed her," he said.

Deborah felt the floor swaying under her feet.

"I—didn't," she said. "Oh, I didn't."

He looked at her. She realized vaguely that his face was white and set and his eyes shining queerly below the brim of his hat. Between them lay that red heap that was unbelievably Mary Monroe. The moment prolonged itself while they faced each other, and it became for Deborah one of those fleeting strange spaces during which time stands still and breathless and suspended and you seem to be on the very verge of making some tremendous discovery about something that goes deeper than merely terrestrial expression and reality.

And immediately, before she had more than recognized that curious suspension of time and space, it was gone and mortal time had started again in its relentless measuring. Time had stopped only for Mary Monroe there at their feet.

Deborah knew that it wasn't the room that seemed

to move a little around her, and she clutched at a chair. It was so hot in the room—so hot and still and——

"Sit down," he said abruptly.

And as she hesitated, he repeated it: "Sit down. Over there. But don't try anything just because you think you can get by with it. Wait!"

She was moving toward the chair he had indicated, but stopped at his sharp command, and he crossed to her and, still holding the revolver in his right hand, ran the left one swiftly over her, not forgetting to touch her smooth skirt beneath which the top of a stocking might hold a weapon.

"I have no revolver," said Deborah. "And I didn't kill her."

His mouth so close to her looked tight and grim and his jaw harder than she had realized it was. He said, not looking at her:

"I know you have no revolver. Sit down, if you want to." He stepped back, away from her a little, and then looked down at her as she sank into the chair. "What did you do with it?"

Deborah's lips moved.

"Go on," he said. "Talk. Get yourself together."

"Was it you," said Deborah huskily, "at the door a moment ago?"

He only looked at her, and she tried again, desperately seeking to make something of it clear to him:

"Was it you, I mean—turning the knob of the door? Just before you opened it?"

He still looked at her, and she leaned forward, her fingers gripping the arms of the chair.

"Don't you understand? The murderer—stood there in the doorway. Stood there and shot her. While she was singing. I—I saw it." The remembrance of the scene was appallingly vivid. She stumbled on hurriedly: "Then whoever did it was gone. The door closed. And she was dead. And a moment before you opened the door—someone outside on the roof turned the knob."

His face was guarded but unbelieving. However, still holding the revolver pointed toward her, he strode swiftly to the door, opened it, stood there a moment on the threshold, and then closed it again.

"It sounded convincing," he said. "But there's no one there." Again their eyes met and held. Then he said shortly: "I know who you are, of course. You're the Cavert girl. I live with another fellow in the flat just below you. Now there's no use crying, you know. I'm going to call the police."

The tight pain in Deborah's throat was thicker. It was all wrong that he should question her like this. She had done nothing. It wasn't just. A queer little surge of anger swept over her and through her veins like a reviving fire.

"I tried to call them myself," she said, "but the wire's cut. At least the telephone is dead. And you have no right to question me like this! I didn't kill her! And I don't know who did!"

After a moment he said, looking into her stormy eyes: "So you tried to call the police yourself. That was clever of you."

The anger in Deborah blazed. She leaned forward, her voice trembling:

"*I tell you I didn't kill her.* I was here—having tea with her. She asked me to accompany her while she sang. And I did. And right there in the middle of the song someone—someone opened that door and shot her and she fell." She struggled and conquered the tremor in her voice and continued: "I didn't even know Mary

Monroe. I know nothing of this—this murder. Except that it is murder. And I think you ought to help me instead of——"

He said, interrupting sharply:

"It was you at the annunciator telephone, I suppose?"

She nodded, staring angrily at him.

"Well, then, if you didn't kill her, who did?"

"I don't know." Deborah was horrified to discover her fine flare of anger deserting her. "I don't know."

Again he looked thoughtfully into her eyes; his own were dark and shining with an expression that Deborah could not read. He slipped the revolver into his pocket, unfastened the collar of his coat, tossed his hat into a chair, and sat down on the arm of a chair opposite her.

She could see his face more clearly now; he had a good forehead and dark hair that looked ruffled as if by the wind.

"My name's Wyatt," he said. "Anthony Wyatt."

She nodded wearily.

"Yes, I know."

"Why did you answer the phone when I rang?"

Deborah took a long breath and leaned forward, lacing her fingers together and determined to make him understand.

"But there was no reason not to answer it," she said. "Don't you understand? I was here, all alone—cut off from help—the telephone dead. The roof——" Her voice became unsteady again, and she said: "I needed help—someone—anyone——"

"Well," he said, "that's one answer." He paused, and she wished she could read the look in his inscrutable face. Then he said consideringly: "I didn't know that you ever came up here."

Again Deborah tried to explain calmly, coherently, holding terror in check.

"I have never been here before. I didn't even know that there was a house here. I met Miss Monroe in the vestibule downstairs. I was about to open the inner door, and she'd forgotten her keys, and I let her in. Then she asked me to come up to tea with her. She—I don't think I can make you understand—but somehow I didn't exactly want to come, and yet I came. And— then she was killed. Just as I told you."

"How long ago was that?"

"I don't know. It isn't long. Perhaps ten or fifteen minutes actually. It seems much longer."

"No one else was here?"

"No one. I was alone. I don't think there are any servants in the house or they would have heard the shot. It was—so loud."

"Then what did you do?"

"I—saw that she was dead. I went to the telephone. I tried to call the police. The wire must be cut; I couldn't get an answer. It was just then that you rang. And I waited—thinking you would ring again because I hadn't pushed the button that releases the lock of the door below."

"I had my own key," he said shortly. "Why didn't you try to escape? If you were afraid of meeting me on the fire escape you could probably have hidden on the roof until I had passed and then got away. Why didn't you?"

The roof. Deborah flung her hands over her face.

"*The roof!*" she cried in a muffled voice that held a very passion of rejection. "*Oh—no——*"

"Look here," he said. "I—I would hate to think I hadn't given you a chance. Tell me who killed her."

"I don't know," cried Deborah. "I don't know. It

happened just as I told you. And I think you'd better call the police."

"And hand you over to them?" he said and stood. Without looking she knew he was moving restlessly about the room, pausing here, pausing there. Finally he said jerkily: "Do you know what it is you are facing? What it is to be dragged through a thing like this—sordid, terrible—with God knows what at the end of it? And if you didn't kill her——"

"Oh, I didn't," breathed Deborah shakily through her fingers.

He flung toward her.

"Look here," he said. "You've got to get out of this. You don't understand what it is." As Deborah looked up, his shining dark eyes plunged deeply into her own. He said after a moment: "Don't you see that I—I can't do it? I can't——" He took a long breath. "You'd better go right away," he said.

"Go?"

"Certainly."

"You mean——"

"I mean I'll try to keep you out of it. I'm not sure I can. So you'd better leave."

"Then you don't think I killed her?"

He looked away from her.

"I don't know who killed her.—Does anyone know that you are here?"

"No. No."

"Have you left anything? Your—hat? Bag? Anything to show you've been here?" He glanced at the door, as if to be sure it was still closed, and then toward the windows. "You must hurry."

"I had no bag. No hat. I——" She was breathless, incoherent.

"All right. Anything else? Handkerchief? Fingerprints on things?"

Fingerprints! But she'd left fingerprints galore. He saw the quick flare of panic in her eyes and turned quickly toward the telephone, whipping out a handkerchief as he did so.

"You say you had the telephone. Anything else?"

"The cup," cried Deborah shakily. "The spoon."

"Wipe them off," he ordered. "Hurry. Someone may come here at any moment."

He was wiping the telephone rapidly and thoroughly. Deborah took from her pocket a scrap of yellow linen with a big "D" on one corner and worked swiftly. Were fingerprints really as important as they were said to be? The cup tinkled as she put it down. The silver spoon. What else? The drawer of the mahogany table. She wiped the knobs frantically. Anthony Wyatt had finished the telephone and gone to the tiny panel set in the wall that was the annunciator.

"Now what?" he said, turning.

"The music," said Deborah. She crossed to the piano and snatched the sheet of music. Oughtn't they close Mary Monroe's eyes—eyes that continued even now to watch the door? Was the door still closed? Yes. "Elégie" fluttered suddenly from her fingers, and she had to kneel beside the red heap to retrieve it. It fell with cruel irony directly beside Mary Monroe's dead hand, and diamonds winked up at Deborah.

Diamonds—and that wide band of gold which she had turned and turned in her fingers.

"*What are you doing?*" said Anthony Wyatt sharply.

"The bracelet," said Deborah shakily. "There are fingerprints on it, too. I can't—I can't touch it."

He gave her a sharp, cold look, then knelt beside the

dead woman. She watched his bent dark head and his hands working swiftly but with a queer gentleness, as if he were apologizing somehow to Mary Monroe. Then he looked at her and was no longer gentle.

"Is that all?" he said grimly.

But Deborah was looking at Mary Monroe.

"If she'd only said why she wanted me to come," she said slowly. "She never told me. And I had the strangest impression that there was something—some reason, some purpose. Yet there couldn't have been. I didn't know her. I had never talked to her before in all my life. I had no motive for killing her."

She could sense the change in him before she looked up and met his eyes again. And she knew that whereas he had been inclined to help her and to believe her, he was now suddenly and inexplicably disbelieving.

"Why don't you tell me the truth?" he said. "You must know that I know that you had the strongest of motives to murder Mary Monroe."

Deborah was trying to say something, and no sound at all came from her throat. She tried again and said faintly: "I don't—I don't——" She stopped abruptly.

From somewhere at the back of the house came a queer light patter of sound. It was muffled by an intervening door, but in the silence they could hear it clearly. It was like beads rattling on a hardwood floor, except that the beads would have to be very large.

Anthony Wyatt was watching the door behind her and at the end of the room, the door that led toward that mysteriously dark back part of the house. His eyes were narrow and alert, and his hand was thrust in his pocket and pulling out the revolver.

"*Go on,*" he said tensely. "*Hurry. Go on down the fire escape. Don't say anything to anybody. I'll call the police.*"

CHAPTER III

HE STRODE swiftly past her. The door opened upon blackness; then he had closed it very quietly behind him and was gone.

Somehow Deborah moved. Her hand was on the doorknob. Outside the black, windswept roof was waiting—the roof and the open fire escape, slippery and dark and hanging precariously above an unknown depth, with no certainty at all as to what might lie there waiting in the shadows of the court below. But he'd said to go down by the fire escape. He knew, then, about the door to the third-floor corridor and its spring lock.

The fire escape was the only alternative. Down into the court, out upon the street, and around to the front of the apartment house.

He'd said, too, to hurry. What was he doing in that silent back part of the house? Why didn't he return?

She took one last look about the hot, still room. A look that forever fixed it in her memory—it and Mary Monroe.

Then she had opened the door, cold wind touched her face, and the door was closed behind her and darkness was all around her. Darkness and a chill wind that whipped her skirt and her hair and pierced her tweed coat as if it were nothing. She gasped for breath and felt blindly for the wall of the house. She could see nothing at all.

Ah, here was a thin streak of light from the window. She groped her way along, touched solid wall with her fingertips, and then her eyes began to adjust themselves to the darkness. This black bulk at her side was, of course, the house itself. If she followed it she would presently come out somewhere near the fire escape. There were windows all along here, but they were dark. She wondered fleetingly what was going on inside those darkened windows, but her main thought was sheer blind desire to escape, to reach the haven of her own apartment. Later she could think. Not now. Her footsteps were swept away by the wind. No one could hear her. Shapes were beginning to loom out of the darkness, but they were shrouded shapes, and there was no sky over her head but instead impenetrable blackness that seemed to drop down in great swathing veils. She stopped abruptly, her fingernails clutching at the wall of house until they were torn, although she didn't know that, then. For she thought that from one of those swathed black shapes that must be chimneys a shadow had become detached.

But the wind swooped upon her, and the shadow, if it was there, did not move, and presently Deborah went on as quietly as any shadow herself.

By the time she reached the corner of the house her eyes had grown used to the darkness. But even so she could see only dimly that the protecting wall of the house ceased and that she must cross that cleared space and find the opening where the parapet wall broke and permitted entrance to the fire escape. The wind seized upon her as she left the protection of the house. But she crossed that open space cautiously, groping ahead of her, until her hands touched the faint dark outline that proved to be actually the cold metal of the fire escape.

It was again like a nightmare; fumbling in the darkness for a foothold, clutching the railing with her hands and fighting for breath against the wind. But she did succeed in doing it—and was, fortunately, perhaps, more acutely aware of the lurking shadows of the roof and of the peril they might conceal than of the open space below her. Descending the narrow slippery steps that seemed to hang so precariously above a black pit of emptiness, she clung tightly to the cold railing and thought only of the fact that with every step she was farther and farther away from the house above and that hot small room that held so gruesome a secret.

At the third-floor landing she stopped.

There was no light above the small door leading into the corridor. There was, in fact, no light anywhere, although away down below where the court led into the street there was a shaft of twilight which indicated street lights somewhere outside. Across the dark well that was the court the walls of other buildings reared black and detached. There was, except for the wind, no sound, although on the street outside there must be passers-by and motorcars. But it was the ebb hour of evening.

Deborah tried to recall the arrangement of the back part of the apartment building. Did the fire escape go straight down into the court? And how did the other apartments open upon it as they must do? And how were the porches and back entrances arranged?

It was an old building much remodeled and added onto, with consequent irregularities of architecture. Probably no one flat was exactly like any other in the whole building.

Well, she hadn't time to explore. The best course was to follow the fire escape. And quickly. But she couldn't help putting her hand upon that small door. It was locked, of course.

She turned, groping through the darkness to find the railing again and seeking cautiously with her toe for the first step. The wind, at a new angle as she turned, swept her short soft hair over her face and into her eyes and wrapped her coat around the railing. She detached it and found the step.

It was about midway of this flight that the thing occurred that, later, was so important.

At the time, of course, it was important enough, but only to Deborah and only because of her subsequent actions, not because of its real significance.

And that was the footsteps that stopped.

She did not know exactly when she became aware of them—perhaps for several seconds she had been subconsciously noting that the sound of her own footsteps —of necessity deliberate and light—seemed to have a kind of syncopation of beat. But the wind flung her coat outward again, and she paused to snatch it closer around her, and the syncopation did not stop.

She listened, rigid—clutching the railing.

And she heard it again: a dull little beat of sound from far below. And under her hand she could feel a faint tremor and vibration of the railing.

Someone was coming up the fire escape toward her.

She never knew why the sound filled her with such unreasoning terror. Perhaps it was a climax to the horror that she had been plunged into during the last hour; perhaps it was due to something deeper and more primitive and less decipherable.

The sound seemed far below, but owing to the gusts of wind she could not be sure exactly where it was. Indeed, the sound of the footsteps was fitful, and Deborah knew that the continued faint vibration of the fire escape was a surer guide than her ears.

She would not return to the roof. And she dared not fight down her terror and go on to meet whatever was coming up those steps.

She could see nothing; she was surrounded by that black, impenetrable wall.

Her breath caught with a kind of sob in her throat.

Her own flat was just below, and there must be some way of getting from the fire escape to the small rear entrance. But she had no key to that door, and Annie was gone. The Riddle flat was there, too. And some of the Riddles were always at home. If she could make them hear . . .

She grasped the railing and ran, not up toward the roof again, but down toward those eerie footsteps. Panting and stumbling, she reached the second-floor level and had met nothing there in the darkness. Although, having once surrendered to terror, she could not stop even to listen.

It was blind instinct that made her feet certain on the slippery steps.

And as she reached the landing and felt it under her feet, quite suddenly a light sprang up at one side and outlined a wide bright window. It was the Riddles' kitchen window. And her swift glance showed her the Riddles' Negro cook turning toward the stove and Chloe Riddle in the doorway talking.

The area of light fell upon a railed porch divided from the fire escape only by that railing.

Deborah grasped it and swung her legs over and was on the wooden porch. With her hand at the door itself she did pause to listen.

But the footsteps had stopped.

In all the black well of the court there was no sound except the wind.

Her breath was tearing at her lungs and her cold hand shaking as she pounded on the door and then somehow found the little button that was the bell. She could see through the window just beside her; the cook looked at the door annoyedly, because she held a hot dish in her hands, and then Chloe, cigarette smoke trailing lazily after her, strolled toward the door.

"Let me in," sobbed Deborah and knew that the wind had caught up her cry and swept it gustily about. "Let me in—let me in!"

And as Chloe opened the door and light and warmth streamed upon her a queer, inward little voice said: "What are you going to tell them?"

But she could not have faced the darkness of the court below and the thing that darkness shielded.

"Why, Deborah Cavert," cried Chloe's warm voice. "Come in. My God, what's the matter, child? You're as white as a sheet."

She closed the door behind Deborah. The light and the warmth and the cessation of the wind and the smell of cooking were almost overpowering.

Deborah blinked and automatically pushed her hair back from her face. She could not speak, and Chloe's green eyes gave her a sharp look and she tossed her cigarette into the sink where it hissed and went out. The cook shot Chloe a dark look of disapproval, and Chloe said quickly to Deborah:

"You haven't had bad news from your father——"

"Oh, no, no," said Deborah, gasping.

"Oh." Chloe's face cleared and then looked perplexed. "Well, my dear, you certainly look like death. That is—— Oh, I've said the wrong thing again! Do you want to borrow something, or is this a social call? If the former, anything we have is yours except the baby's milk. If the latter, I'd better warn you that the Riddles are in a bad way, and Gibbs is in a very devil of a sulk. Everything possible has gone wrong this afternoon, and I went out to tea and just got back to find the whole family at odds. Kids shut up in one room shrieking, dogs in another howling, and Gibbs in a black tantrum and deliberately spoiling the best portrait he's ever done. Come in, my dear. I think it's safe, because Gibbs went out to walk it off. At least, he was going."

Deborah was somehow wafted toward the front of the apartment, through the butler's pantry and dining room and toward the narrow hall running through the long flat. In the dining room Chloe paused to push some electric trains out of the way with her foot. Chloe's feet were beautiful—slender and high-arched— and she always chose very high-heeled pumps. She was wearing some kind of bronze-green silk which clung to her narrow waist and full breast and curving hips, and swished around her feet, and had long flowing sleeves that were slit somehow, so that her white arms showed now and then, and because Chloe wore it it looked glamorous and romantic. It was, however, if you looked closely, faintly wrinkled, with the loop at the neck gone and the sash twisted. Chloe lifted one white hand to push back her untidy but handsome tousle of dark hair, quirked one sleek curved eyebrow at Deborah, and said:

"What's the matter, Deb? Tulip can't hear now."

Deborah hesitated and then said simply:

"There was someone in the court."

Chloe's shining green eyes plunged into her own. After a moment Chloe said:

"Scared you?"

Deborah nodded.

"Why? What did he do?"

"Oh—I just heard someone. It's nothing really. Nerves. I was alone."

"He didn't—try to get in or anything?"

"No," said Deborah. "It's all right, Chloe."

Chloe was, of course, not satisfied. She gave Deborah another long gleaming look that made Deborah feel as if she were a specimen on a pin. Deborah looked back at Chloe steadily, but was chagrined to find herself trembling. Chloe's look suddenly softened and at the same time intensified.

"But Deborah, darling, you are actually shaking with fright. Here, let me give you something——"

"I'm perfectly all right," said Deborah. "It was cold, that's all. And I was nervous. And I do want to borrow."

"What?" said Chloe, her eyes still gleaming.

"Something to read," said Deborah at random. "Anything——"

Chloe gave her a long shining look before she said: "Oh, all right, Deb. Anything I've got. I think it's safe to go on past the studio. Gibbs is still out. At least, he ought to be."

Deborah followed her along the narrow hall. The doors were closed, bottling up children and dogs after the Riddle fashion when both grew too wildly noisy for Gibbs's nerves.

Chloe, so far as Deborah knew, had no nerves.

The studio, a workroom, bare except for easels and tables, a sitting platform and a piano, smelled vehemently of turpentine and was empty of human presence. Beyond it was an untidy drawing room, and from a welter of things on a table Chloe extracted a book and thrust it into Deborah's hands.

"Here's something," she said. "You'd better stay

for dinner, Deb. Although I must say the roast looked rather tough."

Deborah took the book without quite realizing that she had it and murmured something of letters and found her way through a litter of toys and footstools and cushions to the door.

"I'll cross the hall to the front door," she said. "Thanks, Chloe."

Chloe's green eyes glittered amusedly.

"I'll find out what it's all about some time, Deb. You needn't think you've put me off so adroitly."

Oh, yes, you'll know, thought Deborah wearily. She said: "Thanks for the book, Chloe."

Chloe stopped smiling.

"If you get—scared again," she said with abrupt earnestness, "come back—I don't feel any too gay myself."

The thought flickered across Deborah's mind that Gibbs had been drinking again.

She said aloud: "Anything special?" and opened the door.

"Oh, no," said Chloe. Her shoulders rippled in a shrug. "It's just that it's—a queerish sort of night somehow." Her green eyes fastened on the elevator shaft and seemed to widen and flatten like a cat's. Behind the elevator a rather narrow, carpeted stairway wound upward and downward, and just across the hall was the wide oak door leading to the haven of the Cavert flat.

"Oh," said Deborah. "Well—good-night, Chloe."

Fortunately, in that mad interval of time that had elapsed since, incredibly, she had closed that door behind her, she had not lost her keys. Her hand closed on them in her coat pocket. She was vaguely conscious

that Chloe had said something again about calling her
if she wanted to during the night. Then the door closed
and she was inside the flat.

Her hands were trembling and cold as, in a kind of
frenzy of relief, she bolted the door and leaned against
it and let the grateful feeling of physical warmth and
safety flow over her in waves. She was again in her own
familiar world, and it surrounded her and shut out, at
least for the moment, the strange dark things that she
had touched and had been touched so rudely by during
that intervening hour or two—things that, up to then,
had been mere words to her, entirely incomprehensible
and infinitely removed from the tight pleasant circumference of Deborah Cavert's world.

It was unbelievable that the place had not changed,
but it hadn't. The lamp on the table glowed peacefully;
she had turned it on just as she went out the door,
knowing it would be dark when she returned. On the
table, too, lay her hat and her pigskin gloves where she
had tossed them just before leaving to go up to tea in
the house on the roof. To tea with Mary Monroe.

She left the door and crossed blindly to the drawing
room; her fingers found the light, and in a mirror she
could see a strange, white-faced girl with disheveled
bright hair and dark gray eyes who was, strangely, herself.

She sank down into the cushions of the divan.

Blitz came bouncing suddenly from somewhere in the
back of the flat and leaped upon her with joyous wriggles
and delighted licks of a slobbery pink tongue wherever
he would touch hand or chin.

"Oh, Blitz," said Deborah waveringly, and then the
square little terrier's ecstasy of delight moved her, and
she discovered she was poignantly grateful for it, and

she hugged the dog, who didn't like hugging and wriggled away from her, only to return. And she wanted to cry and couldn't. For there were things that must be done.

But it was out of her hands now. Probably by this time Anthony Wyatt had returned to the room where lay that red velvet heap and had himself called the police. Of course, the wire was cut—but there were other telephones. She wondered how long it had been since she had fled from that hot, death-laden room away up there on the black roof and looked at her watch.

It was then a quarter to seven—not quite that. It seemed much later—but her flight down the fire escape really hadn't taken much time.

Well, then, when would the police arrive? Was it possible for him to keep her out of the thing? After all, people always left traces of some kind, else murderers would never be detected. No matter how carefully a crime was planned, somehow the police discovered the most undiscoverable things.

She began to comprehend more clearly, and with increasing alarm as reason confirmed that comprehension, the dangers of her position.

She had obeyed Anthony Wyatt blindly—because she was confused, terrified; because he had made her obey him. Because he had been direct, certain, altogether compelling. Now she saw that her acquiescence and her escape would make her story, unconvincing at best, still weaker. And she knew that even Anthony Wyatt, and even while he had told her to go, had doubted that story.

What could she do! There must be something.

She sat, a rigid slender figure, staring at the rug, thinking desperately.

Aunt Juliet was out of the question. So was her father. Her father! That was a new anxiety.

It was with the small Cavert family (Deborah, her father, and his sister, Juliet Cavert) as it had been with many other families of once prosperous and dignified background during the period following 1929 and 1930.

Four years before, the firm of Cavert & Company, of which John Cavert was president, had been one of the first of the moderately large firms to crash. That crash, unheralded and inexplicable, then, had left them all bewildered and uncertain. Juliet with a customary energy had rallied; she had managed marvelously to salvage every scrap that could be salvaged, to pull them together, to find a place to live; as marvelously she had managed to send Deborah to a good school, to keep her smartly dressed. She was still Juliet Cavert. And she still clung to her dignity and her jewels as she clung to the inevitable, daily gardenia which she had worn from habit for years and which now became a small white flag, not of truce, but of rigid non-surrender. She was still outwardly unshaken. But inwardly—Deborah shook her head impatiently.

It was impossible to appeal to Aunt Juliet. It was unfair. And John Cavert had been for more than a year an invalid because of an extremely serious heart affection—due directly to illness, really if more remotely to the prolonged strain of the thing that was known as the depression. This trip to Florida (undertaken by Juliet only two weeks ago, as a last desperate expedient to prolong her brother's life) and his illness, with its procession of specialists, had been a strain upon Cavert finances at their present low ebb. Now John Cavert's very life depended to a large extent upon maintaining for him peace and tranquillity.

Deborah was pacing the floor, Blitz following her worriedly.

She dared not turn to her father. She must, indeed, keep the thing from him somehow. She could not appeal to Juliet. Queer how few relatives were actually close. Queer how few friends one could go to and say: "I've just been involved in a murder." How few—why, there was no one! No one at all.

But people must do something. What was it? A lawyer, of course. That was the thing. And there was Albert Steffin, a lawyer and an old friend of her father's. Of course, he was a rather stuffy old person, more at home in entangled estates than murder courts, but still he might know what to do.

She sat down at the telephone desk in the hall, and Blitz bounded after her and sat there with his head cocked on one side and his bright eyes inquiring as to what was wrong.

She found the number, took up the telephone and dialed. And at once was conscious of that dead lack of sound that there had been from the telephone in the house upstairs. But did that mean . . . She tried again impatiently and realized that it did mean that the connection for the whole apartment house must have been cut.

Slowly she replaced the telephone. Funny how oddly relieved she felt.

She had no notion as to the arrangement of telephone wires. Did that mean that everyone in the building was cut off? That she must go outside somewhere—to that little drugstore on the corner of Brahms Street—to telephone?

But that meant, too, that she was actually as isolated in the apartment as she felt. And it was—as all the apartments in the building were—old-fashioned and roomy, with high ceilings and long passages that were rather bewilderingly laid out. It was time Annie was back.

What would she say to her father? What would she say to Juliet? Was there any way in which she could put off her father's knowledge of the thing? Every day would be a day gained in that difficult struggle for his life.

She sat upright. She could warn Juliet of it. Now, before the police came. A telegram.

She snatched her hat and pulled it over her bright hair, and took her gloves and ran into her bedroom to snatch her pocketbook. Her coat again. Her keys.

She did pause at the door to brace herself. It wasn't easy to leave again the peace and security and soft lights and Blitz and go out into the windswept, uncertain streets. It wasn't even easy to go into the hall and ring for the elevator and wait for it. But the turn of the stairway looked dark and unsure, and miraculously she had only a moment to wait. She saw no one in that hall or in the lower hall. The vestibule was brightly lighted, and she hurried through it and into the street. It was lighted adequately, and there were a few pedestrians hurrying along it, and a few automobiles. A rush of wind brought with it the muffled murmur of the traffic of Lake Shore Drive, off toward the right.

Then the wind swept on Deborah again and whirled her against a man hurrying along with his head bent against the wind. She gasped and clutched at his arm, and he caught her and set her squarely on her feet, and swung onward. The little contretemps happened so unexpectedly and was over so quickly that Deborah walked on a few steps before she realized that there was something indefinably familiar about the man who had passed on so swiftly.

She whirled. He was walking rapidly along the sidewalk and had already passed the light above the door to the apartment house she had just left. He was merely a quickly moving, tall black figure.

Odd how much one tall, youngish man in an ulster with a hat over his eyes looked at a distance like any other youngish man in an ulster with a hat pulled over his eyes.

CHAPTER IV

FIVE minutes later she had, with the aid of the boy at the soda fountain, collected the requisite number of dimes and nickles to pay for her telegram at the telephone. In the booth with the door securely closed she had sent a telegram to Juliet. But she could not, with only a glass-paned door between her and the scattered people in the drugstore, telephone to the lawyer.

The telegram to Juliet was simple and would be clear to Juliet once she saw the newspapers, no matter what story of the murder they carried. She had said only: "Keep papers from Father."

That much, at any rate, was done.

Then she was out in the street again. And she walked hurriedly, alert in spite of herself to shadows and the dark figures of pedestrians. Now that she had accomplished her purpose, it was not so easy to be unafraid. It was, however, not much more than half a block to 18 East Eden.

18 East Eden. Up till then a quiet number on a quiet street.

"Geographically convenient," Juliet had said with a sigh. "And socially all right. After all, Eden Street is still a good address."

So they had signed a long lease and chosen the things they loved best and that had been a part of the Cavert background the longest to accompany them.

It was an old building and retained certain elegancies of a more leisurely and graceful era. True, it had been much remodeled. And speaking tubes and telephones, electric lights instead of gas, radios and mechanical refrigeration had followed each other in proper sequence. But the high ceilings, the handsome woodwork, dark and satin-smooth, and an indefinable air of dignity and grace remained. And with them a kind of lingering glamour—a hint of the ghosts of the past, and of the feeling and depth that somehow permeate old walls that have known much living.

It looked enormous, though as apartment buildings go it was, of course, not large. It was not even, properly speaking, an apartment building. All around that portion of the city great new towers reared into the sky and were dotted with regular lines of lights that proclaimed them apartment buildings of the new era. But Eden Street and a few quiet streets surrounding it were almost untouched by the strides of the golden 1920's and except for skyrocketing real-estate values remained quietly and calmly themselves, with their narrow dignified fronts flush with the sidewalk—with rounded plate-glass windows and wide, beautifully paneled doors and spotless marble steps which had known, as Number 18 had known, the tread of many satin-shod feet descending to waiting carriages.

Some of the houses had been made into apartments. Some of them were still residences. All of them maintained an atmosphere that contributed largely to the fact that Eden Street was, as Juliet had said, a good address. It was, too, not far from the Loop and not far from the Lake.

Deborah looked up at the dark bulk of the building rising above her as she approached it. Lights were on now, shining here and there from its high old windows. Owing to the way the houses along Eden Street were wedged together, there was apt to be in the daytime a certain dusk and dimness about the spacious old rooms; it was not unpleasant, and there was an air of graciousness about it, as if sunshine could be brought in at will, as if it were excluded merely as all garishness might be excluded. At night, however, the old building was, as a rule, cheerful, with soft lights, and the windows that faced walls or other windows along either side were thickly curtained in damask.

No one would have known that there was a house on its roof. No one could have known what had happened in that house.

It was not, she knew, visible from the street. Yet she looked, searching the darkness for lights. There were none to be seen, of course. None, that is, except the lighted windows that marked one of the third-floor apartments. The other was, she knew, vacant.

The brief flare of courage that the necessity to act had given her was ebbing. Fortunately, she met no one, this time, along the street. The man in the ulster, whoever he was, had vanished.

Her pulse quickened, though, as she neared the apartment house again. What shadow was that at the curb? Nothing! Were there no clusters of cars parked there— were there no figures hurrying in and out the vestibule —was there nothing of the terrifying confusion of police cars and ambulance and police and curious bystanders?

There was nothing. An automobile or two parked quietly across the street. A pedestrian nearing the corner. It was still quiet, still perfectly tranquil.

The police, then, did not know.

She had walked on a few steps before the implication struck her. There were no police at the door. They didn't know about the murder. *But they ought to have known!*

By this time Anthony Wyatt ought to have let them know as he had said he would do. Why hadn't he?

The impact of the question sent her thoughts racing along a path that had been up till then unexplored. Anthony Wyatt and the man who had telephoned from the vestibule were the same; there was no doubt about that; and there had been no doubt from the instant she heard him speak. But why had he come just then? Why had he telephoned just then? What had he said? Something about everything being all right. It had looked, of course, perfectly all right; he had had some sort of business with Mary Monroe and had happened to choose that time to call. But she had been so confused and so terrified that merely the sight of a vaguely familiar face had induced her confidence. Had he been actually surprised to find her there? To find Mary Monroe dead on the floor?

There was no way to answer these questions—at least not now. But there were two things that were inescapable:

He had certainly been carrying a revolver—and one does not as a rule pay business or social calls armed with revolvers.

And he had not called the police. Why?

That was the important thing, of course—his failure to call the police. Deborah's footsteps became weighted as she reached and turned in at the apartment house.

He had not called the police. He had had a revolver. He had come to the house on the roof. Presuming an earlier presence on that dark roof, he would have had time, after the murder, to return to the vestibule and ring the bell which she had answered. Had he, then, killed Mary Monroe?

It was not a question that Deborah could evade. But

it was one that she must, at least for the moment, reject. He had planned and commanded her escape from what would have been—and might be yet—a dangerous, unjust trap that held latent possibilities of horror which Deborah dared not permit herself to recognize. Her only course, just then, was to follow his plan. She had no choice, for she was caught already in a trap and there was nothing she could do but wait. Wait and watch for the police.

There was no one in the vestibule. She unlocked the inner door, and for a pungent instant Mary Monroe's ghost stood beside her—there was a rustle of maroon velvet and a faint scent of tuberose. She had stood just there—so short a time ago—telling Deborah she'd forgotten or lost her keys, inviting Deborah to tea. Already the dusk of that night had cast gray shadows along the marble floor. But she wasn't there because she was dead—dead and waiting in the house on the roof.

Why hadn't Anthony called the police?

Again she saw no one in the hall.

But again it was with a feeling of relief that she closed and bolted the door of the Cavert flat behind her.

And set herself to wait for the police. To wait for the police to come and perhaps accuse her, Deborah Cavert, of murder.

About ten Deborah realized that Annie still had not returned and made a tour of the whole apartment—making herself needlessly sure that windows were bolted and doors locked. In the kitchen the shining black windowpane reflected her own face eerily, and she thought of that dark court and the fire escape winding upward just outside and reached up hurriedly and jerked down the shade.

She drifted, a white-faced little ghost, back to the library. Blitz had inconsistently curled up on the divan and was sleeping soundly and refused to rouse himself.

There was a sound of a car in the street below, and Deborah went to the window and looked cautiously down. It had not stopped. But as she turned away, her glance fell on the piano and she remembered the mimosa. The mimosa and the green vase that she had left on that piano upstairs.

Well, it was too late now.

Where had Anthony Wyatt gone? What had he done? And *why* didn't something happen?

The waiting, the silence, the complete inactivity began to assume a sinister quality of their own.

Usually there were a few sounds from the Riddles' turbulent household—children wailing, dogs barking, Gibbs's furious piano-playing, or voices in vigorous dispute; occasionally the faint muffled sounds of a radio in the apartment below—the apartment that Anthony Wyatt shared with another man, Francis Maly. But that night there was nothing. The apartment just above was, of course, empty. Deborah might have been entirely alone in the whole great house. Alone except for the thing that lay in the house on the roof. Was it still there? Had no one moved it?

It was, perhaps, midnight, and still no one had come seeking her, and there were no untoward sounds from the halls or the street outside. She couldn't sleep, she thought, but she might rest. So there on the divan in the library she curled up, too. Blitz grunted and reluctantly moved and then stretched his head across her feet.

And from sheer weariness she went immediately and heavily to sleep.

Once during the night she roused enough to wonder vaguely why the lights were all burning, and once she was sleepily aware of some sort of sound—something dull and rumbling, like a piano being moved across the floor above—but she was not fully conscious of either impression, though she remembered both later.

It was morning when she became aware that someone was pounding at the door and that Blitz was barking frantically. She sat up bewildered, trying to orient herself. The lights were burning—she'd been asleep, and Blitz was barking, and the knocking at the door continued.

She got to her feet and pulled her skirt straight and all at once remembered what had happened.

"Hush, Blitz," she said and opened the door.

But it was not the police.

It was a man whose white hair and handsome brown face were familiar. He was Francis Maly, and he was one of the two men living in the apartment below. He had once yanked Blitz from the path of an approaching automobile. He said now, pleasantly:

"I'm afraid I've disturbed you. But you see I remembered that you were alone up here—that is, that your family were gone—and I wondered if you were all right."

And then as Deborah looked at him he added:

"You see—don't be frightened, Miss Cavert—you see last night, sometime during the night, a woman in the apartment house was murdered."

Deborah's throat closed. She couldn't have spoken, and she wondered what his unexpectedly keen eyes were seeing in her face.

"I'm afraid I've frightened you. I only meant to be sure you were all right. She was found when the tele-

phone man went to her place this morning to fix the
telephone. No one knows what happened. Why she was
murdered. . . ." His eyes went past her to the brightly
lighted room—lighted at that hour of the morning—and
noted, could scarcely have failed to note in passing, her
ruffled hair and the wrinkles in her yellow linen blouse.
Deborah thought: "The man to fix the telephone—it
wasn't Anthony Wyatt, then, who finally called the
police."

"The police are here, Miss Cavert," Francis Maly
said. "I expect they'll want to question all of us. Can I
be of any help to you?"

"No," said Deborah in a thick voice that didn't
belong to her.

"Oh, well—if there's anything just give us a ring.
Anthony or I would be glad if we can be of any assist-
ance. How is your father?"

"About the same," said Deborah, still in a choked
voice. "It's awfully good of you——"

"Not at all. Not at all." Had she seemed surprised—
suitably shocked? He was turning away.

"Th-thank you," said Deborah. As he approached
the elevator, the door to the Riddle flat flew open and
Chloe Riddle swirled out in a flurry of floating yellow
pajamas, stopped as she saw Francis Maly, and then
swept on to Deborah.

"My God, Deb," she cried. "Have you heard? Have
you heard, Mr. Maly? When did it happen? Does anybody know anything about it? How perfectly horrible!
Right up there over our heads. The police are up there
now. Gibbs says they'll question all of us—he says——"

"*Chloe!*" It was Gibbs himself in the doorway. Clad
in a huge towel, with his hair wet and slick, he still
managed to look self-possessed but black with anger.

His hard mouth was even harder above the towel and his lean white shoulders. He said furiously: "*Chloe!* Get the hell back in here and shut up."

Chloe swirled around to look at him. Her eyes shot a small flame, and her hands opened and closed in a queer, lithe little gesture that only Chloe could have achieved. She said, however, lazily, with only the flame in her eyes betraying her: "Nonsense. Go and get some clothes on."

Gibbs's eyebrows were a thick, straight black line, and his jaw set itself cruelly. He looked fully capable of dragging Chloe back into the apartment by her hair, but luck as usual was with Chloe. Before he could speak, a bell sounded shrilly from somewhere inside the flat. He hesitated, then vanished, leaving the door open. They could hear his reply:

"Yes—yes, I know. But we know nothing about it. We—— But I tell you we know nothing of it——"

"We knew Mary . . ." murmured Chloe absently, as if she were interpolating at Gibbs's elbow.

"Yes, I know, but—oh, well, all right.—All right. Yes, in ten minutes. You mean in the house on the roof? —Up the fire escape. Yes."

He appeared in the doorway again, clutching the towel perilously.

"That was the police, talking from the vestibule. They want us upstairs in ten minutes."

"To inquire into the murder?" asked Francis Maly.

Gibbs gave him a black look.

"Has anything else happened around here?" he said savagely. "Certainly to inquire into the murder. I don't know anything about it. They'll take a lot of time —upset everybody—everything—question, inquire,

poke their·noses into what's none of their business——"
He gestured angrily with the towel, and Chloe said
detachedly:

"The exposed human figure ought to have more
beauty than yours has, Gibbs."

"Oh, hell," said Gibbs and vanished again. An instant
later his head appeared. "They want everybody up
there. Everybody that lives here. You'd better get some
clothes on yourself, Chloe, and in God's name don't
talk so much."

Chloe smiled rather after the fashion of a sleepy
tigress.

"I expect he's right, at that," she said affably to
Deborah and Maly. "After all, with a murder you never
know." A sudden thought seemed to strike her, and she
turned quickly and purposefully toward Deborah. "Oh,
Deb," she said. "I just remembered. Last night did
you——" She stopped abruptly.

"Did I what?" said Deborah steadily.

"We'd better get dressed," said Chloe. "'Morning,
Mr. Maly. I expect we'll meet upstairs."

"I expect so," said Maly. "I'd better let Wyatt know
about this inquiry before he gets away." He nodded
at Deborah and at Chloe and entered the elevator, and
as it droned downward Chloe said:

"I said we'd better get dressed." Her tone was flat
and meaningless, but she was looking at Deborah's
wrinkled yellow blouse.

"Yes," said Deborah.

Chloe looked fully into her eyes again.

"If I were you, Deb," she said finally in a low, oddly
still voice, "and had seen anything—queer—last night,
I would forget it."

If Chloe only knew how anxious she was to forget a certain thing she had seen!

Chloe did not seem to expect an answer. She turned briskly away, said over one lacy yellow shoulder: "I'll ring when we are ready. You may as well go with us," and was gone.

Well, it had come. As Deborah had known it would.

She was getting out of the tub when there was another knock at the door. This time it was Tulip—La Tulipe Noire, Gibbs called her when he wasn't sulking—carrying a tray with coffee and toast on it. Her eyes were shining with excitement. When she'd gone, Deborah found under the toast a note in Chloe's vigorous sprawling writing: "Gibbs would kill me for meddling, but for God's sake, Deborah, *don't say anything*."

The last three words were underlined.

Deborah drank the coffee and was grateful for the stimulating warmth of it. She went back to finish dressing and looked at herself carefully in the mirror as if what she had experienced might have made some sort of mark upon her face. But she was only a little white and tired, and there were faint black smudges under her eyes. She fastened her dress and looked at it with mechanical approval. No matter how low the Cavert exchequer ran these days, Juliet insisted and, marvelously, managed so that Deborah's clothes were exactly right. The right dressmaker was as essential to Juliet as the right church. And she had guarded Deborah's teeth, carriage, and health as she had guarded her own remaining jewels. The gray wool dress was sleek and expensively simple, and it clung in beautiful lines; and above it Deborah's eyes looked like gray jewels, and her hair shone. There was a red scarf and a red belt and a gay red handkerchief and small gray oxfords.

She thought of the cold fire escape and took the coat that went with the dress—gray, too, with a handsome scarlet lining.

The bell at the annunciator phone from the vestibule rang as she put the coat over her shoulders, and she answered it.

"Miss Cavert." It was Anthony Wyatt.

"Yes——"

"Look here—have you said anything?" His voice was hurried and low.

"No," said Deborah. "No."

"All right—don't, then. Don't—not yet——"

His voice broke off, and a confused sound came to Deborah's ears. Then a door closed somewhere—there was another subdued sound, as of a door closing, and presently the bell rang again.

Was he still there, then?

"Why?" she said into the telephone.

"Miss Cavert," said someone. "Hello—hello——" It was a new voice, heavier and without the clipped consonants that marked Anthony Wyatt's words.

"Y-yes . . ." stammered Deborah.

"This is Lieutenant Waggon of the Brahms Street police station. We're investigating an occurrence of last night here in the apartment building. We'd like your presence, please, upstairs right away. In the house on the roof. Thank you, Miss Cavert."

The voice sounded as if it had said the same thing a great many times.

"Yes," said Deborah again, faintly. But probably he hadn't waited to hear.

For the second time she was to go up to the house on the roof. The first time she'd seen murder done—she'd almost felt the breath of it past her cheek.

Now she was to go up to the crowded room again.

And Anthony Wyatt hadn't called the police and had warned her to say nothing.

She didn't stop then to question, for Chloe knocked at the door and called: "Deb—are you ready?"

CHAPTER V

IF, BEFORE the murder of Mary Monroe brought them so strangely and yet so naturally and inevitably together, anyone had asked Deborah how many people she knew in the whole apartment house, she would have said: "Why, no one. Except, of course, Chloe Riddle."

And she'd known Chloe Riddle only superficially in spite of all those years since they'd gone to dancing school together. And even then Chloe had been sixteen and threatening to elope with the dancing master while Deborah had been a stiff, shy, long-legged eight. Chloe was always disturbing; you were always conscious of lazily banked fires within her. She could have made, Juliet had said tight-lipped, a good marriage. But after a series of more or less dramatic love affairs, she'd married Gibbs Riddle—he was a good enough portrait painter, of course. He might even become celebrated. If he didn't kill a client in one of his sudden black rages, Juliet had added dryly.

After Chloe's marriage and consequent rapid and vigorous baby bearing and tending, Deborah had seen little of her. But she did remember that while affable on the surface, still Aunt Juliet had not been too pleased to discover that the Riddles were comfortably and apparently permanently settled just across the hall when the Caverts came to the apartment at 18 East Eden.

Yet their acquaintance had the quality of intimacy and understanding that comes only from years and similar backgrounds. And Deborah would have said that she knew no one else in the whole place.

Actually she found that she knew not only the names of practically everyone assembled for that beginning inquiry, but something of them. After all, you can scarcely live under a single roof and not know certain small details of the other lives that are going on all around you.

As she knew that the men in the flat below had a radio, so she knew vaguely their names. There was Anthony Wyatt, of course. There was Francis Maly— she remembered him because of Blitz, and because of his white hair and brown, slender face.

So, too, she knew others in the apartment house. Yet as she followed Chloe through that narrow corridor that she remembered so well and out onto the fire escape that she remembered even better, she would still have said, had she been asked, that she knew none of the other residents in that house.

Later she thought that it was strange that murder should have been the link that it was. That it dragged all of them into its terrible circumference. That it actually caught and altered forever certain of those lives.

This was the place where her coat had caught.

Just there below, she had listened to those erratic footsteps.

Gibbs behind her said: "Look out for the railing. You'll get rust all over your clothes. We ought to have a new fire escape. This one's in a terrible shape."

Rust. The word reached Deborah, and she looked down and suddenly stopped there on the narrow step and snatched away her hand. It was only faintly orange, but the other hand, the hand that had grasped that railing so desperately during her descent from the roof, was to her horror still faintly henna-shaded across the pink palm. Most of it had washed off certainly; but there was still a wide bar of faint dark orange, and even her fingertips looked as if she had dragged them over saffron. She recoiled inwardly as if it had been blood, so marked and so hideous the stain seemed. Then she realized that Chloe had gone on upward, her silk ankles flashing, and that Gibbs had stopped just below her, waiting for her to move. Had he seen? If he had, would he guess? His eyes, so keen to color, must have seen. Yet he was below her.

"What's the matter?" he said crossly. "You won't fall."

Deborah went on. She managed to get a fresh and disguising streak of rust on each palm during the remaining steps, but still she felt strongly shaken and marked.

Then they were crossing the opening of the ledge and Chloe was showing a great deal of very pretty legs. They were met by a policeman, and the roof was no longer dark and windy but was instead flat and gray. It was a dismal day; there was moisture in the air, and the smoke hung low. The chimneys and incinerators were just chimneys and incinerators and held no lurking, moving shadows.

Deborah knew she was white as they passed the long line of windows—still closed and dark—and approached the door. But so was Gibbs. And even Chloe looked a bit pale, and the heavy crimson paste on her mouth stood out.

Then they were in the crowded drawing room—crowded with the accumulation of Mary Monroe's vivid life.

The spirit had gone out of it as completely as it had

left Mary Monroe's body. Deborah's glance went swiftly and involuntarily toward the rug beside the piano. But the body had been taken away, and a lighter patch looked as if the rug just there had been scrubbed recently.

Had anything else been changed in that terribly familiar room?

There were the teacups, there was the litter of small objects beside the table and empty drawer—there was the telephone—there was the piano. Someone had picked up the sheet of music that had fluttered out of her hands as she had bent over Mary Monroe. And the green vase with its yellow load of mimosa was gone.

It was not on the piano. It was nowhere about the room.

The police . . . fingerprints . . . could they discover who owned a plain green Charnwood vase? Deborah's mind leaped to a hundred possibilities, all of them incriminating. Why had she forgotten the vase? And what else had she forgotten?

Above all things she must not let anyone know what she felt.

There were others in the room. Policemen who were for the first time in Deborah's life figures of menace and threat. People—herself, Chloe, and Gibbs. The man Brocksley, fat and shifty-eyed, and his little blonde wife. The janitor. Several men silhouetted in a confused group against a window. There was a faint acrid odor of smoke in the air, and an intangible impression that many men had come and had done what they had to do and had gone.

And there was about the whole thing a casual, workaday atmosphere that vaguely surprised Deborah, who had thought that an inquiry into murder would be something quite different. She was not, however, deceived by that businesslike attitude, although she did not then know that Lieutenant Waggon had an axiom. It was, "Give 'em enough rope."

A big, uniformed policeman who might have had a murder served up with his oatmeal every morning for all the excitement there was in his bearing thrust chairs politely at Chloe and Deborah, which they accepted. Gibbs stood scowling at the fireplace, and Deborah became gradually aware that a tall, loose-jointed man, also in a uniform, was talking in a conversational way with the janitor.

"And then what?" he said pleasantly. His face was long and pale, and he had calm blue eyes and a patient, motherly manner. He was Lieutenant Waggon, and that motherly manner had been known to produce the most sinister results, but Deborah did not know that, either.

She was, instead, caught by something out of the ordinary in the janitor's attitude; for he was positively placative. Even his red hair was unwontedly smooth; his freckled, belligerent jaw was uttering respectful phrases in honey-sweet Irish accents. His name, mysteriously, was Juanito, and he had velvety black eyes that could become ugly.

"Well, then the telephone repair man yelled, 'By God, she's dead' and I saw she was. And that's all."

"Who had reported the telephone trouble?"

Juanito shrugged. "I don't know. Somebody trying to call her, I suppose."

"And you left things exactly as you found them?"

"Yes, sir. I've told you that——"

"Certainly. I wanted to check a few things in your first statement." Lieutenant Waggon's calm eyes swept around the room, and he said: "Is everybody here?"

"Well," said the janitor with a shade of reluctance, "just about. Yes, sir."

"Just about?" said Lieutenant Waggon. "Who's not here yet?" He took a slip of paper from his pocket, and Juanito said:

"The men from the first-floor flat. Mr. Wyatt and Mr. Maly."

There was a commotion at the door, and voices, and the janitor said quickly: "Here they are now."

Anthony Wyatt. Deborah looked swiftly and met his eyes for a fractional second as he glanced about the room and nodded unsmilingly to her and to the Riddles. Then the two men went to stand beside Gibbs, and Lieutenant Waggon murmured something to one of the policemen, and Juanito was mopping his freckled forehead with a handkerchief, and all at once Lieutenant Waggon was saying in the pleasantest way in the world:

"Well, folks, it's good of you to come straight up here. We thought it might save us a little time and help us if we'd see you together—that is, if you'd all come up here at the same time. I guess you know that a woman by the name of Mary Monroe was murdered here last night. We don't know who killed her. Not yet, that is. Now what I want to know is whether any of you saw anything or heard anything that you think might have some bearing on the murder. Anybody prowling around the place last night—or any shots—or anything like that. Now you needn't any of you be nervous about telling anything you know—if you don't want to say anything here you can tell me in private. Which one of you's Brocksley?"

The inquiry was unexpectedly sharp and sudden. Brocksley, who'd been leaning against the piano, cleared his throat twice before he could say: "I am."

Lieutenant Waggon looked at the slip of paper and then at Brocksley again.

"What's your full name?" he asked mildly.

Brocksley cleared his throat again. He was a large man, with small light eyes and small features and a somewhat pompous and theatrical manner. Deborah had often heard him practising scales and bits from opera through the door of the Brocksley flat.

"Alfred," he said. There was a note of indecision in his voice.

"Alfred?" said Lieutenant Waggon.

"Well," said Brocksley, with pink crawling into his fat cheeks. "It's really Alfred Lord Tennyson Brocksley. I use Alfred in private life."

"Private life?"

"Yes. Lord Brocksley for professional purposes. It's more euphonious."

"I see," said Lieutenant Waggon gravely. "What is your profession, Mr. Brocksley? I thought you were the renting agent for the apartment house."

"Well," said Brocksley, "I am. That is, I consented to see to the leasing of the apartments in order to accommodate the owners. However,"—he swelled out his somewhat prominent stomach and chest, and his voice became important—"however, I am an opera singer. Perhaps you've heard of me."

"Perhaps," said Lieutenant Waggon doubtfully. "But I don't know as I hear much opera."

"Oh," said Brocksley with more than a touch of condescension. "I understand. Well, I was about to tell you—if you *had* heard opera that for instance in *Mignon*—if you had heard *Mignon*—when the castle is set on fire the guests are there in the garden watching the terrible spectacle and the—er—attendants rush out of the house carrying buckets of water and save the whole story by putting out the fire—a crucial point, you can see—well, I carry the first bucket. And then in *Carmen* I lead in the scene where——"

Dolly Brocksley lifted her head wearily; she looked, as always, thin and cold, and her small blonde face was tired, with hollow circles around her red-rimmed eyes. "She's been crying," thought Deborah, and Dolly said, in a clear, tired voice:

"He means he's a chorus man."

Brocksley repeated: "—in the scene where—" and shot a malevolent look at Dolly, and Lieutenant Waggon said:

"Are you a singer, too, Mrs. Brocksley?"

"No," she said, giving the lieutenant a long weary look and then returning to stare at the tips of her worn little pumps. "I'm a dancer. In the opera ballet. When there is a ballet."

"Ah," said the lieutenant. "Well, Mr. Brocksley, I suppose you leased this place to Miss Monroe."

"Yes." He looked away from his wife and drew himself up again in an important way.

"How long ago was that?"

"About—four years ago, I guess."

The janitor said: "Four."

"Did Miss Monroe live here alone?"

"I already told you——" began the janitor and stopped as Lieutenant Waggon gave him a slow, patient look.

"Yes. That is, I—I believe so," said Brocksley.

Dolly said: "You know it," without looking up from her pumps, and Lieutenant Waggon went on:

"Do you know anything of Miss Monroe's circumstances, Mr. Brocksley?"

"Why, I—I don't know what you mean."

"Well—how did she live? Any facts at all about her way of living that might help us."

"Oh," said Brocksley, looking less tense. "I'm afraid I don't know a thing, Lieutenant."

There was a little pause. Then Lieutenant Waggon's patient eyes wandered around the room again.

"Does anyone?" he said softly.

Deborah thought: "This is the time for me to speak." And immediately Anthony Wyatt was saying quietly: "We don't know much about this, Lieutenant. When do you think the murder occurred? Perhaps to know the time would help us remember something——"

"You can't tell to the minute, Mr. —" he looked at his slip of paper, and the janitor whispered audibly: "Wyatt."—"Mr. Wyatt," continued the lieutenant. "But they think the murder occurred not less than twelve hours before its discovery—not more than eighteen. However, I received only the first report from the medical examiner a few minutes ago. There may be something more definite later."

"It happened some time last night, then?"

"Probably between six o'clock and midnight. But that's not fixed."

"Aren't there any clues at all to the murderer?" asked Anthony Wyatt.

Was he going to tell?

Deborah was so still and rigid that her very heart seemed to have stopped, too.

"Well," said Lieutenant Waggon, "depends upon what you call clues. Has anybody lost a key lately?"

Again the unexpectedness of the question touched them as a small electric shock might have done. There was, however, complete and utter silence. If anyone had lost a key, he did not apparently intend to admit it. The lieutenant shook his head gently and said rather sadly:

"I guess none of you want to know what key it was. Well—I wonder if, just for form's sake, you'd mind telling us something of where you were last night. Each of you."

There was another silence. Then Anthony Wyatt said: "Do you mean you found a key?"

Lieutenant Waggon looked at him.

"No. I just wondered if there was any way for an outsider to let himself through that door from the vestibule into the apartment house. I guess there ain't."

"Oh, you mean that possibly one of us lost a key and the murderer found it and thus got into the apartment house?" asked Francis Maly.

"Well—yes," said Lieutenant Waggon. "But I guess that's out."

Something was tightening in the air of that little room. Something was making itself felt—something obscure but something important. Deborah was staring fixedly at the police officer. And she knew that Chloe was watching, too, and that her hands were clutching the arms of her chair and that Gibbs was grim and angry and Dolly Brocksley had stopped looking at her pumps. And Brocksley was oddly pasty, too, and his eyes had retreated into the fat folds of flesh. Something was going to happen, and Deborah did not know what it would be, but there was a queer little tingle of fright running along her nerves.

"But," said a mellow voice from the corner near the window, "there's the fire escape."

Deborah's head jerked that way.

"Yes, Mr. Tighe," said Lieutenant Waggon agreeably, "there's the fire escape."

The man in the corner moved forward in an oddly lunging way. He was thick and heavily built, with arms and legs that seemed to spread outward from his thick body like spiders' legs, and a heavy-featured, loose-lipped face.

"Anyone," he said huskily, "could have walked up that fire escape and got into this house. Look here, Lieutenant, I'm a busy man. I can't stand around here all day. If you want to see me, you can find me any time—not that I have anything to say about all this. I don't know anything of it at all."

"Oh, all right, Mr. Tighe," said Lieutenant Waggon. "Certainly. I just thought that, since you live directly beneath this house, you might have heard something."

"Well, I didn't," said Mr. Tighe. His voice was throaty and thick but oddly pleasant. He added: "However, I'll send up my—my secretary. Although he knows nothing of it, either."

"Your secretary?" said the lieutenant, looking at the slip of paper. "I thought I'd got everybody that lives here. Does he live here, Mr. Tighe?"

The janitor was a soft, brick red.

"Sure, I forgot the little man," he said. "I forgot him, Lieutenant."

"Oh," said the lieutenant. "*Did* you? Well, what's his name?"

"Pigeon," said Mr. Tighe blandly. "I'll send him right up. No objections to my going, I suppose?"

"Oh, not at all," said Lieutenant Waggon. "What was this you were telling me about the fire escape, Juanito?"

Juanito moved restively, and Tighe halted to listen.

"I was only saying when you asked me, Lieutenant, that it was up."

"You mean——"

"You know good and well what I——"

"I'm asking you again, Juanito," said the lieutenant in a motherly fashion. The janitor's fists opened and closed, and he swallowed.

"Yes, sir," he said tamely. "Well, the bottom of the fire escape is a kind of ladder. Down the last fifteen feet to the ground. Weighted so it can be put up and let down if anybody wants to use it.—Oh, you all know this——"

"Go on, Juanito."

"Well, anyway, sometimes Miss Monroe would ask me to put it down. But yesterday——" He stopped, and Lieutenant Waggon said kindly:

"You mean, the fire-escape ladder can be put up so that no one from the court below could reach it, and yet someone coming down from above could swing it down and continue their—er—descent."

"Lots of them are like that," said Juanito.

"Thus anyone could get out of the apartment house if he wished by means of the fire escape?"

"Yes, sir."

"But nobody could use it as a means of access to the roof?"

"Well, not while it was up. Not without——"

Lieutenant Waggon cut into his words sharply: "And was it up yesterday?"

It was so silent in that room—that crowded room where Mary Monroe had sung and where she had died. No one moved. Probably no one breathed.

"It was up, Lieutenant," said Juanito. "It was up

all day, sir. And it was still up this morning when we found the murder."

There was again silence—a strangely taut and breathless silence. And it was just then that Pigeon appeared in the doorway. He did not speak, he did not make a sound. He simply appeared—a little gray man, with no eyebrows and no hair to speak of, and eyes that were set very close together in an altogether undistinguished face, and that glittered and yet did not seem to move at all.

His appearance was soundless, but Tighe knew somehow that he was there, for he whirled with astonishing lightness and rapidity.

"Oh, there you are, Pigeon," he said and turned again to the lieutenant. "Do you mean to say that you are accusing us of murder! I want to tell you, Lieutenant, you can't get by with stuff like that. I have influence, and I'll see that you——"

"I'm not accusing you," said Lieutenant Waggon. "Just looks like whoever murdered Mary Monroe had to go through the apartment to gain access to the roof. That's all. And since he had to have a key to get into the apartment house——"

"There are a hundred ways to do that," said Tighe. "And you know it."

"No," said Lieutenant Waggon peaceably, "I don't know it. But under the circumstances maybe you folks won't mind telling the boys just where you were last night around seven o'clock. Say from six till—oh, morning."

"Alibis, huh?" exploded Tighe.

"Oh, I wouldn't call it that," said Lieutenant Waggon. "Just a matter of form."

"Form nothing. You're threatening us."

"All right, all right. Have it your own way. Go ahead, boys. Get their names—try to make complete statements, folks. That's always a help."

A little confusion arose as two policemen moved forward; there was a murmur of voices and a shifting of groups. Lieutenant Waggon turned to speak to one of the policemen, and Gibbs Riddle and the men from the first-floor apartment joined in a low-voiced conversation. Deborah found herself standing in the curve of the piano while a policeman asked Chloe her full name and if she had an alibi.

"Five children," snapped Chloe, and Deborah discovered that the tip of one gray oxford was just touching that scrubbed place on the rug and moved rather hurriedly away.

Dolly Brocksley was still sitting in the chair that Deborah had sat in the night before. She was staring dismally at her hands and did not move. Deborah could see Anthony Wyatt's dark head above the little group by the fireplace, but he did not look at her.

What was she going to say when one of those blue-uniformed figures with its pad of yellow paper turned up, questioning, at her own elbow?

She looked rather desperately around her, although she knew there was no way out.

The gray little man with the moveless eyes was all at once beside her. She was sure she had never seen him before, yet there was in his look the strangest quality of recognition and knowingness. Then, though his lips did not move at all, he said in a kind of husky whisper that was still very clear:

"Wonder if they looked for fingerprints on the piano keys."

Deborah could not move or speak. Waves were surging about her, beating in her eardrums, and the room and all the people in it seemed to waver and move away from her.

She said finally in a tight queer voice: "What do you mean?" and the sound of her own voice seemed to come from miles and miles away.

No one was near them except the group of men by the fireplace, and they were talking. Pigeon's mouth did not move at all, yet Deborah heard his thin whisper.

"You know what I mean," he said.

CHAPTER VI

"WHAT'S your name, please?" It was another voice, businesslike and a little bored, and Pigeon slid away as unobtrusively as a little gray spider.

Deborah dragged herself back to a realization of the immediate need. The policeman beside her was chewing a pencil meditatively and studying the pad of paper in his hand. Out of the confusion and terror in her mind she snatched one thought—two. One was that if Pigeon knew of her presence in the house at the time of the murder and had been going to tell, he would have done so at once. The implication in his words and the threat must wait. The second was that Anthony and Chloe had both warned her to keep silent; Anthony because he knew, Chloe because—well, perhaps she guessed or perhaps she knew something that Deborah did not know.

But she could not permit herself to be at the mercy of that little gray man they called Pigeon. The thought was intolerable.

Afterward she realized that she would have gone then and there to Lieutenant Waggon and told him the whole story had not Anthony Wyatt crossed suddenly to her and said:

"What's the matter, Miss Cavert? You look ill—may I——"

The policeman had stopped chewing the pencil and was looking rather sharply at her, and Anthony Wyatt's dark eyes plunged straight into hers and held a message that she could not resist. Yet away back in her mind a doubt of Anthony stirred again. Was she only, in some obscure way, playing into his hands? But again his eyes were imperative and her need was urgent.

"I'm quite all right," she said. "It's—so hot in here. My name is Deborah Cavert."

"How do you spell it?" said the policeman and addressed himself to writing. Anthony's eyes warned her across the pad of papers.

"You live in flat number three?"

"Yes."

"That's on the second floor."

"Yes."

"All right. Now, Miss Cavert, can you remember where you were and what you were doing last night—beginning about six o'clock?"

Deborah was held as if fascinated by Anthony's dark, shining eyes. They warned, they advised, they all but put words into her mouth.

"Why, I—I was here. In the apartment house, I mean. At home. Oh, yes, I went out about seven—just to the—" her thought flashed to the telegram and the possibility of tracing it, and she said: "To the corner. I'd intended to take a walk, but it was windy and I came straight back. I don't suppose I was gone more than five minutes."

"Anything else?"

"Oh—yes, I went across to the Riddles' apartment. That's just across the hall. To borrow a book. Then I spent the whole evening at home."

"Anyone there?"

"Why—why, no. I was alone."

The pencil poised itself over the paper, and the policeman looked at her sharply again.

"Nobody there at all?"

"No. It was the cook's evening out."

"H'm. Well—did you know Mary Monroe?"

Did she? Anthony's eyes shone, and Deborah said:
"Slightly. I'd often heard her sing."

"Lately?"

"I—believe it's been some time since her singing
days," said Deborah carefully and stifled a swift memory of Mary Monroe singing, "The gay sun, the laughing days have gone." She *must* not permit herself to
think of things like that.

"When did you first know of the murder?"

"I was told of it this morning," said Deborah, evad-
ing and hating herself for it and yet thankful that she
could find a way. "Mr. Maly came up to tell me of it
and to see that I was all right."

He wrote "Maly" laboriously and then, surprisingly,
said: "Thank you, miss. That's all now. How about you,
Mr.—er—Wyatt, is it?"

"Anthony Wyatt." His eyes shot Deborah an ap-
proving look and then became guarded.

"All right. What about your alibi?"

"I don't think I have one," said Anthony. "Let me
see. I got home around six—went out again for dinner
and to do a few errands—had dinner at Brascotti's,
but I doubt if anyone would remember me——"

"What time was that?" asked the policeman, scrib-
bling busily.

"About—I don't know exactly. Around seven-thirty,
I expect. Maybe earlier. And I dropped in at a
movie——"

"Where?"

"The Moonbreak, I think they call it. Around the
corner of——"

"What film?"

Anthony hesitated and then said with an effect of frankness:

"I don't know. I simply don't know what the title of it was. A very handsome blonde girl was in it——"

The policeman chewed his pencil thoughtfully.

"Was there a Mickey Mouse?" he said, after a moment.

"Yes, there was."

"What about?"

"He was in a haunted house. A skeleton came up from the——"

A subterranean rumble from the policeman interrupted him.

"Oh . . ." said he indistinctly and with a very pink and bursting face. "That's a good one. Remember the owl? I guess you were there, all right." Anthony was smiling, and the policeman conquered his seizure but remained affable. "Let's see, that show lets out about ten. Then what did you do?"

"I came straight home," said Anthony in an easier tone. "Francis—that is, Francis Maly—was at home, too. We spent the evening in the flat."

"H'm. Let's see now. Oh, yes, did anybody see you when you came home about six?"

The curtain dropped again over Anthony's face.

"Why, no," he said. "I don't think so."

"What's your business, by the way, Mr. Wyatt?"

"I'm a chemist. I work for . . ." He mentioned a large drug-supply company.

"Did you know the deceased?"

"Slightly," said Anthony pleasantly. "She had lots of friends."

"Looks," said the policeman with truth, "as if she

had some enemies. I guess this is all the lieutenant wants right now." He looked at the paper and shook his head regretfully. There was a faint air of comradery about him when he spoke to Anthony that had been entirely missing in Deborah's case. "This ain't much of an alibi," he said. "But then, I guess it's better than these alibis that are too good. There ain't nothing that gets the lieutenant down on anybody quicker than one of these air-tight alibis."

"What's this alibi business for, anyhow, officer? Have they got something definite?"

"Well," said the policeman, "that ain't for me to say. But I guess it's no secret that somebody was up here with Miss Monroe drinking something. There was teacups and things laid out on the table. Two cups."

"But that might not mean a thing."

"Maybe not," said the policeman thoughtfully. "But one of the cups was wiped clean of fingerprints. You can see for yourself what that means." He glanced cautiously around him and lowered his voice, although the murmur and confusion of other voices and movement all around them already masked it sufficiently. "That means that somebody had a reason to wipe off the fingerprints. Therefore that whoever was here drinking tea with her knew something he shouldn't have known about the murder. That's the way it looks, anyhow."

"I see," said Anthony. "Do they have any clues?"

It was too leading a question. The little friendliness remained in the policeman's manner, but he became at once circumspect and businesslike again.

"I wouldn't know about that," he said. "Thank you, Mr. Wyatt." He looked at his notes and moved away. Across the room Chloe was talking to Dolly Brocksley and Alfred Brocksley was posing mountainously against the piano. The man Tighe had gone. Francis Maly's slender brown face and white hair was visible beyond Gibbs Riddle's square shoulders. And as Gibbs Riddle moved suddenly to one side and made an impatient gesture with one square sensitive hand, Deborah saw Pigeon, gray and silent, his eyes still and glittering and yet seeing everything.

Anthony moved nearer her. "Don't let your face give you away," he said in a voice that barely reached her ears.

"But I must know," whispered Deborah jerkily. "What are you going to do? What am I to do? What did you mean when you said I had a motive——"

"*Stop that.*" It was low but as sharp as a lash. It did, however, check incipient hysteria. He continued: "It's a terrible thing to happen, of course. Poor Miss Monroe. . . . What do you think of it, Francis?"

Francis Maly was beside them, looking almost spectacularly handsome with his silver hair and brown face.

"Hello, Miss Cavert," he said. "Why, I don't know. Poor old girl. Was she robbed, do you know?"

As she spoke he glanced idly away. And Deborah thought she alone saw the queer little change in Anthony's face. It was so slight that it was not actually perceptible—yet it was there, and Deborah was conscious of it as one is conscious of a deep-flowing undercurrent below water that is, on the surface, almost still. Perhaps the muscles of his face were suddenly set a bit more firmly; perhaps something only moved and flickered away back in his dark eyes. He said coolly enough: "I don't know. I've heard of nothing."

"Well," said Francis Maly, "it's too bad. But I

don't know—maybe she would have wanted to go swiftly—dramatically. That's the way she must have lived."

"I don't think anybody wants to be murdered," said Deborah crisply, trying not to remember Mary Monroe's face. "I think it's—dreadful." Her breath caught in her throat, and Francis Maly looked at her quickly.

"Yes, of course," he said. "There's always the macabre aspect of the thing. I often wondered just what they think—there must be a second or two of recognition—of——"

"You're frightening Miss Cavert," said Anthony.

"Oh, I say, I'm sorry," said Francis. "You see, Miss Cavert, I write—do feature stories and stuff for syndicates. Also advertising. I keep thinking of the advertising side of it. For instance, just suppose after the publicity this affair will have if it's played up right, Mary Monroe could stage a come-back. That is——" He caught himself quickly as Deborah uttered a little gasp. "Oh, I do beg your pardon, Miss Cavert. Don't mind me. I was only thinking what a waste it was. What——"

"My God, Francis, shut up," said Anthony impatiently. "How much longer will they keep us here? I've got to get to the office some time."

"Well, they don't seem to be accomplishing much. I didn't see any sense to having all of us here, anyhow. Unless Lieutenant Waggon wanted a nice little get-together. Just to get into the spirit of the thing. Still they do say he's pretty good. He——"

Lieutenant Waggon was speaking. He held in one long hand a sheaf of yellow papers, and he was looking fond and motherly. He said:

"I guess that's all for the present, folks. Thanks for

coming up and giving me this information. I expect maybe"—his voice became so kind that it very nearly veiled the meaning his words held—"I expect maybe I'll be seeing some of you later."

That meant, thought Deborah, that each of them was to be interviewed at length—questioned, harried, trapped perhaps into damaging admissions. Under that kindness and back of those calm blue eyes was a living threat, infinitely the worse for being so disguised.

She moved confusedly toward the door.

As she reached it, Pigeon brushed by her and went quietly out onto the roof. He did not look at her, yet she knew that he meant her to see him.

"Come on, Deb," said Chloe's vibrant voice at her side. It sounded, however, a little taut. "Let's get out of this horrible place. Honestly"—they were out the door and on the roof; Anthony was not in sight, but Francis Maly and Gibbs Riddle were just behind them —"honestly," said Chloe with a shaky little laugh that was not one of mirth, "I kept seeing Mary Monroe as plain as life. I believe she was wearing that maroon velvet dress of hers when she was killed."

"Why——" It stuck in Deborah's throat, but Chloe understood.

"Oh, I don't know. Maybe because it's the dress that —she liked. Anyway, I could just see her in it stretched out on the floor. Did you notice that spot on the rug that had been washed? I didn't know that policemen clean up things like that. I expect Juanito had to do it, when they got all through with their examination. I hope it was Juanito."

"Some time, Chloe," said Gibbs Riddle's voice harshly behind them, "you'll realize that you talk too much. You sound ghoulish."

Chloe's eyes hid a little lambent flame. She said: "Look out for the step, Deb. It's slippery."

"I didn't know you knew Mary Monroe," said Deborah. Chloe had gone ahead down the fire escape, and Deborah could see only the thick curls and the turn of her cheek.

"I didn't much," she said composedly over her shoulder.

The door to the third-floor corridor had been propped open. Francis Maly stopped and bent over the lock. His white hair and handsome face was profiled against the light.

"Queer," he said, examining the lock. "This has a spring lock. Nothing was said about how the murderer escaped. He couldn't have come in this way."

"Maybe he went down the fire escape," said Gibbs. "He could do that and swing the thing back up again."

"I suppose so." Francis Maly straightened. "This is, providing it was a man. A woman couldn't have done so. Anyway—I don't think the police were telling all they knew. It seemed to me that there was something underneath all that talk."

Gibbs scowled.

"What?"

"Oh, I don't know." Francis Maly lifted one nicely tailored brown shoulder. "But the general public, even the suspects themselves, seldom know much of what the police are actually doing. They only know the results."

Gibbs's eyes looked black and angry; he said: "Well, I've got to get back to work."

The long narrow corridor echoed their footsteps so intricately that one could not tell which were echoes and which were footsteps. The little old elevator creaked, and the hall and the stairway were dark and empty-looking in spite of the lights that had been turned on. None of them felt inclined to linger and talk.

There was no telegram from Juliet waiting, though Deborah had more than half expected it. And Annie was still inexplicably missing. Blitz inquired with polite earnestness about breakfast, and he and Deborah shared what she could find in the refrigerator and the milk that was waiting on the back porch. Again as she reached for the milk and cream bottles standing there, Deborah was conscious of the fire escape winding upward to the house on the roof, and again she closed the door sharply and bolted it.

Surely Anthony Wyatt would somehow manage to communicate with her. There was nothing she could do, no course she could plan until she had talked to him. Until she had asked him certain questions. But the slow morning dragged on, and no one came and no one rang the bell.

About noon, in order to get away from the endless circle of conjecture and questions that haunted her, she took Blitz for a walk. Leaving the apartment house, she was a little surprised at its quiet. There were no police, no reporters, no ghoulish clusters of sight-seers. She was to learn later that the reporters had come and gone hours ago and that Lieutenant Waggon was known and liked for his fairness to the press. Now the only indication of the seething activity that, unknown to Deborah, that dignified entrance had witnessed earlier in the morning, was Juanito mopping up the prints of many feet on the marble steps. He nodded surlily at Deborah's word, and she turned toward the lake with Blitz tugging at the end of his leash.

It was cold and gray and cheerless with, now, a hint of snow in the air. Christmas shoppers were pouring along the Drive toward the bridge and Loop, and passing limousines already had holly wreaths dangling in rear windows. It was one of those still days when every sound is muffled and every motion is made quietly and a bit sluggishly and the very air seems to wait. Deborah felt remote and distant from the world that flowed quietly and serenely past her; as if she were viewing it enviously from a strange and distant planet.

18 East Eden loomed darkly above her as she turned in again at those marble steps. Its weather-stained gray stone looked heavy and somber, and the shreds of ivy clung to it raggedly and without much spirit. A few lights were on here and there, owing to the darkness of the day, but they did not lessen the look of grimness and of secret brooding. It had changed overnight, thought Deborah. It had become subtly and intangibly charged with the violence it had known. Or was the change only in her own feeling? Perhaps; yet in the strangest way those old walls seemed to know what had happened. They seemed to know and, even, to wait with hushed, dark expectancy for what was going to happen.

It was not a pleasant thought.

Neither was it pleasant to stand there at the top of the steps in the vestibule with the maroon velvet ghost of Mary Monroe again at her elbow while she unlocked the inner door. Blitz pulled at the leash and as usual wrapped it around Deborah's ankles as they entered. The hall was dim, and a heavy silence lay over it. Not a sound came from either of the tall, dark oak doors that led to the Brocksley apartment on the right and the apartment on the left that was shared by Anthony and Francis Maly.

The telephone was ringing when she opened the door, and she reached it in time to reply. It was Annie, and the little mystery of her absence was explained, for Annie in worried Irish accents said she was quarantined. She'd gone to spend her day out with her daughter, and baby Annie had the scarlet fever and Annie had to stay and Holy Mother of God, what would Miss Deborah do with Miss Juliet gone and all?

"I'll be all right, Annie," said Deborah, over a sudden lump in her throat. "Don't worry."

But Annie did worry and told her of it at length. She had promised Miss Juliet to look after her. But how was she to know that little Annie would go and take the scarlet fever?

"Sure and she's terrible sick, the poor lamb," said Annie, choking.

Deborah said everything comforting that she could think of and put down the telephone. That meant, then, that she and Blitz were to continue to be alone. She would miss Annie's cheerful presence and the knowledge that someone else was in that long, too roomy flat. She took off her hat and strolled aimlessly into the drawing room. And it was there that she saw the mimosa and very nearly screamed.

The soft yellow plumes glowed above a green vase which stood nonchalantly on a table. Deborah stared incredulously.

It *was* her green vase. It was certainly the mimosa that had stood on Mary Monroe's piano.

How had it got here?

And how had it got here while she was out and the door locked?

Her knees were shaking, and she sat down, staring at the mimosa and paying no attention to Blitz who was whining at the crack of the outside door.

She strove to think clearly. When had she last looked

in the drawing room? Not that morning—not since the night before. Then it could have been returned during any of the time since. She'd been out just twice. Once during the inquiry that morning. Once, just now, for the walk with Blitz. Both times the door was locked securely behind her. And the mimosa couldn't have been returned during the night before, because she would have known it. She felt chilled at the fleeting thought of someone's entering the flat while she slept and did not know it, and she dismissed it at once, because, had that happened, Blitz would have barked.

He would have barked, too, had anyone entered while she was in the house on the roof during the morning. But no one would have heard and come to investigate, because they were all on the roof. Then if they were all on the roof there was no one to return the mimosa—she caught herself quickly, for that was to assume that the murderer of Mary Monroe was among that all too limited number who lived in one house, separated from each other only by walls and corridors. And besides, it was not, certainly, the murderer who had returned the mimosa; there would be neither rhyme nor reason in that.

Probably it had been returned while she was out with Blitz. But then, where had it been in the intervening time? It had not been in Mary Monroe's crowded room that morning.

And *who* had brought it back to her? Who had known it belonged to her? The janitor might have a key to the apartment. Chloe might have recognized the vase. But that would mean that Chloe had been in the house on the roof, too, that night. Or at least that she knew something of the affair. Of course, there was Anthony Wyatt, too.

Blitz whined again, and a queer, vague feeling that there might be someone or something in the place then seized Deborah, and she rose and Blitz preceded her. They searched together every square foot of the apartment, Blitz sniffing and standing by eagerly, ears alert and eyes bright and tail quivering, while she looked in closets and—half ashamed—under beds. There was no one there.

Perhaps it was the police—who had brought it in order somehow to trap her into admitting what she knew of the murder.

But that didn't seem sensible, either. Blitz sat down and scratched his ear absorbedly and the telephone rang again.

She knew it would be Anthony before she replied, and it was. And he wanted to know if he could come up to see her. "Right away," he said. "I've not much time."

He arrived a moment later and she led him into the drawing room and they sat down, each eyeing the other rather after the fashion of polite duellers sizing up each other's strength and skill.

"Have a cigarette?" said Anthony, leaning forward. His dark soft hair was now smooth and unruffled. His eyes were lowered to the light he held and were shadowed and inscrutable. His mouth was unexpectedly sensitive, seen so close; yet firm enough, too, above a slightly obstinate and square chin. He was about the same height as Gibbs Riddle, but where Gibbs was hard and square Anthony looked elastic and unbelievably quick.

Then he looked into her face, and Deborah caught the gleam of small gold lights, warm and sherry-colored now, away back in his eyes. He seemed about to say

something when the small flame of the match reached
his fingers and he moved and dropped it in an ashtray.
When he turned toward her again, a kind of curtain
had dropped somewhere over his face, and Deborah felt
faintly but curiously disappointed.

Then the full realization of what his presence there
meant swept over her, and she leaned forward and said:
"Tell me. Tell me everything. I must know."

A little cloud of cigarette smoke drifted between
them.

"There's not much to tell," he said thoughtfully,
watching her. "Except that the police do not know that
you were with Mary Monroe when she was killed.—Of
course," said Anthony, "that's not fair at all to the
police. It's—well, it's pretty bad from that viewpoint.
So you'll have to give me your word not to—escape."

"I won't escape," said Deborah coldly. "But if you
think I murdered her, how can you trust me to keep my
promise?"

"I don't," said Anthony Wyatt. "But I'd rather take
the chance than—well, I'd hate to see any girl dragged
through murder if she had nothing to do with it. Especially when she wouldn't have a chance in the world.
And, of course, I'd better warn you right now that if—
if it seems the thing to do I shall be obliged to tell them
what I saw."

"And produce me?" said Deborah in a still voice.

"Exactly," said Anthony Wyatt.

It sounded honest. Yet—in protecting her he had also
protected himself. In all this talk of police he had not
offered to tell them of his own presence. Yet if, later, he
told that she was there, it was automatically an admission that he was there, too. She was confused and

perplexed. There were so many things she must know. So many questions she must ask. She leaned forward. "Do you——" she said and stopped. After all, looking at him, realizing that so far he had shielded her, it was altogether impossible to say in effect: *Did you murder Mary Monroe?*

Her face was suddenly hot, and he looked at her and knew what she had been about to say. He smiled unexpectedly.

"No," he said calmly. "I didn't murder her. That's what you wanted to know, isn't it? I didn't murder her, and I didn't call the police because—because I thought it best not to. I couldn't help things, and I could do—a great deal of harm by calling them. That may not sound sensible, but it happens to be true."

"Why—why were you there——"

His face hardened, and he avoided her eyes.

"I had to see Miss Monroe about—about some business. I don't blame you for asking, but it really had nothing to do with all this. And if it's the revolver I had that you are worrying about, why, I assure you I didn't murder Mary Monroe with it. Of course—you may not want to believe that, and I can't, now, prove it to you, but it's—well, it's true. Anything else?" finished Anthony in a lighter tone which sounded a little forced.

"Yes," said Deborah slowly, "there is something else. Why did you tell me that I—had a motive for killing Mary Monroe? What did you mean? Is that why you said I wouldn't have a chance in the world? You must——" She choked a little in her earnestness and had to repeat: "You *must* tell me."

She could not read his face except that, again, she

knew somehow that something in his manner had swiftly changed. His eyes looked cold and removed. He took the cigarette from his lips.

"See here," he said abruptly. "We'd get along a lot better if you'd tell me the truth."

CHAPTER VII

In DREAMS one beats one's hands against doors that will not open, against walls that remain impassable, against gates that are bolted. But Deborah was not dreaming.

"But I am telling the truth," she cried futilely. "I don't know what you mean. I had no possible motive. You——"

"Let me ask you a few questions." Anthony rose abruptly, his clipped voice cutting into Deborah's scarcely coherent protests. He went to the window and lounged against the window casing, his hands thrust in his pockets and little wreaths of blue and beige cigarette smoke floating around his head.

"What did you do after I left the room last night—in the house on the roof, I mean?"

"I came back here."

"Then what?"

"Well—that's all. And waited for the police."

"Are you sure that's all?"

"Yes. Except that I did go out for a few minutes. About seven o'clock."

"Why?"

Deborah hesitated.

"To send a telegram. I thought I met you there near the entrance. At least, it was someone like——"

He had swung around, his face looking suddenly grim and white.

"*To send a telegram? What about?*"

89

"To my aunt. I was afraid my father would read the papers and——"

He strode toward her, towering above her and looking angrily down into her face.

"What did you say? In God's name, what did you say?"

"I said—I said to keep papers away from Father. That was all. I signed it Deb." It had seemed so safe. No one had known. She said aloud: "No one knew."

He uttered a sound that was like a groan and pushed one hand furiously through his hair so it was ruffled again.

"No one knew! Oh, my God—I ought to have told you. But you didn't give me time. Don't you realize— oh, of course you don't." He stopped, stared down at her, and then said with a touch of exasperation: "You must be innocent. You'd never do such darn fool things if you weren't."

"You mean they'll trace the telegram?"

"They'll trace everything. I know something of Lieutenant Waggon."

"And my telegram was sent before the murder was discovered. That's what you mean?"

"That's what I mean."

"But papers," said Deborah slowly, "might refer to anything. Might be—stocks, or letters, or—or financial news."

"Might be," said Anthony. "But I don't suppose Waggon will think of anything but newspapers. Look here, have you done anything else like that?"

"No——"

"Out with it? What?"

"It's nothing I did," said Deborah. "I want to know if it was you or the police that returned the mimosa."

"Mimosa? Where?"

She pointed, and watched his face as she explained.

"You're sure it's the same?" he said after a moment.

"Oh, yes. At least it's my vase. And I left it in the house on the roof."

"When—how was it returned?"

She told him.

"I didn't do it," he said. "And I can't think who—— Does the janitor have a key to your flat?"

"I suppose so. I don't know."

He looked at the soft yellow feathers thoughtfully.

"Well, that's a crazy sort of twist," he said finally. "I can't think how on earth—or why—— Of course, it might be the police, but even so there wouldn't be any reason——" He sheered abruptly. "Look here, does anyone else know that you were in the house on the roof last night?"

"Yes." Deborah's hands clutched together, but she said steadily: "I think the man they called Pigeon knows. He——"

Anthony had whirled back, pouncing toward her again.

"Has he said anything to you? What makes you think he knows?"

"He told me. He said—said something about finger-prints on the piano keys. And when I said, what did he mean, he said—well, he only said that I knew what he meant. And, of course, I did know. But I can't ex-press—— The words themselves—just the words—don't mean what he meant. That is, I felt—threatened. As if he's going to do something about it. As if——"

Anthony's jaw had become as hard and tight as Gibbs Riddle's in one of his worst tempers.

"Oh, so he's going to do something about it, is he?" he said. "We'll see about that. Is that all he said?"

"Yes. There wasn't a chance for more. There were people all around."

"You've not seen him since?"

"No."

"He didn't——" Anthony hesitated and then said: "He didn't mention knowing that I was there, too, did he?"

"No."

He looked down at her for a moment.

"You know who he is, don't you?" he said finally.

"They said he was secretary to the man who lives on the top floor."

Anthony looked impatient.

"Does he look like a secretary to anything but a sawed-off shotgun?" he demanded. Deborah was obliged to admit that he didn't, and Anthony went on swiftly: "He's Tighe's bodyguard. Everybody knows it. And there's not a wilier little snake in existence. He's also a dead shot, as quick as an eel, and, unfortunately, smart. Otherwise Tighe wouldn't hire him."

"Who's Tighe?"

Again Anthony looked at her with a mingling of exasperation and solicitude.

"My dear child," he said, "Tighe is Tighe. No other description need apply. He's just one of the mysteries of a great city. Don't try to understand. Just whisper his name to the policeman the next time you are held for a traffic violation."

"Do you mean he's a gangster?"

"No." Anthony shook his head sadly. "Listen to me. He's smooth and he's smart—not quite as smart as little Pigeon, maybe, but smart. And he's got his fat fingers in a lot of pies and he's . . . well, he's Tighe. And he's always on the side of the law, somehow. He lives quietly up there on the top floor. Pigeon cooks for him and keeps the flat in perfect order, and they say it's something of a sight to see Pigeon beating up a nice cake, with a revolver in his apron pocket. What's the matter?"

"I was only thinking of Juliet," said Deborah rather faintly. "And what she would say if she knew."

"Juliet. That's your aunt."

"Yes." She thought suddenly: "How did you know that?" His face, however, had hardened faintly, and there was all at once that subtle barrier between them again, so she did not say it. She said instead: "If Pigeon knew that I was there he must have been on the roof, too. Perhaps it was he——"

"Who murdered Mary Monroe?—I don't know." He was frowning. "Look here," he said. "Is there anything else you haven't told me—I mean anything that seemed, oh—unusual. After you ran away last night did you do anything that you haven't told me—or hear anything or see anything? It might be some very small thing but still be significant."

"Yes," said Deborah. "There was—when I came down from the roof, you know—there was someone on the fire escape——" Remembered terror clutched at her throat, and her voice wavered and caught.

"On the fire escape?"

She told him briefly, and her own feeling must have communicated itself to him, for he went suddenly rather white around the mouth. But he walked away to the window again and stood looking into the street and said in a queer voice: "You ought to have waited for me. I ought not to have let you go down alone."

"Do you think," said Deborah, trying to steady her voice which distressed her by shaking—"do you think it was the—murderer——" The last word was whispered, and Anthony whirled.

"No," he cried loudly. "Certainly not! No—but look here." His voice was rough and his face still very white. "You've got to be careful. I mean—don't take any chances with—with anybody. Understand?"

Deborah did understand.

She said hurriedly: "Where did you go? What did you do?"

"There was someone in the back of the house. I'm not sure who it was. We played a ghostly kind of hide and seek among the"—he hesitated briefly and then said: "among the rooms, and then he got away from me. I went back and you were gone, too, and then I hurried down the fire escape and through the apartment house and made a kind of circuit of the whole neighborhood but couldn't find anybody I thought looked suspicious." He glanced at her sharply. "I expect that sounds a little lame, but that's what I did. I was terribly relieved to meet you on the street but didn't—didn't want to stop."

"You told the police you went to a movie," said Deborah slowly.

"Yes. And I really did. But not for long."

"And you don't know who was in the back room?" asked Deborah.

"No. That is—no."

"It might have been Pigeon—mightn't it?"

"Yes, it might have been. But—a sort of queerish thing happened. I—— Do you know this tune? Listen——"

He began to whistle softly. Blitz came trotting in and sat down and watched him appreciatively. But all at once Blitz and the mimosa and the long, green damask

curtains and the polished mahogany of Cavert heir-
looms dropped away and Deborah was back in a
crowded room with the wind whispering around a black
and shadowy roof outside. She stood, her hands at her
throat.

"You know it," said Anthony and stopped whistling.

"It's—it's the 'Elégie,'" said Deborah with stiff lips.
"It's the song Mary Monroe was singing when she died.
She had just sung—'*Les jours riants sont partis*——'"

"And they were gone for her," said Anthony rather
grimly after a moment. "Do you—— Are you a mu-
sician?"

"No. I can—oh, play a little on the piano—as I can
speak a little French and drive a car adequately—that
sort of thing."

"You didn't go to the piano, did you—while I was
in the back of the house, last night?"

"No."

There was a little silence. Outside in the hall was the
faint clang of the elevator door, and Blitz barked once.

"Well," said Anthony Wyatt, "I—— You see, I
heard someone at the piano. And I thought it was you.
And whoever it was, was playing 'Elégie.' It was light
and soft and sort of hesitant. Like a ghost touching the
keys." He did not appear to hear Deborah's muffled
little gasp. "I thought it was you, of course."

"But it wasn't! I didn't touch the piano!"

"I didn't see who it was, I only heard that sound. It
stopped before I—could get back into the room. When
I did come back you were gone and there was no one
there. Except, of course, Mary—the body."

Deborah said something breathless and incoherent,
and he looked quickly at her.

"Don't be frightened," he said. "Don't look like that.

Hadn't you better—sit down—or do you want a drink or something——"

He was above her again, his warm lean hand upon her wrist.

Deborah's eyes were dark in her white face. "But it couldn't have been Mary Monroe. She was dead."

"Of course. Here——" He pulled her toward the divan and sat down beside her, holding both her cold hands in his. "I didn't mean—you mustn't—don't tremble like that, Deborah. It's all right. It's just that somebody was there and I want to know who it was. It might help, you see."

"The song——" began Deborah shakily and stopped because she couldn't say anything more, and he said something indistinct and put his arm around her drawing her close against him. Her cheek was pushing into his shoulder, and his arms slowly tightened and there was a queer silent moment that was still somehow full and confused.

Then quite suddenly he was standing.

"See here," he said abruptly. "Have you had anything to eat? Any sleep?"

"Yes. All I wanted."

"You don't look it. You're as white as a little wraith. Nerves like wires. Well, I don't blame you." He was lighting a cigarette with elaborate care while Deborah sat back among the cushions and her cheek felt hot and pink where it had pressed against him. He flicked the spent match into the ashtray and said as if he'd come to some decision:

"I've been thinking a lot about this, of course. And I don't know whether I'm right or not, but I want to ask you to—trust me."

"Trust you?"

"Just that. I mean—well, you asked me what I meant by saying that you had a motive for murdering Mary Monroe."

Deborah was sitting abruptly erect.

"*Yes*——"

"Well, that's one thing that I think we'd better not go into. There's a good reason for it. In fact, I—— There's no other way that's safe."

"I don't understand you."

He gave her a long look. Then he stooped and patted Blitz and turned toward the door.

"I've got to go," he said. She rose and stood there clutching the polished arm of an old chair. Her hair shone brightly, and her eyes were dark and she looked very small and pale. He paused with his hand on the doorknob.

"I'd like to believe you," he said. "Good-bye." He opened the door and then closed it as if in afterthought. "If you get scared or—want anything, give me a ring, will you? I'll come straight up." He looked at her again, paused and said: "Shall I come up tonight—or maybe you'd go to dinner with me? After we've got the newspapers and know more about where we stand."

"Yes. Yes, I'd like to," said Deborah.

He nodded without smiling and was gone.

But she had no motive at all for murdering anyone—certainly not a woman she hadn't even known.

She ought to be able to convince him of it. She ought to be quite cool and calm and reasonable about it but very firm. So that he would listen. And believe.

He'd said he wanted to believe her. And he'd asked her to trust him. Perhaps he actually knew more of the thing than he had let her know. Perhaps, even, he could see a clear way out of it for both of them.

She'd said or implied that she would trust him, but there wasn't much choice in the matter. And she did feel gradually a little relieved and hopeful, though certainly there was no real reason to do so. She thought again of a lawyer but decided, again, to wait. A secret such as she possessed was better shared as little as possible.

Pigeon, of course, remained an uncertain quantity. But she could do nothing about that, either, just then.

Again she could only wait. And travel that already well-worn path of fear and doubt and question. There were even then certain gates that, in her mind, she left unopened. Labyrinths whose dark entrances she passed hurriedly.

That afternoon of December 7th was to loom in the memory of all the people living in 18 East Eden an oasis of calm. A breathing space. An interval of quiet and a kind of static peace.

They ought to have been grateful for it. Instead, they went their usual ways, concerned about the murder of the previous night but not, for the most part, deeply. They did not know, and there was no way to know, what had been let loose in the dim spaces of the old house. It was only later that they understood how terribly and with what directness it concerned them—and then it was too late.

Later Deborah was to remember almost incredulously that after Anthony's departure she had felt a little relieved and as if things might smooth themselves out after all. And that she had slept a little there on the divan where Anthony had sat beside her, and waking had romped with the dog and pretended not to see the mimosa. Once, it is true, when she heard the clang of the elevator door she had gone to her own door, and hearing Chloe's voice outside, had opened it. Chloe in a dark hat and coat—which on Chloe immediately became, somehow, daring—was herding four small children and two weary-looking spaniels into the elevator, and Tulip, also ready for the street, was standing beside her holding a fat and ruffled baby.

"We're going to the country," said Chloe. "Put your hat on, Mary—take your thumb out of your mouth, Junior. No, no, don't touch the electric button. Stand in front of the panel, Tulip, so they can't reach the elevator switch. How are you, Deb?"

"Are you all going?" asked Deborah.

Chloe glanced sharply at her.

"Oh, no, I'm taking the kids to Mother's. She's heard of the m-u-r-d-e-r——"

"Murder," said Gibbs Junior hardily.

"Not at all," interpolated Chloe swiftly.—"So Mother called up and demanded that they be removed. She said there was no telling what might happen. I'm taking them out to her. And the dogs."

The dogs looked sad and sought a corner of the elevator.

Beyond Chloe, Deborah caught a glimpse of Tulip's eyes showing whites as they roved uneasily toward the stairway and dim shadows back of the elevator shaft. She said hurriedly:

"It'll be a nice change for them."

"Yes," said Chloe. "That's why I'm sending them." She glanced at Tulip with a touch of defiance. "You see, Tulip, Miss Deborah agrees with me. I'm sending them only because the change will be good for them."

Tulip, who had had time to forget the rather pleasur-

able excitement of the morning, said, "Yes'm" skepti-
cally and looked over her shoulder.

Chloe appeared faintly baffled. "Well, there's certainly nothing to be afraid of now, Tulip," she said
sharply.

"No'm," said Tulip, and looked over the other shoulder.

Chloe bit her full lower lip, and some of the dark
crimson paste stayed on her teeth.

"I wish Mother had thought to send a car for us,"
she said to Deborah. "However, I intend to taxi all the
way out and then simply walk into the house and let
Watts do what he will about the bill."

"Watts," said Gibbs Junior with an anticipatory look,
"is Grandmother's butler. He has corns. We have no
butler. We have only Tulip. Hurry up, Chloe, before the
twins get to fighting."

Chloe separated two brooding four-year-olds whose
incipient wriggles had been detected by her oldest son,
and regarded her offspring helplessly.

"Just look, Deb," she said. "A whole elevator full of
progeny. That's what happens to romance. Unbridled
motherhood——"

Tulip put out a firm black hand to close the door,
and as the little elevator droned out of sight, Chloe's
voice floated upward:

"I'll be back in an hour or two, Debbie."

The hall was very quiet after they had gone. Chloe's
voice hadn't seemed quite natural. And she was hurrying the children away. Why? The murder had already
happened. Deborah went back to the quiet drawing
room with its gleaming mahogany and thin old rugs.
But something had happened to the false calm of the
afternoon, and when Blitz brought an old slipper and

pushed it at her hand she hadn't the heart to play with him. It was growing late and would soon be time to turn on the lights. Just about this time the previous day she'd met Mary Monroe.

She plunged again into the macabre speculations that lay in wait for her whichever way she turned. And for the first time she began to try to answer certain questions. To most of them there was no answer. And there was not even a conjecture about the most important one, and that was, who had stood on the roof in a twilight like the one now falling, and fired the shot that had killed Mary Monroe? Again Deborah could see the tall red figure crumple and fall and become empty and drained of life.

Was that why Mary Monroe had watched the door and watched the window? Had she known what was coming?

But if she had known she could have stopped it, somehow—she wasn't obliged simply to stay there waiting for it.

After all, why had she insisted upon Deborah coming to take tea with her? Had she something to say to her —something perhaps to do with that mysterious motive that Anthony imputed to her? And that he wouldn't talk of—and that yet made him withdraw from her when she asked him—as she surely had a right to do— what he meant by it.

Deborah shook her head impatiently and went back to Mary Monroe.

Perhaps she had only been frightened and had wanted Deborah's company—had wanted anyone's company. And then she sang the "Elégie." And died.

Who was it who had played that melody after Deborah had gone?

Light and soft, like a ghost touching the keys, he'd

said. But there was no one in the room—no one but Mary Monroe. And Deborah had seen no one on the roof. And there was no sensible reason at all for anyone to enter that death-laden room and touch the piano—actually play the accompaniment for a song. And a song that Mary Monroe had been singing and now would never sing again.

It was as if some untetherable echo had lingered in the room, repeating itself. But that was, of course, impossible. Human fingers had to touch those keys.

Gradually it began to seem important and significant, chiefly for its utter lack of logic. If Anthony only had discovered who dared sit at that piano immediately above the dead woman and touch the piano keys! And there were so many things she hadn't asked Anthony and that she must know. With him she had been somehow defensive; she'd felt, which was all wrong, as if he were weighing everything she said, questioning it, balancing it in his mind against other things she said. Didn't he yet believe that she had not murdered Mary Monroe? Was he still not quite convinced?

Deborah rose and moved to the window. Below, the street was growing darker, and soft blobs of yellow radiance that were street lights were beginning to glow here and there. Directly across the street was a decorous row of brick and brownstone fronts, their windows correct and inscrutable. She wondered whether the people living so quietly behind those curtains were, some of them, looking out toward 18 East Eden—wondering what was going on in its dim, roomy flats.

Odd how silent the place was. It lay all around her, secret and still and brooding.

There was some scrap of melody repeating itself over and over in the back of her mind, and suddenly it came

to the surface. "*Oh, doux printemps, d'autre fois. . . .*"
The "Elégie," of course.

Almost violently she rejected the errant musical
phrase, and Mary Monroe's voice came up out of the
confused and terrible tangle of memories and it was
saying huskily: "It's a queer thing that you should have
chosen that particular song. You see, the last time I
sang that——" What had she said, then? Deborah
couldn't remember, and she sought for it, and then
knew that Mary Monroe had looked at her as if she
were conscious of her, Deborah's, presence and had
forgotten it while she had talked of the song. And she
had stopped abruptly and said: "Oh, well—I'll sing it"
and had added something about being a child of fate.

But a song couldn't do murder. Mary Monroe was
shot. A song . . . Deborah fumbled blindly along strange
avenues of thought. A song could have some sort of
significance. Could have meant something to Mary
Monroe, as it certainly had reminded her of something
that had happened the last time she sang it. And then
she'd sung it for, literally, the last time.

A car drove up below and a woman, foreshortened and
only a dark figure in the rapid dusk, got out and entered
the apartment house. Chloe, probably. Returned already.

What sound had taken Anthony so quickly into those
back rooms of the house on the roof? It had indicated
certainly that someone must be there, but what had
that curious little sound been? And exactly what had
he done and where had he gone? He had said so little,
really, during their talk; but there'd not been time for
everything that needed to be said in those short moments. She thought of one moment during which nothing at all had been said and then sheered swiftly away

from it. He'd felt sorry for her, of course; and he was sensitive and probably kind and certainly must hate the position in which she had placed him.

The doorbell rang, stabbing shortly through the silence. Blitz bounded upward, barking, and Deborah went to the annunciator telephone, set in its small panel in the wall of the narrow entrance hall.

It was Francis Maly, and he wanted to know if she had the newspapers or cared to look at them.

He came up at once, a great bundle of newspapers under his arm. She turned on the lights nervously and hoped he had forgotten or had failed to note her betraying confusion of the morning when he had told her, expecting it to be a shock, of the murder of Mary Monroe. She must be very calm—guarded, but calm. His first words, however, while innocent enough, were not exactly conducive to calm on Deborah's part.

"The mimosa's nice," he said idly. "First I've seen. Well, I've got all the available papers. But you don't need to look at them all, for they've practically the same story." He sat down at her gesture and pushed the bundle of newspapers from him and looked at her. His eyes, Deborah discovered, were actually so dark a blue that she'd thought them brown. His fine face with its peaked chin was brown, and his hair looked startlingly white above it. The lamp spread a soft glow downward, and she perceived that he was older than she'd thought him; older and there were fine patient lines at the corners of his mouth and eyes. He leaned a little nearer, and Deborah had an uneasy fear that he was looking straight through to the ugly secret that lay behind her own gaze. She lowered her eyelids protectively, and Francis Maly said directly:

"What's the matter with Anthony?"

CHAPTER VIII

IT WAS the last thing she had expected. Juliet's training, however, was thorough, and Deborah thought he didn't know that the abrupt question had startled and confused her. She said slowly:

"Anthony? Why, I don't know. Why?"

She tried to make her own eyes open and candid under the thrust of those direct blue eyes opposite. Did he know? Did he suspect?

"He's not himself," he said, watching her. "He's worried about something. I thought you might know what's wrong. He—— I'm terribly fond of Anthony, you know. I'd hate to let him get involved in something that would——"

"Would what?" said Deborah steadily.

"Oh . . ." Francis Maly's slender brown hands moved. "Oh, that would be bad for him," he said lightly.

He waited, and presently Deborah said:

"I think you'd better say what you mean."

"Oh, my dear child, don't look so stern. I meant nothing. I only asked because I know you and Anthony are friends and I thought he might have said something —or that you might know—— You see, he's so frightfully worried about something. Not at all like himself."

"Have you asked him?" said Deborah.

He looked at her and laughed. "I did, and do you know what he said? He said 'Oh, go to hell!' And I

think he meant it," added Francis Maly rather rue-
fully. He was suddenly likable. "I do assure you that
I'm not trying to pry into my friend's affairs. You see,
Anthony and I have shared the same apartment for
two years. We've learned to know each other pretty
well, and I'm enough older than he to feel a kind of—
I suppose you'd call it protective instinct. It's silly, of
course, for certainly Anthony Wyatt of all people is
fully capable of taking care of himself. My excuse is
that I'm rather a lonely sort of person. And he——
Well, as I said, I'm pretty fond of him. I thought he
might have told you——" He paused and then added
slowly and with a kind of reluctance that was in itself
alarming to Deborah: "It's just last night and today
that I've noticed it."

The words lay between them in a small, too meaning
silence while Deborah wondered what she could say.
Evidently his suspicions had been aroused; as evidently
there was more than a tinge of disapproval in his bearing. She was not sufficiently worldly to weigh and measure the possible effect of that disapproval. But she did
recognize that faint, troublesome suspicion. What did
he know—what had he guessed—what could she say
that would shatter his doubt? All at once Blitz was
whining somewhere—whining and scratching and Deborah was aware of it. She said:

"Something's the matter—I'd better see——" and
rose, thankful for the interruption. Francis rose, too,
quickly and was at her side as she entered the hall.
Blitz looked up and growled and then thrust his nose
against the crack below the outside door and again
listened.

"Odd," said Francis. "What's the matter, old
fellow?"

Blitz scratched at the door once again and listened.

"Something's out there," said Deborah in a queer voice that was not her own.

Francis Maly looked at her in a startled way.

"In the hall, you mean? I wonder." He put his slender brown hand on the doorknob and swung the heavy old oak door wide open. Blitz bounded out on stiff white legs, but the hall beyond and the descending stairs were empty.

"The door back of the elevator?" said Deborah. And Francis Maly gave her one sharp look and then went quickly across the hall. As he disappeared behind the elevator Deborah followed and was in time to see him open the small door leading to the narrow corridor that ran the full length of the apartment house, as on the third floor.

"No one there," he said, closing the door and returning. "I think Blitz was having a dream."

But Blitz, puzzled, insisted upon sniffing furiously along the carpeted floor to the stairway until Deborah coaxed him into the flat again. And then he was sulky and growled a little and retreated into one of the bedrooms.

"What's in the papers?" Deborah asked as they returned to the drawing room. "Anything we don't know?"

"Well," Francis Maly said pleasantly, "I don't know how much you know. But there's not really much there. A résumé of Mary Monroe's career, but that's public property anyway and nothing that offers much reason for her murder. So far they've been really very decent to us all and have, in most of the papers, soft-pedaled the police department's suggestion that somebody living in the house murdered her. At least, there's no mention of the point about the keys that Lieutenant Waggon made—and not very successfully, I thought. However, I expect they aren't telling all they know. The police, I mean. And then the news about the new strike broke today and has rather crowded everything else off the pages. Want to look at them. Here's the best . . ."

They were still looking at papers when Anthony arrived. And somehow, Deborah never quite knew how, Francis went with them to dinner.

She could hear the two men talking when she went to put on her hat, and she gave the small gray thing a rather vicious tug over her right eye as she realized that in all probability he would do so.

Blitz, looking worried and unhappy, refused to watch them leave.

"I'll leave lights on for him," thought Deborah and knew that it wasn't for Blitz that she was turning on every light in the long flat before leaving it and while she could hear the comforting murmur of men's voices coming from the drawing room.

They went around the corner to Brascotti's and sat at a small table next the wall, surrounded by shaded red lights and the din of an orchestra and clouds of cigarette smoke.

Anthony sat across the table from Deborah and looked withdrawn and thoughtful, and Francis Maly, after cocktails, was pleasant and urbane, and made conversation—rather desultory conversation owing to the spasmodic submerging of themselves and everything around them in waves of music.

It was Francis, too, who demanded café royale and burned the brandy and sugar himself for it, his brown hands steady and adroit above each cup and the tiny blue flames reflecting themselves in his intent eyes.

And it was very good and cheered what had been a somewhat somber dinner, and later they danced, Deborah dancing first with Francis, who was light and graceful as a feather and barely touched her as they moved, and then with Anthony. Anthony wasn't as good a dancer as Francis; Deborah was oddly conscious of his arm around her body holding her rather tightly against him as the floor became crowded, of her fingers in his hand. There were more and more dancers all around them on the dim, crowded space.

The orchestra became muted, and someone took a megaphone and began to sing softly: "Let's—fall in love. Why shouldn't we—fall in love. . . ." Queer, thought Deborah vaguely, how wistful and strangely stirring popular dance tunes contrived to be. How poignant so that they got into you as if through little chinks in your armor and you were suddenly wistful and longing and wanted—oh, something—you didn't know quite what. But that wasn't original. Hadn't somebody said something like that in a play one time—only much less sentimentally? Deborah couldn't remember. And anyway it was probably the pleasing effect of the café royale. She lifted her eyelids. Anthony was looking over her head, his chin just about at the scarlet feather in her hat.

And then the dance stopped and Anthony said: "You look awfully—awfully sweet." He hesitated and added quickly: "That's a nice little hat—where's our table . . ." He was guiding her through the maze of tables and dancers, and Francis Maly was getting to his feet and smiling, but suggesting their departure. Deborah would have liked another dance.

They left her, still collectively, at her door, and there

was no way in which she could tell Anthony that she wanted desperately to talk to him.

"Give us a ring," said Francis, "if—oh, if anything frightens you—and we'll be up in full force. Not that you won't be all right."

Anthony frowned at that.

"You aren't all alone, are you?" he said. "I thought there was a servant here——"

Deborah explained Annie briefly and said she would go to Chloe Riddle if she felt lonely. She didn't add "or nervous," and said good-night too brightly.

And she hadn't more than closed the door behind her and heard the drone of the descending elevator outside it than she knew that during her absence someone had been in the apartment.

Yet there was nothing changed. And there was no one there now, because Blitz would have been barking furiously.

She thought of calling someone—the Riddles perhaps, or the men who'd just left her.

But nothing had been moved—the drawing room was exactly as she'd left it. The library. The bedrooms. The lights were all burning brightly.

Why, then, was she so sure of someone's having recently been through these rooms—as one is sure from the trailing waves in the wake of a ship on the ocean that that ship has passed? Were there waves, too, left in a room when someone had passed—impalpable but nevertheless there—little disturbances of the ether that made that small electric impact upon one's consciousness?

There was no sound at all, and nothing was changed. She reached the kitchen, and Blitz was sitting in the middle of it dejectedly looking at the door that led out to the porch and the black fire escape. He turned, however, and yawned without much interest, and the door was not only locked but bolted on the inside.

Encouraged by Blitz's bored attitude, Deborah made the rounds of the place again and was sure that now, at any rate, no one was there.

And she still had nothing definite upon which to base her feeling that someone had been there. Nothing at all had changed except—what had happened to the newspapers which had been spread out on the divan and spilling over onto the floor? There was no newspaper at all there now. And she was sure that neither Anthony nor Francis had carried the papers away with him.

It was that trivial change, then, that she must have noted subconsciously as she entered. Noted without realizing she had noted it, and her tense nerves had telegraphed a quick message of alarm.

After a time she convinced herself that one of the men had carried the newspapers along with him and she had failed to see it.

And that no one had been in the apartment.

It was not so much instinct as nerves, she told herself. But nevertheless, thinking of the mysterious return of the mimosa which proved that certainly at some time that day the apartment had been entered, she pushed a dining-room chair under the knob of the door to the outside hall. It was a beautiful old chair and would probably be marred and Juliet would want to know what had happened to it. But Deborah felt safer. She wished parenthetically that she would hear something from Juliet and knew that she must write to her explaining what she dared of the story that Juliet would soon be, if she wasn't already, reading in the newspapers. True, it would be some time before Chicago newspapers could reach Florida, but there would be Associated Press dispatches.

That night, too, was quiet.

Lights burned all night in the great old house, but whatever its occupants thought or did during those long quiet hours, there was nothing to be seen or heard. If the policeman on that beat gave it a little more than his usual attention there was no one to know it. No one, that is, except perhaps a few dark figures, which seemed mysteriously to be strolling along at the corner of the alley, or under the light at the entrance, or, even, loitering along the street, dark and muffled, with hats over their eyes and only a word or two as the policeman passed them again and yet again.

Morning was gray and cold, with Chloe coming to the door about nine to ask how Deborah was getting along. On hearing about Annie and the quarantine, she observed flippantly that Annie didn't live there any more and carried Deborah off to breakfast in her own apartment.

"Gibbs," she said as they crossed the hall, "is still sulky and Tulip is scared of her shadow. Seems cold in the hall, doesn't it?"

"It's your pajamas," said Deborah. But it wasn't. The hall did seem chilly and too empty.

It was a somewhat difficult meal, with Gibbs scowling over the morning papers, Chloe chattering when she remembered to do so, and Tulip slapping down plates and snatching them away again as if the devil himself were sitting at the table. As, indeed, she may have felt, for if ever a man looked hagridden it was Gibbs Riddle that morning. He was white, and his thick black eyebrows made a dark slash across his face; it was his eyebrows, thought Deborah, that made him look so sullen and black; his eyes were actually a very light, cold blue-green with hard black pupils.

"Well, Mary Monroe wasn't robbed," said Chloe. "'When found the former diva was dressed in red velvet, real lace displayed a cluster of diamonds at her throat, and she wore a diamond-set bracelet which (in conjunction with the fact that the jewels and money in her safe were not touched) leads the police to believe the motive for the murder was not robbery. Her gown and diamonds also suggest that she was expecting or had been entertaining a guest. This was borne out by the used tea service—one cup wiped clean of finger-prints—Mary Monroe's fingerprints on the other ...'" Chloe's voice trailed away as she read. She swerved to another column and said cheerfully, "Well, there are no clues. At least so the papers say."

Gibbs pushed his newspapers away.

"The papers!" he said scornfully. "How do we know what's actually happening? The police say they expect a disclosure within twenty-four hours, don't they? Well, how can they say that if they actually have no clues?"

"They always say that." Chloe snatched the paper he had thrust away. "Oh, look, Deb, here's a picture of her as Elsa. Lovely, wasn't she? That must have been a long time ago."

"Can't you," said Gibbs, "talk of anything else?"

"Oh, yes," replied Chloe pleasantly, reading the closely printed columns. "Lots of things. But this is so interesting. I think the police must be embarrassed by the wealth of information. She must have known simply millions of people. There's the postman, Gibbs."

He rose as the bell rang and flung out of the room. But it wasn't the postman. It was Dolly Brocksley, thin and looking cold in a sleazy little silk negligee with a coat tossed over it. Her eyes were wide and frightened, and her hands looked large and bony and red.

"Why, Dolly," said Chloe. "Come in. What's the matter?"

She came forward slowly and with the queerest, loveliest grace. Her cheap little silk and her dry hair and her ugly bony hands faded away into nothing when Dolly Brocksley walked, and you felt for a breathless moment as if the sky had opened and something ineffably lovely and light and gentle were coming toward you.

Then she sat down and put her elbows on the table and slumped forward, and her hands were red and bony again and you knew that the calves of her legs would be hard and muscular.

"It's Brocksley," she said. Her short blonde hair was curled only on the ends. Her skin was dry, and there were tiny, fine wrinkles around her mouth and her eyes and a hard line that marked the beginning of a double chin—fought, probably, doggedly. But her eyes shone and were alive and vital and, now, full of something like desperation.

"What's Brocksley done?" said Chloe calmly. "Tulip —bring coffee for Mrs. Brocksley, please."

They must have known each other rather well in a curiously intimate and yet impersonal way. Probably they had done much talking and much sharing of everyday affairs, of family, and trivial illnesses and worries about money—yet Chloe wouldn't have thought of asking Dolly to one of her parties, and Dolly wouldn't have thought of being asked, although she might have discussed the kind of sandwiches and cakes with Chloe for days before the affair took place—which would be,

since it was Chloe's, unpretentious and somewhat impromptu in effect and yet very amusing. It was not at
all because Chloe's somewhat haphazard and lively
social pretensions excluded little Dolly Brocksley. It
was simply that her acquaintance with Dolly began and
remained on its own small plane.

Now Dolly looked at her worriedly.

"Something's terribly wrong," she said. "Tighe's
down there in our flat, and that little devil they call
Pigeon. They're all quarreling"—a long shiver ran
down over her thin shoulders and she added: "*Horribly.*
And Brocksley's going to call the police. I heard that
much before he—threw me out."

She winced faintly at the recollection and looked at
her arms. Deborah had a sudden and rather appalling
vision of Alfred Brocksley's fat hands twisting cruelly
those painfully thin arms.

Gibbs made a sudden step toward her and said
harshly:

"Why is he going to call the police?"

"Because," said Dolly looking up wearily, "he's got
some evidence about the murder of Mary Monroe."

CHAPTER IX

Tulip pushed forward the swinging door, paused to give the still group around the table a brief, dark look, and then came forward, a silver tray gleaming against her green bosom and white apron.

Chloe made a mechanical gesture with one lithe hand, and Tulip put coffee before Dolly and, somewhat reluctantly and rolling her eyes backward, departed. The swinging door creaked a little, and Deborah swallowed with a dry throat, and Gibbs Riddle said harshly:

"*What kind of evidence? What does he know?*"

Dolly looked at her coffee. For one barely perceptible second she hesitated, and her air of weary candor vanished. Then she looked up with an effect of frankness:

"I'm not sure that I know. But I think he heard something, perhaps that night. Or knows something."

"About Tighe? I mean that involves him?"

Her slight hesitation was gone at once, and her air of candor was real again.

"I don't think so. I mean—they're quarreling about calling the police—all of them. But somehow I didn't think that it was Tighe that the evidence would be against. That murdered her, I mean. That is—I just heard a few words, you know, and——"

"What were they?"

Dolly looked at her coffee again.

"Let her get her breath, Gibbs," said Chloe, but she, too, had a still, tensely waiting look on her face.

"Well," said Dolly, "I heard Brocksley shout: 'I'll

116

call them—I'll call the police!' He said that, oh, a number of times. Kept saying they ought to have the evidence. And Tighe and Pigeon kept trying to talk him out of it. I couldn't hear what they said, much, except the tones of their voices, you know. I——" She hesitated. "It's possible that Brocksley's holding out for money. I don't know. But I think"—terror flashed into her face and stiffened it, and she spoke in a queer hoarse whisper—"*I think something awful's going to happen.*"

"But, Dolly——" began Chloe.

"Why do you think that?" said Gibbs. "*Why?*"

"I don't know," whispered Dolly.

Chloe gave her a long look and reached across the table and patted one of her hands.

"You are frightening her, Gibbs," she said.

"But, my God, Chloe, she comes in here and makes statements like that and then won't explain what she means."

Dolly lifted her head.

"Would you say more?" she asked. "I've said too much already. I don't want to be——" She stopped and then went on jerkily: "Anyway, that's all I know. Except that I don't think the evidence was actually against Tighe—I mean, I don't think that Brocksley had evidence that Tighe had anything to do with the murder because—well," concluded Dolly simply, "if that was it, Brocksley would have been afraid to tell Tighe about it. He's an awful coward, really."

Gibbs whirled savagely and paced the floor while Dolly stirred coffee mechanically and Chloe stared at the tablecloth and kept patting Dolly's idle hand and Deborah sat rigid and unmoving, trying to stifle a conclusion to which she had leaped, and that was that Pigeon had told Brocksley of her presence when Mary

Monroe was killed and that that was the evidence Brocksley wanted to turn over to the police. Yet, in that case, Tighe would have no reason, certainly, to try to dissuade him.

Gibbs pounced back upon Dolly.

"Why did you come up here?" he demanded suspiciously, the hard black pupils of his eyes like pin points. "Tell me that."

"There wasn't any other place to go," said Dolly wearily. "I'll go back as soon as they leave."

"You'll stay as long as you like," said Chloe warmly but absently.

"Well, look here, Dolly," said Gibbs. "How well did you know Mary Monroe?"

Dolly stared downward.

"Pretty well," she said in a queerly sullen way. "I knew her pretty well." She was blinking, and her eyelids were reddening. "She—she gave us money for food more than once." She looked up suddenly. Her eyes were scarlet-rimmed, and there were heavy tears in them, but she glared defiantly at Gibbs and spat out protests like a small, cornered cat. "What's it to you? What's any of this to you? You've no right to question like this! We'd have starved if it hadn't been for her. The only jobs Brocksley's had during the last few years, she's got for him. Me, too. That's how well I knew her. She was good. Good, I tell you. And I loved her! And, I could kill with my own hands the man that murdered her." She was sobbing heavily, catching her breath between phrases. "I could kill him myself," she sobbed jerkily, her little face distorted and wet. "With my own hands. Law's too uncertain! The chair is too slow! I could kill him. . . ."

She put her head down upon her arms and cried

violently and dreadfully with great retching sobs. Tulip opened the swinging door an inch and peered in, and Gibbs stared downward, and Chloe patted those thin heaving shoulders.

"Keep right on crying, honey," she said. "It's good for you. Get it all out. Don't stop."

Gibbs gave Chloe one black look, glanced down again at Dolly and flung himself out of the room, and Deborah heard a door somewhere slam.

"Keep right on crying," said Chloe again, and presently Dolly stopped.

She went away shortly after; Chloe went to the door with her, and if she said any more Deborah did not know it.

And apparently the quarrel had settled itself one way or another, for she did not return, and during the morning there were no evidences of any untoward happenings in or about the Brocksley flat.

And when Deborah returned from walking Blitz later in the morning, she met Tighe lunging down the steps in the direction of the limousine pulled up at the curb.

In the clear light he looked very dark and liverish, though he was grossly fat, with pendulous stomach and trembling yellow chins. He stopped as he saw Deborah, took off his derby hat, and said pleasantly:

"Oh, good-morning, good-morning, Miss Deborah."

His eyes were yellow brown and knowing, and his whole bearing was unexpectedly suave and somehow very subtly flattering, so that she actually had that pleasant little feeling of being herself an attractive and interesting person. It is an effect which only the very experienced can achieve, and even then there must be a special gift for it.

Deborah found herself replying almost cordially to a

man she would rather have disliked. A man she did dislike.

"I do hope your father is better," he said, and again Deborah had an extraordinary little glow of self-appreciation.

"Thank you," she said. "He's about the same, I think." Blitz wished to explore various points of interest he had already thoroughly explored and tugged at the leash, and she became aware suddenly that Pigeon, silent and unobtrusive, with a chauffeur's cap over his eyes, was sitting at the wheel of the car.

"I think the change of climate will do a great deal of good for him," said Tighe, and Deborah felt inexplicably sure of it, too. "Don't let this affair of the—er—murder worry you. It will clear up all right."

Feeling rather stunned, Deborah saw him lunge into the car and bow pleasantly to her as the great shining thing moved away. Or at least as near a bow as was physically possible. Pigeon had not moved, except, presumably, to engage the clutch. If she could only know what was going on under that visored cap!

That and Anthony Wyatt's unheralded call about noon were, as Deborah recalled it later, the only incidents that marked that slow, dreary day, during which, again possessed of a hideously restless spirit of waiting, Deborah did practically nothing but listen for the elevator and footsteps on the stairway and try to come to some decision. Several times, as evening and morning newspapers were read and discussed, friends of Juliet's and of her own began to telephone. For the most part they were kind, if ghoulishly inquisitive, and one and all (with what struck Deborah as rather sinister expectation) advised her to go to her father in Florida, blissfully ignoring the fact that she might not be free to do as she liked. Old Mrs. Northly invited her kindly to come to her, and Helen Mickle somewhat excitedly said that Mother had said she must make Deborah come straight to their house and added that they were terribly keen to hear all about the murder.

There were not, however, so many calls that Deborah found it difficult to evade them. And even if the police had permitted it, which somehow she doubted, she could not have gone away.

Once, at least, during the morning, the police were in the apartment house, for she saw a police car outside, but no one came to question her and she did not know what they were doing, although she wondered again if Brocksley had given them his evidence. She was inclined to believe, thinking of Tighe, that he had not.

When Anthony came she told him at once of Dolly Brocksley and what she had said. He listened thoughtfully.

"Do you think Brocksley saw you?" he said at once.

"I don't think so. But—I don't know. Anyone could have seen me without my knowing it. I talked to Mary Monroe in the vestibule—I went up to her house while there was still enough light so that I could have been seen. And Pigeon must have seen me—some time."

He nodded.

"Perhaps Pigeon told Brocksley."

"I thought of that, too—but it makes no sense. Tighe wouldn't have tried to dissuade Brocksley from telling the police on my account."

"She didn't," said Anthony, looking at Blitz, "say anything about me, did she? Dolly, I mean."

"No. Do you suppose Brocksley has given his evidence to the police? They were here this morning."

"What for?"

"I don't know. I didn't see them."

Anthony groaned.

"Well," he said, "if they do come to question you, just keep your shirt on. Pigeon is the only witness against you."

"Perhaps," said Deborah, "we ought to tell——"

He laughed shortly.

"You're damn right we ought to tell," he said. He looked at her thoughtfully. "Still trusting me, are you?"

"Yes," said Deborah. "I can't help myself."

"Well, that's right, too," he said. "I've got to get back to the laboratory."

He hesitated. "We've got a lot to talk about. But I'm not sure—I've got to think of some way——" He broke off abruptly, gave her another long thoughtful look, and said: "We'll talk later."

It was after he'd gone that the telephone rang again. It was, said a voice blandly, ignoring the very unusual ability it claimed, the drugstore on the corner. And Western Union was trying to return her telegram.

"Return it? Why?"

"I don't know," said the voice. "I just thought I'd let you know. In case you wanted to send another. This *is* Miss Deborah Cavert, isn't it?"

"Yes," said Deborah. Was it someone from the drugstore? Or was it the police? "Thank you," she said. "It doesn't matter."

"Well," said the voice, "if you'll stop you can have your money back. Seventy-six cents."

"Thank you," said Deborah again.

It was convincing. Too convincing and too pat.

It added to her uneasiness when the late afternoon post had still no word from Juliet.

Chloe brought her an evening paper.

"Dolly was up again," she said without preamble. "And says she thinks Tighe talked Brocksley out of his notion that he wanted to give evidence to the police. I imagine he bought him off."

"*Why?*" said Deborah. "*Why* would Tighe——"

"I don't know," said Chloe coolly. "Unless he murdered Mary Monroe himself. But if that's it, Alfred Brocksley had better watch out for his fat throat. I don't feel that Mr. Tighe is a man to be trifled with. To say nothing of that wily little wretch they call Pigeon. I'd hate to meet him on a dark night just on general principles. And as for Tighe, it honestly gives me gooseflesh just to pass him in the hall. He's like an enormous brown spider, lunging along."

She opened the paper.

"It's just come," she said. "I wonder—— Golly, look at this, Deb."

The newspaper rattled eagerly, and Deborah leaned forward.

The strike had that day been settled, and the murder leaped at once to great black letters running across the top.

Murder Arrest Expected, it said pungently. Police Active in Monroe Case. Arrest of Murderer of Opera Singer Expected Hourly. Sensational Development in Murder.

Murder—murder—murder. Deborah plunged on past the headlines.

Presently she found it:

"'While a direct statement was not forthcoming, we are reliably informed that the police are in possession of a clue which will lead promptly to arrest.'"

"Well, of all things," said Chloe. "They say this

clue leads to a woman. I wonder who." Her green eyes
squinted thoughtfully. "I wonder if it was a woman
who had tea with her. They've said a lot about there
being two teacups."

A phrase out of the columns of print leaped at Deborah: ". . . the arrest of the woman is momentarily
expected . . ."

Deborah shut her eyes, and fine type went across her
eyelids: ". . . the arrest of the woman is momentarily
expected . . ."

Chloe darted a quick green glance at her.

"Turn on the light, Debbie. It's too dark to see. You
look as white as a sheet."

Deborah went to the lamp and pulled on the light.

Her face felt hard, as if it had been set in wax and
chilled, and Chloe looked at her and then at her dress
and then back to the paper.

"You look about sixteen in that little crimson wool,"
she said. "I suppose you paid a dreadful sum for it. But
do put on a little rouge when you wear it. Who do you
suppose this woman is? Well, there's one thing, it can't
be anyone in the apartment house, for there's only me
and you and Dolly. That will relieve Tulip. That is, if I
can make her see it. It would be exactly like her to walk
out on me, and it's so hard to get somebody who'd put
up with the Riddles." She was reading avidly, and her
voice trailed away as if she thought little of what she
was saying. Yet there had been something careful and
calculated about it, too.

"Well," she said at last. "I guess that's all. I'll leave
this paper for you, Deb. Gibbs shouts every time anything is said of the murder."

She went away, trailing green silk across the silent
hall.

Fifteen minutes later she returned.

"He wants the paper after all," she said. The little lambent flame was in her eyes again, and even her thick tousle of black hair looked alive and vibrant. She gave Deborah a long look as she took the folded newspaper.

"You're behaving very well, my dear," she said enigmatically and turned away. Over her shoulder she added: "Juanito ought to put larger bulbs in these lights."

"*Chloe!*" She turned and Deborah said: "Chloe, what do you mean by that? What is it that you—have hinted at?"

"*Hush!*" Chloe's eyes were suddenly narrow and fiery, and she glanced swiftly around the hall and toward the stairway and the elevator shaft. "Don't you have any more sense, Deborah—shouting like that!" She herself was whispering sharply. "I don't mean anything. Not anything at all!"

Deborah said slowly: "You've got to tell me, Chloe."

Chloe's eyes were shining slits of light. Her lithe hands were opening and closing oddly. She said, still whispering: "Not here, Deborah. And it's nothing. Believe me, nothing."

She wrenched herself away from Deborah and disappeared inside her own flat. The heavy oak door closed and remained closed and blank.

The shadows of the hall were somehow forbidding and seemed to move, although of course they didn't.

But no one could have heard Chloe. There was no one to hear. The elevator shaft was empty, the padded stairway stretched up and down into the blank shadows, the little door back of the elevator shaft was closed.

She shivered under her crimson wool and went back into her own apartment.

And it was not twenty minutes later that Anthony Wyatt came to make his amazing proposal.

It was just that.

For he stood in the shadow by the window, staring down into the dusk of the quiet street below, with his face rather white and his hands plunged into his pockets, and asked Deborah to marry him.

"Don't think I'm crazy," he said. "And don't scream. And in God's name, don't giggle. But I think we'd better get married. Right away."

Deborah didn't giggle. Indeed, she made no sound at all, although she sat down, because her knees dissolved under her. Anthony stared into the street and said after a moment:

"How old are you?"

"T-twenty-one."

"That's all right, then," said Anthony with forced briskness. "Well—what about it?"

"But," observed Deborah with great presence of mind.

He said rapidly, still without looking at her: "I'm not making love to you, and I won't. And I want you to understand perfectly, too, that the—the marriage can be annulled simply and easily later. Do you understand that?"

Deborah grasped the arms of the chair in which luckily she found herself.

"Why?"

He did not reply for a moment. Finally he turned toward her.

"Because," he said, "sooner or later the police are going to discover what really happened in the house on the roof—that you were there and that I was there. People have been hung on much less conclusive evidence."

"Yes," said Deborah, "I know. But—still——"

"A husband," said Anthony, "can't testify against his—his wife in a grand jury case. Nor a wife against her husband. It's been done before this—a marriage, I mean, like this one."

Deborah was on her feet. Queer how often their eyes had met and clung like this. Even in that first strange moment in Mary Monroe's house there had been something oddly compelling in that long exchange. She said: "You mean that you are afraid you will be obliged to testify against me?"

"I mean," said Anthony, "that each of us would be the star witness against the other. I am—if you didn't kill Mary Monroe—the only other suspect. Your testimony against me is almost exactly as convincing as mine against you would be."

"Oh," said Deborah simply.

Anthony shrugged.

"You were considerably more at a disadvantage than I. But you must have realized that I will be in exactly the same position that you are in when the police discover, as they will, that we were there."

"Then it isn't just for me and my own—safety——"

"Not at all," said Anthony briskly. "It's for both of us. I don't want to have to go to the chair for something I didn't do. And you don't want to. And one or both of us are in—well,"—there was a note of forced lightness in his voice that did more to convince Deborah of the grim truth of his statement than anything else could have done—"we are in considerable danger of being the center of interest in a murder trial. And one of somewhat short and conclusive duration."

Deborah stood quite still, and he walked toward her.

"And I'd better say again," he said gravely, "that I

didn't murder Mary Monroe. I want you to know that."

"Do you believe that I did?" said Deborah. "I can't possibly marry you if you—believe that."

"You see, then, that it's the thing to do?"

"I don't know. I don't know." She put her hands over her eyes, and lifted them to push her hair back, and put up her chin. "I don't know," she repeated. "I must think. But I must know first that you believe me."

He was standing very near her and unexpectedly he put his lean warm hands around her face, cupping her chin and lifting it so he could look directly into her eyes.

"I do believe you," he said. "Now . . ."

He was looking suddenly at her mouth, and there was something glowing back of his eyes. Then all at once the glow vanished and he thrust his hands into his pockets again and said rapidly:

"It's the only thing I can think of to do. And, please believe me, it's not at all an effort on my part to protect you. I'm keenly interested in saving myself. It's a selfish impulse, although since we are both in the thing it happens to benefit both of us. They'll suspect us, and there'll be trouble, but if they can't introduce our own stories in court they'll have a hard time getting any jury to bring in a verdict of—— *Don't look like that, Deborah!* After all, things may be perfectly all right. Something may happen—something may break so that we won't be suspected at all."

"He's saying that to reassure me," thought Deborah. "He doesn't believe it."

"It's only to be on the safe side," said Anthony quickly, watching her. "But it's the only thing that I've been able to think of that would give us a measure of safety at the last. And since you told me of Pigeon——"

"Pigeon?"

"He knows. And there's no telling what he's going to do with what he knows. I don't know of any other possible way to save ourselves."

Deborah's lips were trembling, and she tried to steady them. This, she adjured herself sternly, was no time for tears. Not when she was about to be—oh, what? said Deborah to herself. Married? What utter madness!

A car passed outside with a low mellow wail of a horn. Blitz trotted busily into the hall bent on some private business of his own. Anthony looked at her and without warning grinned.

"I've got the ring," he said and dug it out of his pocket and looked at it before he extended it on his palm so that she could see it.

"I guessed at your size," he said. "Do you like it?"

Deborah looked. And the slender little gold circle—yellow gold with a fine tracing of leaves upon it—became all at once and in the strangest way a magnet, and it held them both silent and engrossed for a long moment. Then Deborah made herself look away from the slender gold thing and say:

"You must have been rather certain of your bride." She said it with an attempted lightness which fell very short of being light, and at once she wished she hadn't said it.

But Anthony put the ring back in his pocket and said gravely:

"Maybe it will prove an entirely unnecessary precaution. Maybe we won't need it at all. But I think we'd better be prepared. Now then—think it over. I'm going

away. If you decide to do it—well, we can do it right
away. We'll get away from the police somehow, for if
they know it now they'll wonder why. We'll only let
them know when—I mean in case the—in case it does
prove necessary. I'll go now. And I'll telephone in—oh,
half an hour or so. That's not much time. But every
moment we wait increases your—the danger from
Pigeon. We'll drive straight to Crown Point, get married, and come back. Well,"—he was at the door now
and Deborah somewhat dazedly had followed him; he
looked down at her and laughed a little—"believe it or
not, I've just asked you to marry me. It's now six-
thirty. At seven I'll telephone for your answer. And "—
the smile vanished—"and don't be worried about the
marriage," he said in a different voice. "It's only a
parachute. In case of trouble."

He was gone, then, and Deborah sank rather limply
into a chair. It was very still now that he'd gone. And
she was again alone in the heavy, chill silence that was
somehow threatening. She sat without moving. Queer,
she thought presently, how the whole thing resolved
itself into a question of Anthony Wyatt himself. Or
did it? Was the question one that concerned Pigeon—
and what Pigeon knew?

She had not moved when the telephone rang.

But it couldn't be the telephone, thought Deborah,
or at least it couldn't be Anthony. Not already. Not——

It rang again.

She looked at her watch. And there was a queer tight
feeling in her throat when she saw it was seven o'clock
exactly.

It was just then, too, that she was vaguely aware that
the elevator had stopped and that there was the muffled
faint clang of the door. At least, she must have been

aware of it, for she remembered it clearly later. But at that moment she knew only that it was Anthony at the telephone expecting her to have come to a decision. An impossible, a fantastic decision.

She was at the telephone.

"Deborah," said Anthony's voice.

"This is Deborah."

"Well——" he said. "I—— What's the answer?"

Someone that was certainly Deborah Cavert was speaking. And she was saying huskily: "The answer's, yes."

There was silence from the other end of the wire. Then Anthony said:

"Wait a minute, Deb. I can't hear you." She heard his voice shouting, away from the telephone: "Turn down the radio, Francis. It's making a hell of a racket." Then he was back again.—"It's now or never," thought Deborah rather frantically. —"What do you say, Deborah?"

"I said yes," said Deborah again.

"Oh—that's—that's what I thought you said. Well—my car's outside. Shall we start?"

"Yes."

"Put on a warm coat. When will you be ready?"

She paused, thinking.

"In five minutes," she said, and then from an obscure and trivial feeling that she must start things in a suitably unsentimental way she added: "I'll meet you in the hall of the first floor. Will we have any trouble about the police? Or do you think anyone is—watching?"

"I don't know." She could feel a quality of hesitation in his voice. "But I don't think so.—In five minutes, then. And be sure to wear something warm, for it's a—er—rather cold for even a short walk."

"What?—oh,"—that was for Francis's ears. "Oh, yes, of course. I will."

The telephone clicked softly under her hand. She wished somehow that she hadn't thought of Francis and his observant, suspicious eyes, and she hoped he wouldn't have to know of and wouldn't discover their marriage.

The word caught at her and she pushed it away. It was not a marriage at all. It was a mere arrangement for safety. A precaution. A—what had he called it?—a parachute in case of trouble.

But he'd been so sure that the trouble would come.

Blitz came along the hall, something odd in his attitude. But Deborah did not note that oddness.

She went into her room and selected a fur coat—a mink coat that miraculously Juliet had contrived to produce by means of an old coat of her own and some added skins and the best furrier in Chicago, and Deborah had never understood how it had been paid for. She ran a comb through her shining gold hair and pulled on a small crimson hat and then leaned over to look at herself doubtfully and, presently, with small chilly fingers, to add a touch of rouge and some soft crimson lipstick. She looked so terribly pale even for a bride. No, no, not a bride. A parachute jumper. Well, that was worse.

Her eyes were dark and shining, and there was now a flame of pink in her cheeks, and her lips were soft and red and half smiling, and Deborah was somewhat surprisingly conscious of the fact that she had never looked better in her life.

Well, why not, at her own wedding! But it wasn't a wedding. She turned hurriedly away from the mysteriously beautiful girl in the mirror. She snatched gloves and a bag and slipped into the coat and refused a

last glimpse of herself in the mirror, as she turned into
the narrow passage that ran along the whole apartment.

The five minutes were up. She started toward the
door.

Blitz was there.

He was stretched out along the floor with his nose at
the crack below the door.

He was sniffing and making the queerest, most horrible little sounds. And the hair all along his neck stood
up straight and stiff.

Deborah opened the door.

CHAPTER X

CHLOE had said: "Juanito ought to put larger bulbs in
these lights." And Blitz was pushing past Deborah's
ankles and was growling queerly. And there was nothing
in the hall—nothing, that is, that moved. There was
only a thick dark blotch that lay as if flung heavily upon
the floor.

Then Deborah stirred and forced herself to move
slowly like a sleep walker, out from the doorway and
across a few short steps to the huddled bulk that lay so
queerly just in front of the door to the elevator. Her
coat dragged upon her shoulders—her hands were at
her throat, and she thought she had screamed, but she
hadn't. The lights were not bright enough. They were
too dim, too weak, too—but there was enough light to
see it.

It was Alfred Brocksley.

And it was a very ugly thing to see, because there
was something queer about his throat. And about the
angle of his head.

Chloe had said: "Juanito ought to put larger bulbs
in these lights." And Chloe had said also: "Alfred
Brocksley will get his fat throat cut."

Deborah thought she closed her eyes, but she couldn't
have done so, because the whole scene was indelibly
photographed upon her vision. Long, long afterward
she could still see the hump of his thick fat shoulders—
his hand supine upon the carpet, the way his green tie

was pulled to one side—and the unmoving shadows along the stairway.

Unmoving shadows—silence—the closed door to the Riddle apartment—the small door back of the elevator shaft—murder. Murder again.

Were those shadows unmoving! *Was* there actually nothing alive—nothing moving in that hall? Did nothing watch from the elevator—from the door—from the shadows? Were there no furtive, soft steps on the padded stairs? The strange, primitive sense of being under observation seized upon Deborah, and with it the instinct of self-preservation that sheer, mad terror induces, and she began to creep backward, silently, breathlessly—an inch at a time. Her heart was pounding in her throat—her coat like a weight—her body detached from herself and utterly involuntary.

She never knew how she removed her eyes from that thick black thing that had been Alfred Brocksley, how she got the door closed and bolted. But somehow, after eons of time, she was sitting on the edge of a chair shaking, with something that was exactly like a horrible, soul-shattering chill, except that she wasn't cold.

She wrapped her coat around her, and then Blitz was whining somewhere, and all at once, with a rush of comprehension, Deborah started to her feet.

Brocksley was dead. Brocksley was murdered. That's what that thing in the hall meant. That's what had happened. And she was sitting there with her teeth chattering and doing nothing—saying nothing—calling no one.

And Anthony was waiting downstairs.

She had been going to meet him. That was it. That was why she had on her coat and hat. She'd been going to meet him and they had been going to do something— to drive to Crown Point. To be married.

She shook her head, and things cleared suddenly, and the stark numb paralysis of horror left her with the need to act.

The telephone—she couldn't possibly go out into that dreadful, shadow-laden hall—she couldn't bring herself to look upon the thing that lay there again. But she could telephone—what was his number?

She had stripped off her gloves and was fumbling, with fingers that were shaking, through the telephone book. Blitz's whining worried her, and she said sharply: "Hush, Blitz. Hush——" and listened for sounds in the hall.

Wyatt—Anthony Wyatt. She reached for the telephone and dialed the wrong number and Blitz growled and growled so that she was distracted and she forgot the right number and had to look for it again.

The telephone clicked and clicked and then finally she heard the welcome sound, periodically repeated, that meant that it was ringing. It rang and rang and then stopped.

"Yes?" said a voice.

It was Francis Maly.

Deborah, on the verge of hysteria, pulled herself up shortly.

"I want to talk to Anthony, please," she said.

There was a very brief hesitation at the other end. Then Francis said:

"I'm not sure he's here. Will you wait a moment?"

He had turned from the telephone, and she could hear him shouting above a babble of sounds from the radio: "Tony—hey, Tony . . ." His voice diminished as if he were walking away from the telephone.

Tony was, of course, waiting in the hall. The hall—it was dangerous to wait in the hall—the whole great place was charged with secret danger—with something that killed swiftly and horribly like a beast—like a lurking, man-killing tiger—like a——

"Hello," said Anthony crisply.

"Anthony!" said Deborah as if she had sobbed.

"*What is it*——"

"Anthony," she cried incoherently, "something— don't leave—don't go into the hall—don't—" She knew she was talking wildly and stopped and tried again, slowly, deliberately: "Anthony. There's a man—it's Brocksley. He's dead. He's in the hall. He's been killed."

"I'm coming——"

"But you don't understand—he's been murdered——"

"Listen." His voice was very low yet taut. "I'll come the back way. Wait . . ."

He had hung up. It was incredible, but he had done just that right in her ear. And with a resounding click. Deborah looked unbelievingly at the receiver and finally herself hung up and then, blindingly, knew why he had been so guarded. It was on account of Francis's listening ears. And Anthony was protecting her. Deborah. Because she'd been alone and she had opened the door of the hall and walked straight upon Alfred Brocksley whose throat had been cut.

But Anthony was coming—up the stairway that connected the rear entrances of the flats.

She hurried along the hall, through the dining room, with Blitz at her heels, into the kitchen. She was at the door listening, and yet when she heard him she called: "Who is it?" and waited for his answer before she unbolted and opened the door.

It was Anthony, however, who closed and bolted the door again before he looked at her and took her into his arms as if he weren't altogether conscious of what he was doing and said shakily:

"Are you all right?"

And Deborah, her face buried for a second time against his shoulder, murmured something and felt terribly grateful for the warm shelter of his arms and the tremendous, important fact of that human presence.

"You're not hurt? You're sure?" he was saying rather hoarsely, and Deborah cried jerkily:

"It's Brocksley, you know. He's dead. He's been murdered. I found him. When I started to meet you. And there wasn't anybody—anybody———"

"All right—I know—I understand—it's all right now, Deborah. I'll see to things. Don't shiver like that. Stop it."

She couldn't stop shivering. Suddenly Anthony's hands went to her shoulders and gripped them and forced her to look at him.

"Deborah, you must control yourself. Listen to me. Oh, I know it's horrible—but you absolutely must listen and do as I say. We've got to get out of here. Things were tight enough for us before, but now—well, there's not a minute to be lost. Now, see here—sit down here on this chair. Don't move, don't think, don't feel."

"*Where are you going?*"

"I'm going to look———"

"*Anthony———*"

He was gone. The door into the butler's pantry was swinging, and Blitz hesitated, looking anxiously at Deborah and at the door, trying to decide what to do.

"Stay with me, Blitz," said Deborah, and the little dog trotted to her.

Anthony was right, of course. She must control herself, stop this nervous shuddering. And he was right, too, when he said that their danger was increased.

The door opened, and Anthony came into the kitchen again.

"Lord," he said and sat on the table and stared unseeingly down at Deborah. His face was white, and there was a look of horror in his eyes. He took a long breath and said: "Gosh."

"Who did it?"

"I don't know—I don't know." He stared at her and then suddenly comprehension came into his eyes again. He got up, gave himself a queer little shake, and said shortly:

"Come on. We've got to get away. Where's the light switch?—I'll turn it off so that no one in the court can see us leave. Here it is. Take the key out of the lock, Deborah, so we can lock the door from the outside and get in again this way if we need to. Now then—all set?"

The electric switch snapped, and the kitchen was in darkness. Deborah felt Blitz nudging softly at her ankles and stopped and scooped him up under one arm.

"Now then," Anthony was saying in a whisper, "out the door—give me the key—there we are. Hang onto my hand, Deborah. We'll go down these stairs. Quietly——"

The court was dark except for that rectangle of twilight from the street. It was, too, windy again, and they made little sound on the wooden stairway. At the bottom of it Anthony paused and put his mouth close to Deborah's ear.

"We can't go out to the street where there's a light. The place is being watched—has been since yesterday. But there's a way out that they may not know about.

It's just a chance, but we'll try it. Don't say anything and keep hold of my hand."

They were edging cautiously along, close to the building and keeping well within the darkest shadow it afforded. They rounded a corner, followed a blind wall, and were presently across the well of the court and still in deep blackness. Deborah glanced toward the apartment house and could see lights in the Riddle flat and lights in the Brocksley flat. Had they found him yet? The house was still, and there was no evidence of any commotion. But then it had been really only a few moments. She looked again at the dark bulk of the apartment house. Tighe's lights were glowing, too; probably Pigeon was out there in the kitchen preparing dinner.

Then she became aware that they had stopped before the wall surrounding the great building that reared darkly and mysteriously ahead; the building whose blank tiers of windows had watched her descent from the fire escape the night Mary Monroe had been killed. Mary Monroe. And now Brocksley.

Anthony was fumbling at something that scraped and creaked.

"Ah!" he whispered. "Here is the place. I was afraid it had been closed—go ahead, Deborah."

Deborah gasped. A section of the fence had opened like a gate. It was a gate, and she stepped through it, and Anthony followed and closed it very gently after her.

The shadow was deeper on that side, and Deborah surmised from Anthony's quicker movements that he felt that they were safer from detection.

"Now then," he breathed in her ear. "Just a few steps and around a corner and we'll be on Vine Street. All right, Deb?"

"But that—gate. What is it? Why——"

"Oh, it's been there, forever. I'll tell you later. Don't slip—the pavement up this alley's a bit uneven."

It was uneven. Deborah's heels caught, and she had to walk with care on the worn old bricks. Buildings hedged them on either side, and away up overhead the sky was only faintly lighter than the surrounding walls. But they turned a corner and then another and a light appeared—a street light on Vine Street.

"Nobody in sight," said Anthony. "So far so good. Now for the car. It's parked just around the corner on Brahms." Under the light he looked down at her scrutinizingly and said: "That's a good girl. Hurry along now. Once we are in the car we'll be all right. I haven't heard any police cars, so nobody's reported the murder yet. Am I walking too fast?"

"No," breathed Deborah a bit jerkily. "Anthony— why was there a gate in that fence?"

"Oh—I don't know." He was uninterested.

"But how did you know about it?" It was a little thing, of course; trivial, of no significance. Yet it was sufficiently unusual to permit Deborah's thought to fasten upon it and speculate about it and thereby shut out a picture of that dim hall back at 18 East Eden and the thing it held.

He did not reply at once. Then he said: "Juanito showed it to me once. I don't suppose the police know of it. They wouldn't be looking for it. It was luck for us that the fellows watching the house didn't happen along just as we left. I suppose they were watching the entrance to the court. Here we are. Into the car with you, Deborah. There's no one in sight—at least I can't see anybody. My God, you've brought your dog!"

"Well—yes." Deborah climbed into the long coupé

and put Blitz beside her. "Now what?" she said as Anthony took his place behind the wheel.

He reached over to unlock the ignition and put on the dashlight. In the little glow she noted the quick look he shot up and down the street before he pressed the starter. The engine turned over with a hum that seemed dreadfully loud, caught, and the car slipped away from the curb.

Anthony did not speak until they were about to turn onto Michigan Boulevard. Then he glanced over his shoulder.

"Nobody at the apartment house yet. Well, that's that, Deborah. We did get away and not a minute too soon. And now," he said—"now for Crown Point."

Crown Point. And—incredibly—marriage.

CHAPTER XI

ANTHONY said: "This thing—Brocksley's murder, I mean—has made—marriage—almost imperative, Deborah. And the sooner we can get it done the better for—for us both. I don't want to hurry you into anything you might regret, but I do think it's the only thing to do. After all, it's not as if it were a real—I mean a permanent thing."

He stopped for a red light, waited in silence, and then continued:

"You see, Brocksley's murder is going to tighten up the police investigation. That is, there are implications; people in the apartment house will be seriously involved, and I doubt very much if any of us will have a moment's real liberty. And the police have almost got to make some arrests."

"I suppose we ought to have called a doctor——"

"No," said Anthony. "Brocksley was dead. There wasn't any chance of saving him. And unless I'm badly mistaken there was no great chance of discovering the murderer. I don't know—it's hard to know exactly the thing to do when there is so much involved. Your safety. And mine, too, of course. But I knew if we didn't get out then and there and get this marriage over with, there'd be no chance of it later. However . . ." He was turning off the Boulevard. "I'm going to stop a moment at this drugstore and telephone——"

"To the police?"

"Yes, of course."

He parked expertly and vanished into the brilliantly lighted maze of advertising placards in the windows of a small drugstore. Five minutes later he emerged.

"Now if they don't succeed in tracing the call!" he said. "All set, Deborah?"

Deborah had had a few minutes to think.

"You mean," she said, "that I'm in danger? Because I found Brocksley? That was why you hurried me away?"

He was suddenly very busy with gears.

"That *is* what you mean," she repeated. "Tonight's papers said that the arrest of a woman was momentarily expected. Was that—does that——"

"Yes, I saw that. I don't know what it means. It can't be anything very definite or they would have your apartment guarded at least. But I do know that it's better for you to stay entirely out of this Brocksley affair. God knows what it is going to mean in the end. I may be making a mistake in practically compelling you to take this course of concealment, but—but I think I'm right."

"But there doesn't seem to be any sense to it. Who would murder Alfred Brocksley?"

"Maybe somebody heard him sing," said Anthony gloomily. "Why was Mary Monroe murdered, if you come to that?"

"I suppose they were somehow connected," said Deborah. "Mary Monroe and Brocksley. But I don't see how."

"Murder breeds murder," said Anthony laconically. "And besides there's Brocksley's evidence. The evidence he wanted to give to the police. There's a motive—and he'll certainly give no evidence now."

"He couldn't have killed himself," hazarded Deborah.

"No," said Anthony with convincing terseness. "Besides there was no knife."

"No clues?"

"Well," said Anthony, "nothing I'd call a clue. Place deserted, door to the Riddles' flat closed and silent, door back of the elevator closed, elevator at some other floor—I don't know where, but it doesn't matter. But there's the evidence he said he had for the police. Who knew of it?"

"I knew," said Deborah. "And Dolly Brocksley. And Tighe and Pigeon."

"And Chloe and Gibbs Riddle, and that black cook of theirs——"

"Oh, yes. Tulip. Yes, she probably listened."

"Exactly. And I knew it. And Francis, for I told him. Not a secret by any means. I daresay Juanito knows it, too; there's very little that goes on in the house that Juanito doesn't know."

Deborah hesitated, then said somewhat diffidently: "Does Francis know about—about this? I mean, our going to Crown Point?"

"N-no," he said slowly. "I thought it was well not to tell even Francis. He might not have taken my view of it, and since I felt this was the only thing to do, I didn't see any use in discussing it with him."

"He wouldn't have approved," said Deborah. "He would have said you were sacrificing yourself for me."

"Perhaps," said Anthony. "But if so it would be because he wouldn't understand. That isn't at all true. I'm busily engaged in saving my own skin. But Francis is—well, we're friends, you know. And he would have taken a one-sided view of it. And he's just enough older than I to feel a kind of responsibility about me."

"He doesn't trust me," said Deborah slowly. "He suspects something. I'm sure of it. Do you think"— Deborah hesitated—"do you think he would go to the police?"

"Of course not. Don't be silly."

"But if he did——"

"He won't. Forget it. If necessary I'll tell him."

"Oh, no. Please don't," cried Deborah sharply. "It would only convince him. He—he already makes me feel as if I were an adventuress. Trapping you, somehow."

Anthony laughed.

"That's a thought," he said. He turned to look at her, still laughing. "I hate to disappoint you, Deborah, but you couldn't be an adventuress if you tried. You don't know the first rules." His face sobered suddenly, and he took one hand from the wheel and put it over Deborah's. "Don't worry, Deborah. Francis doesn't suspect you— or if he does he has no real reason for it. And don't mind my very poor jokes. And don't look so—so little and white and scared."

His hand was warm and strong. Blitz sat up and regarded it with interest and poked a cold nose against it, and Anthony said: "Things will come out all right," and the light changed and they swept along on the stream of motion. Yet somehow, in the middle of throbbing motors and police whistles and swishing tires, they were altogether alone and isolated. A girl in a crimson hat and mink coat, with a square little Irish terrier alert beside her, and a man with an intent profile, and darkly shining eyes shaded by his hat, all shut into the small world that was the car. They had turned again and were speeding smoothly along toward the South Shore. On the left and beyond a high wall the Sky Ride towers loomed ghostlily upward, and the great, light bulks that were the Century of Progress buildings looked cold and bare under the winter night.

Anthony said suddenly:

"Look here, Deborah, before we marry there's something I want you to know. I mean about Mary Monroe. You've taken me on trust and maybe because I've—oh—made you believe me. You would be very easy to lie to, you know, because you are yourself a truthful person. However, I want you to know why I came up on the roof that night and why I was coming to see Mary Monroe." He paused as if to assort his thoughts, and Deborah said irresistibly:

"You said something cryptic about everything being O. K. And that you had something——"

He frowned. "Yes, of course. That's what I came for. We'd got our salary checks that day, and I owed—well, I owed Mary Monroe something. Some money, I mean." He hesitated. "It was, really, a matter of business. But I was, naturally, a little reluctant to say anything about it; the amount of money wasn't much, but the idea—well, I wasn't just keen to——" He stopped again and finally said with an effect of choosing his words: "I had—spent—more than I had intended. Not much more, but some. And I owed her some money and was coming to pay it, and that is all there is to it. Except that I do hope you'll believe me."

So that was it. Oddly, perhaps, she did believe him. There was a tinge of half-ashamed defiance in his confession that made it convincing. And after all, according to Dolly Brocksley, Mary Monroe had been the kind of person sought by people in difficulty. The explanation was simple; it covered everything. Or did it?

"Is it your custom to carry a revolver when you pay your debts?" asked Deborah rather sweetly.

He looked at her briefly, slowed down, maneuvered to the curb, and stopped.

"Deborah Cavert," he said, "I'm anxious to save my own skin. And yours. But I'll be damned if I'll have a wife who says things like that. Not even temporarily. Not even for a night. Not even," said Anthony firmly, "for five minutes. God deliver me from an ironic wife."

The thing was, he meant it. And he waited somewhat grimly for her to say something.

Deborah wriggled a little and looked at the street ahead and patted Blitz.

"Oh, all right," she said.

He took it as a contract and got into gear. From his voice she thought he was smiling, but she refused just then to look. He said: "That's good. I'm glad we have an understanding."

"But after all," observed Deborah, "you did have a revolver."

"Yes," he said soberly. "And I think I had the clue to the murder—to both murders—right in my hand. And lost it."

"Lost it!"

"Literally. You see (and I warn you this may not sound true at all. But it's what happened)—you see, I picked up that revolver just outside the door of Mary Monroe's house. Stepped on it and picked it up. That's why I—I wasn't exactly surprised to find a—scene of violence when I opened the door. That is, I didn't expect murder. I didn't in so many words expect anything.

But after all, finding a revolver does give you a sense of alarm. Well, then, after I left you and went into the back of the house I—lost the revolver. I know how that sounds," said Anthony lamely. "But nevertheless I managed to do it. Tripped, dropped it, and couldn't find it without turning on lights. And the person I was after was getting away from me, and it seemed to me more important to pursue the person than the revolver."

"And you discovered neither?"

"No," said Anthony, and a mask came down over his face again. "And so far as we know, the police didn't find the revolver, either. So you see—somebody must have found it. And that somebody—could have been—must have been the murderer."

"You can't be sure of that."

"No. You can't be sure of anything. The circumstances of both murders seem—oh, not premeditated. They suggest a kind of emotional explosion. As if the murderer killed first and then tried to cover· up the crime and escape. There doesn't seem to be much evidence of careful planning. Of anything at all cautious or elaborate about it. For instance, it looks as if whoever murdered Mary Monroe simply grabbed a revolver, came up to the roof, heard her singing 'Elégie,' opened the door, and shot. Then he cut the wires—there at the corner of the roof where they enter the house—obviously to delay anyone desiring to call the police. Then he escaped. All right. The way of escape was open; it would be simple for a man to go down the fire escape and swing the thing back up again. Or he may have had a key to the third-floor door——"

"That would mean someone in the apartment house," said Deborah.

"Yes, perhaps. But there's that tune, later, being

played on the piano. I can't get that out of my head. At exactly the time when I was in the back rooms—and you were just about entering the Riddles' apartment, or already there."

"That gives time for whoever was on the fire escape to go up to the house."

"Time, yes. But there's no rhyme or reason for an escaping murderer to return and sit tranquilly down at the piano and play a tune." Anthony threaded traffic expertly, turned and said: "I wonder what's going on back at Eden Street."

"What did you say when you called the police?"

"Just told them there was another murder at 18 East Eden. I suppose Lieutenant Waggon is on the job by this time. He's pretty near infallible, you know. Look here— how did Brocksley and his wife get on, do you know? I've a sort of feeling that he was rather a brute with her."

"I don't know," said Deborah slowly. "I had rather that impression, too. But if the evidence Brocksley said he had about the murder of Mary Monroe was actually the motive for his own murder, why, that would mean that it was done by someone whom that evidence would involve."

"Yes."

"Then if Tighe and Pigeon were trying to talk him out of it, obviously the evidence involved one or—or perhaps both of them, then obviously——"

"Obviously Tighe or Pigeon may have murdered him," finished Anthony briskly. "Either one looks to be more or less expert, though perhaps Pigeon would be the betting favorite. He's terribly dexterous, wily as a little eel. Silent, quick—yes, he could have done it. But somehow—I can't quite explain—but he would have done it more efficiently, I think. This murder, too, has a queerly impulsive aspect. Not ·planned." Anthony paused thoughtfully. "After all," he said, "it's not a particularly neat way of disposing of anyone. In fact it's decidedly unpleasant. And Pigeon—you may think this is absurd, but I've been told that he really is fanatically neat."

Deborah made a gesture of dubiety, and Anthony said quickly:

"Oh, I know that's not conclusive. But you see—there's something irrational about it. As there was about Mary's murder. Something impromptu. Just a quick, silent killing. Perfectly simple and direct. It's—well, it's as if something had got into the house; some queer detached force that meant murder. And I suppose murder always is incomprehensible, a kind of fact standing alone that it is difficult to connect with real people. But after all, there's always a human agency. And if the police are the men I think they are they'll discover it. The only thing is," said Anthony, "I don't want them to make any mistakes about it."

He always returned to that, his fear that she, Deborah, would be charged with the murder of Mary Monroe. That was because of that mysterious motive he imputed to her. Yet how could she have a motive that she didn't even know about! It was not possible. But all sorts of things had been happening that, a week ago, she would have called impossible. And he had been so certain. A strange little doubt blew across Deborah's thoughts like a chill, revealing wind. Was it even faintly possible that he was right?

"Anthony—ever since the night of Mary Monroe's death you have talked as if I might be, somehow, involved in her death. I mean—about motives. You've put me off when I've asked what you meant. You——"

"Deborah——"

"No, no. Please let me talk of it. You see, you are so very convincing about it that I'm almost ready to believe it myself. And yet I—it is exactly as I told you. I didn't even know her. I had no reason to wish for her death. No reason at all. You must believe me."

He drove on silently. It was a long three minutes before he spoke, and then it was with an effect of having chosen his words carefully.

"We thrashed that out once, Deborah. At least I thought we had it settled. You see—I asked you to trust me. I've simply got to ask it again. If you really don't know——"

Deborah made a half-pleading, half-impatient little murmur and he said quickly:

"Oh, of course I believe you. That is—yes, I believe you so far as fundamentals go. I mean by that," he continued hurriedly, "I thought at first that—well, never mind what I thought. You—oh, can't we call this settled? We've said all there is to say. Besides I may have been altogether mistaken, you know. There's always that. Why not call it that and forgive me and let it go?"

It was an odd mixture of boyishness and a determination that was not boyish. Out of it one thing was certain and that was that, mistaken or not, he had said all he would say.

Deborah said stiffly: "Well, at any rate, I certainly had no motive for murdering Alfred Brocksley."

He looked at her again, negotiated a corner, and said:

"I've got to do what seems best to me. Do you mind a little speed? We are getting out of traffic now, and I'm going to let the car out a bit."

It was considerably more than a little speed. Deborah clutched Blitz and braced herself against the rocking of the car as they shot past telephone poles and culverts and occasional automobiles, following the long lane of lights that traveled ahead of them.

Crown Point and marriage. Her thoughts went to the long silent apartment to which she would be returning. Last night when she had returned she had been so sure that someone had entered the place during her absence. Last night—— She sat upright abruptly.

"Did you take the newspapers with you last night when we went to dinner?" she said.

Anthony swerved perilously, slowed down, steadied the car, and said:

"Newspapers? You mean those you and Francis and I were looking at just before we went to Brascotti's? No. Why?"

She told him briefly.

"You are sure Francis didn't take them?" he said.

"I don't know. I simply can't remember. But there were quite a lot of papers, you know. I think if you or Francis had carried them away I should have noticed it. It would have made a pretty bulky roll."

"Then do you think someone was in the apartment while we were gone?"

"I don't know. There was the mimosa, you know. Yet——"

He said abruptly: "I don't like your staying alone there."

"I don't like it either," admitted Deborah. "But I can always go to Chloe."

"Oh," said Anthony in an odd voice. "Yes. There's Chloe." He said nothing further, though he looked thoughtful, and again the rush of motion submerged them and made conversation difficult. Once the lights of a small town rose, and Deborah thought it was Crown Point, and a queer stifled throb was suddenly in her throat, but it wasn't and they flashed past. And once Anthony glanced at his watch and frowned and pressed his foot harder on the gas throttle.

When they actually arrived the thing was done in the simplest, most matter-of-fact way in the world. The courthouse, of course, was closed, but telephoning brought not only the clerk but a justice of the peace and the boy from the filling station near by to act as the extra witness. The room was filled with benches, and they stood before a long pine table, and there was a definite smell of sweeping compound which lured but puzzled Blitz. The voice of the justice of peace sounded hollow, and the boy from the filling station started to light a cigarette and stopped himself guiltily. It was only the familiar yet poignantly unfamiliar phrases of the ceremony that gave Deborah a sudden sense of solemnity and all at once a queer, clear flash of realization of what she was doing.

These promises could not be made lightly; you could not enter upon these compacts and mean, in your heart, no single word of it. Well, then she must stop it. Now, before it was too late. She looked at Anthony in a sudden strange panic, and he caught her slight motion and turned to look down at her soberly, and all the cogent reasons for this thing swept over her again and it was too late then to stop it. The ring fitted, and Anthony's hand was not too steady. The justice of peace looked at them beamingly over thick eyeglasses and said briskly: "'. . . do pronounce you man and wife . . .' It's customary to kiss the bride, and I don't know who has a better right than her husband."

He waited. The clerk waited. The boy from the filling station waited.

Then Anthony turned to Deborah and put his arms around her and kissed her mouth. Kissed it fully, completely, deliberately.

When he had stopped, the justice beamed a bit mistily, the little clerk sighed, and the filling-station boy said, "Gee" under his breath and grinned joyously at Deborah. So it must have been, thought Deborah confusedly, a fairly satisfactory kiss. But her lips stung from that hard pressure; and the man who had kissed her was, madly, her husband.

CHAPTER XII

SOMEHOW they were in the car again. Deborah had a confused memory of Anthony's shaking hands with each of the three and of their hands going immediately thereafter to their pockets; of their friendly farewells and good wishes; of Blitz barking furiously at a cat who was sauntering along the street; of the filling-station boy appearing again at the window just as Anthony started the engine of the car.

He opened the door.

"It's a flower," said the boy, looking at Deborah. "A geranium. It bloomed this morning just in time." He held out the red blossoms which he had set carefully against two large green leaves. "For the bride," he said and grinned.

"Th-thank you," said Deborah. She took the geranium, and Anthony thanked the boy, who waved happily after them, and they were off. Headed this time back toward Chicago. Deborah sniffed the geranium and pinned it to her coat and felt something like tears in her eyes and looked up to find that Anthony was looking at her in a still, intent way. It was as if they were speaking, and yet neither moved nor actually spoke until Anthony quite suddenly smiled in the friendliest way and Deborah smiled, too, and the little constraint vanished.

Then the roar and motion of the car gathered them up again into a sort of hollow of speed and steady sound

that was hypnotic. Deborah, deeply thoughtful, sat for
the most part in silence while Anthony drove and at
intervals looked at his watch. The ride back to where
the lights of Chicago made a dull glow in the sky seemed
very much shorter than the ride out.

"I meant," said Anthony as they neared the city,
"to have stopped for dinner. Seems as if we ought to be
a little festive. But now—with this new development,
I believe we ought to get back to the apartment house
without delay. We'll have to tell a straight story. One
that's the truth—if not all the truth. And our stories
must agree. From the looks of Brocksley I'd say he
hadn't been dead very long. Of course, he must have
been killed between six-thirty and seven—or five after
seven. He certainly was not in the hall when I left your
place at six-thirty. That leaves thirty-five minutes.
Francis will alibi me. He was at the radio the whole
time; kept changing stations while I was talking to you
till I could scarcely hear you—so he couldn't hear what
I said to you, I'm sure, but he could hear my voice."

He paused and smiled rather mirthlessly. "I telephoned to the Brownstone to order a—a wedding dinner, just after I talked to you."

"Oh," said Deborah, and Anthony went on rather
hurriedly:

"But he had got an orchestra just then. I'm sure he
couldn't hear what I said. And if he did there's nothing
exactly incriminating about ordering a dinner for two.
The point is, I have an alibi. Have you?"

"No," said Deborah soberly. "I was alone, and I
didn't even hear a sound from the hall outside."

"You didn't hear—don't think I'm out of my head—
but did you hear a song?"

"A *song!*" It was an instant before she understood.

"No, I heard nothing." She pulled her coat tighter around her.

"Oh—well—it simply can't mean anything. 'Elégie,' I mean. Yet somehow—it's got to. Mary Monroe was singing it when she was killed. And then, later, I heard the melody being played on the piano. Nobody would have taken such a chance without a reason for it; sitting at the piano directly above the body of Mary Monroe, calmly playing 'Elégie'! Even if whoever played that song thought he was alone in the house it was still a risk. No—there's got to be a reason. Well," he returned abruptly to the immediate question, "the police will be there when we reach the apartment house. I think we'll be able to stick to the truth except about your finding Brocksley. We left the house about seven. Went by the back way because my car was parked near there. That's not very good, but it will have to serve. Then we went for a ride. They'll ask where were we riding all this time. So what?—Just riding is the only answer to that. Doesn't seem exactly sensible to ride so long on a winter night, but the nearer we stick to the truth the better it is for everybody—even aside from any fondness for truth telling!"

They stopped at the bridge and went on northward. In a very few moments now they would be at home. What would they find? What had happened during that interval of time?

Anthony was edging over to the inside lane of traffic. He was turning into Eden Street. Deborah's heart had got up into her throat and was pounding there, and she leaned over Blitz to stare anxiously along the short street.

"They are there," said Anthony grimly. "Now for it, Deborah."

It was a changed street. No longer quiet, no longer dignified, no longer deserted. Even now, hours after the murder had been reported, it was choked with cars—with lights—with figures clustered here and there—with police. Anthony pulled into the curb half a block from the entrance to the apartment house because there was no space farther along. He turned off the engine and looked at Deborah for a moment before he took her bare left hand. He held it thoughtfully, looking at the hand and the ring on it before he said rather gently: "I expect you'd better take the ring off. I don't know why I got it except that—oh, a marriage isn't a marriage without a ring, is it? That is,"—he caught the implication swiftly, flushed a little, and said quickly: "That is—of course, this marriage—that is, I mean—oh, hell. Come on, Deborah."

But he paused to watch with an odd, thoughtful look while she slipped the ring off her finger. She put it in her bag and gathered up Blitz, and then suddenly they were in the cool air and threading their way through brawny policemen and alert groups of men talking in low voices and clusters of curious passers-by.

They reached the vestibule before they were stopped, and then it was the bulky policeman who had questioned them the morning after Mary Monroe's murder.

"Hey," he said and recognized them. "Oh, it's you. Thought it was somebody trying to get into the house. Say, the lieutenant's been looking for you."

"For us!" said Anthony. "Why? What's happened? What's all the excitement about?"

"Haven't you heard?" said the policeman. "Gosh, from the way people've been hanging around watching, I thought everybody in Chicago knew. There's been another murder here. That Brocksley fellow. Throat cut."

"Brocksley!" cried Anthony. "Who killed him?"

"I don't know who killed him," said the policeman. "Nor how. But he's sure dead. Come on. The lieutenant is in here."

There were groups in the hall, too. Anthony and Deborah were towed through them and toward the Brocksley flat. The door was open, and there were people in the front rooms, but the policeman led them straight along the hall to the dining room.

It was a queer confused picture of which Lieutenant Waggon, long and pale and very calm, was the central and dominating figure. Dolly was there, huddled despairingly in a chair, with her small face hard and still and her bony hands twisting themselves together on her lap. Chloe was near her, and Gibbs. Francis Maly stood beside Gibbs and looked relieved when he saw Anthony and Deborah enter, and moved forward at once.

"Gosh, I'm glad you've turned up," he said in a low voice to Anthony. "Where've you been?"

"Riding," said Anthony laconically.

"You've heard——" began Francis, and Lieutenant Waggon said: "Ah, Wyatt. Come over here, please."

Numbly Deborah heard Anthony tell their story and heard her own voice subscribing to it. The lieutenant's eyes were deep and blue and searched her own until she felt there was something unearthly in the far-seeking gaze.

He asked a few questions, accepted, or seemed to accept, their replies, and was interested only in the exact time at which they had left the apartment house.

"It was very close to seven," said Anthony. "Perhaps five or ten minutes after."

"You and Miss Cavert left by the back way?"

"Yes—my car was parked around on Vine."

Lieutenant Waggon meditated.

"You saw no one in the court?"

"Not a soul," said Anthony.

"No one in the street?"

"No one."

Lieutenant Waggon glanced at a man at his side whose sleeve wore stripes and said in a markedly gentle manner: "Who let 'em get by?"

The man with stripes looked far more uneasy than the lieutenant's manner seemed to justify.

"Corran, sir. And Briggs."

The lieutenant nodded once, and Deborah would not have wanted to be either Corran or Briggs. He said:

"How about you, Miss Cavert? See anybody in the alley or court?"

"No," said Deborah steadily.

"Do you know anything of this murder?"

The words themselves were general and easily evaded: all one had to do was say, broadly, no. But when spoken by the blue-eyed man opposite, they became very direct and inclusive, and Deborah was horribly impelled to reply fully and openly. She bit back the words on her lips, replied briefly that she knew nothing of it, and was for a dreadful moment perfectly sure that Lieutenant Waggon's calm, motherly gaze had plumbed her thoughts so accurately and thoroughly that he had no need for further questions. This unwelcome conviction was strengthened by the fact that he did not at the moment question her more but glanced once at Blitz (who, impressed and awed, was for once content to trot sedately at Deborah's heels), and turned his attention to a hurrying policeman who was whispering in his ear.

Deborah, feeling herself dismissed, turned, caught
Chloe's eyes, and drifted to her side, the little dog
following closely.

Chloe was very white, and her green, shining eyes held
something still and terrified in their phosphorescent
depths. But she was still Chloe. She pushed back her
tousle of black hair with one lithe hand, took a long
breath which moved the folds of green silk at her breast,
and said:

"Where'd you get the geranium?"

Deborah glanced down at the fragrant red blossom.

"A filling-station boy," she said and felt her face
growing pink.

"Secret?" said Chloe uncannily. "Or just a tribute
to your bright eyes? My God, Deb, you were lucky to
have missed all this. Alfred Brocksley——" Her throaty
whisper broke off abruptly, and a shudder rippled her
shoulders. "*I saw him*," she whispered. "*So did Dolly.*"

"Who did it?" said Deborah.

Chloe's eyes became fixed. She said in a faint, sharp
whisper:

"They don't know who did it. But Deb—they do say
this. That it was someone in the apartment house. You
see, the place was guarded. And they say that nobody
from outside—nobody, I mean, except us who live here
—was in the building when the murder was done."

Deborah's lips moved, and she broke through a curious paralysis of speech that gripped her.

"When was he murdered?" she said. "What happened? Who——"

"Who found him? I don't know. First thing I knew
was the noise in the hall. Dolly was with me. And Gibbs.
We ran to the door and into the hall, and there were
policemen already and—well, there was Brocksley."

Chloe's eyes went over Deborah's shoulder to the shifting groups near Lieutenant Waggon. The confusion and talking in the room covered her whispered conversation with Deborah, yet Deborah felt that Chloe was, for the first time in all the years she had known her, reluctant to speak.

"What time was that?" asked Deborah irresistibly.

"Exactly seven-twenty." (Seven-twenty. Then it was Anthony's telephone message, probably, that brought the police.)

"Dolly was with you?"

"Yes. She had just come upstairs to see me. They questioned her—questioned me—questioned everybody. Dolly's story is straight enough. She says Brocksley was in the living room reading the paper when she saw him last. That was just before seven; she was sure, because she looked at her watch. She came up to see me. Used the elevator but saw no one on the stairway. She saw nobody in the hall—and nobody was in their flat but Brocksley. We—that is," said Chloe slowly, "Dolly and Gibbs and I—talked until the police came twenty minutes later." Chloe's shoulders lifted again. "That's all we know. Brocksley was murdered some time during that twenty minutes—at most twenty-five."

"Do they know who were here in the apartment house?"

A small flame glowed away back in Chloe's eyes.

"Apparently all of us were here," she said. "Juanito included. Everybody, that is, except you. And Anthony Wyatt." Gibbs, white and angry-looking, with the pupils of his eyes like hard black agate points, strolled toward them, and Chloe said suddenly: "I wish they'd find the knife."

"*Knife!*" said Gibbs.

"Well," Chloe shrugged, "his throat was cut. And nothing was found. Therefore, the murderer took it away with him. And I must say I don't relish the thought of that knife being loose somewhere in the place." Gibbs's black eyebrows came together.

"You'll be lucky if you get to stay here at all," he said. "I wouldn't worry about knives if I were you. Looks very much as if they are just going to arrest us all."

"On the theory that one of us is the murderer?" said Chloe. "Well—after all—with the house guarded every minute of the time."

"That didn't seem to stop Tony and Deborah from leaving," said Gibbs, watching Deborah. "I don't see why it would stop someone from entering. Anyway, everybody in the house has got an alibi."

Quite suddenly Anthony was at Deborah's elbow.

"Alibi?" he said in a low voice. "What's that about alibis, Gibbs? You say everybody's got one? Then that ought to let us all out."

"Everybody's got an alibi all right," said Gibbs. "But whether Lieutenant Waggon accepts them or not's another matter. You don't notice him letting up on questions any, do you? How did you get away so simply, Tony? All these guards about the house and still nobody saw you leave!"

Anthony did not look at Deborah. He said: "We just walked out. Never even saw a guard. See here, what about these alibis?"

"Well, first," said Gibbs, "the Riddle family is out. Dolly was with us, so she's out. Francis Maly and you were together—according to Francis, that is—up till the time you left."

"Of course," said Anthony. "That's right."

"And just after you left, Juanito came to your flat to fix the plumbing in the kitchen, and he and Francis were together till the police got here."

"Yes, Francis told me that. That still leaves Tighe— and Pigeon."

Francis Maly had quietly joined the small group. Across the room Lieutenant Waggon, policemen, various men in plain clothes, went on in a matter-of-fact way with their business, engrossed, unheeding for the moment the little murmuring huddle of suspects. Suspects! It was an unpleasant word. But that was exactly what they were. Apparently free to move about and talk, they were actually under the closest, tightest restrictions.

The overhead light shone garishly down upon the shifting, busy groups, upon the shining veneered walnut chairs, upon the heavy, built-in buffet with its green glass bowl of wax water lilies, upon the glistening, round table. There were crocheted doilies on the buffet, and a large crocheted piece on the table had been pushed back and wrinkled. Deborah glanced at Dolly, who sat as if altogether unaware of the motion and murmur of voices around her. Her small face was blank and set; the hands which had made so painstakingly all those doilies, and which kept the cheap furniture glowing from polish— hands which could dissolve into serene and flowing grace when Dolly walked or danced—were now awkwardly, wearily supporting her small, lined chin.

The only possible kindness was to leave her in the seclusion which her withdrawn attitude proclaimed. Again Dolly's sobbing words of that morning drifted across Deborah's memory: "I could kill with my own hands the man that murdered her," Dolly had sobbed. But she hadn't killed Alfred Brocksley. She had been with Chloe at the time he must have died. Or had she? Wasn't it possible that she had killed him there in the hall before entering the Riddle apartment—possible, that is, if time, and not Dolly herself, were the only consideration? What was it Anthony had said about murder? Something to the effect that it must stand alone as a fact—that it was difficult to link with real persons. Persons you knew. There was murder. And there was Dolly Brocksley. But Deborah could not link the two.

Yet if time alone were to be considered, Dolly could have done this murder. Was Chloe sure that when Dolly arrived there had not been a dark, soggy-looking figure sprawled there before the elevator? Deborah turned to Chloe. Francis and Gibbs were talking of police procedure, and Deborah, under cover of their low voices, whispered to Chloe:

"You are sure that Brocksley——" She caught herself on the verge of saying, betrayingly, "—wasn't already lying there before the elevator," and substituted: "—wasn't already dead when Dolly arrived?"

Chloe's eyes became green slits.

"You don't mean that as it sounds," she whispered sharply. "Dolly didn't do this. And there was nothing—nothing, you understand me?—in the hall when Dolly came. I know, because I opened the door for her. Dolly didn't kill him."

"I wanted to be sure," said Deborah honestly, and the little flame died from Chloe's green eyes.

"I know," she said quickly. "I felt the same way myself. But it—well, it just couldn't have been Dolly. If you are thinking of what—" Chloe's eyes slid toward the group around Lieutenant Waggon there at the table and then, nearer, around their own small circle. Gibbs,

Anthony, and Francis were murmuring together, intent only on what, at that instant, Francis was saying, and Chloe whispered in Deborah's ear: "—what Dolly said this morning about—well, about what she'd like to do to whoever killed Mary Monroe—if that's what you're thinking of, so did I. Couldn't help myself. But it simply couldn't have been Dolly. She and I and Gibbs were there in our flat when Brocksley must have been killed."

Lieutenant Waggon's mild face came into view as the broad shoulders of a policeman standing beside him moved. He was sitting at the table, and the light fell full upon him, and his blue eyes traveled slowly around the room. Under that motherly regard, Chloe fell quickly silent.

Francis, however, continued talking, and Deborah heard his low words:

". . . so it does seem strange that whoever reported the murder won't admit it. They can't trace the telephone call, you know."

"When was it reported?" That was Gibbs.

Lieutenant Waggon's pallid gaze rested upon him, and Deborah felt oddly sure that the lieutenant knew what Gibbs said, although, owing to the ever-changing confusion of voices and motion, he couldn't have heard Gibbs's low tones.

"I gathered the call came at about a quarter after seven. At least they inquired very particularly about that time. It was sheer luck for me and Juanito that we were working at that kitchen tap when the thing happened."

"Scared, Francis?" asked Gibbs with a disagreeable smile.

"Certainly," said Francis. "It's a nasty business. And the police have got to get somebody."

"They'll get the murderer," said Anthony shortly, "if I know anything of Lieutenant Waggon."

"He's supposed to be pretty good, isn't he?" said Francis.

Gibbs's face darkened.

"Too damn good," he said. "He'd send us all to jail rather than risk losing the murderer."

"Well," said Francis, "after all—it does look rather bad for us. Guards all around the house. Only ourselves here. And another murder—right under our noses. Not at all pretty, Gibbs, old thing."

Gibbs's eyebrows were a lowering black line across his face, and the pupils of his eyes were small and hard and black.

"That's rather a largish margin, though," he said. "Remember that it includes such shining examples of our citizenry as Tighe. And Pigeon. And that they very accommodatingly alibi each other; Tighe swears he was eating dinner and Pigeon that he was serving it." Gibbs laughed mirthlessly, and Francis said with truth: "Well, yes—it does sound a bit accommodating," and there was a commotion at the door.

Several policemen were ushering in someone who was a sort of nucleus to the whirlpool. And one of them said: "Got it, Lieutenant," triumphantly, and the circle parted and the nucleus was Juanito, his eyes smoldering in a sullen face. "We had to break the door down. There's a lot of stuff stored there. You'd better take a look at it, Lieutenant." The voice held a note of repressed significance and excitement.

They had pushed themselves and Juanito forward to meet Lieutenant Waggon. Juanito's smoldering eyes went from one side to another like those of a trapped animal, and another policeman said:

"This fellow here still pretends he's lost the key. Says he don't know a thing about the vacant apartment. Says he don't know when the stuff was stored there. Says the apartment's been vacant for months. But somebody's been there and not very long ago."

With a triumphant air he extended something toward Lieutenant Waggon. Lieutenant Waggon looked at the small object in the policeman's broad hand for a moment before he put out, himself, a long hand and took it up. Then Deborah saw what he held.

It was a gardenia. It was crumpled and limp but not withered. The edges of the petals were brown, but their inner depth was still the color of thick smooth cream.

CHAPTER XIII

SLOWLY Lieutenant Waggon lifted the flower to his long nose and sniffed it. No one moved.

He looked up. Looked all the way around the room. His slow regard lingered upon the group of suspects that included Deborah and Chloe, Anthony, Francis, and Gibbs Riddle.

He said quietly to a sergeant:

"Let 'em go. But keep 'em in the house." He addressed them more directly: "Please to remember, folks, that there'll be a strong police guard about the place —for your own protection," he said fondly. "Now then, Mrs. Brocksley, if you'd like to retire there'll be a police matron here in a few minutes. I think you'll rest better if we keep a woman in the place with you."

Dolly did not move but seemed to agree passively.

Lieutenant Waggon's gaze returned to Juanito. After a moment he said:

"Guess I'll take a turn at him myself. Clear the room, Sergeant."

Chloe went to Dolly and patted her still hands and would have remained, but Lieutenant Waggon looked at her and she lifted one shoulder and trailed out after Deborah with her hand on her hip.

In the hall, Francis said: "Come in, won't you? We'll have cocktails. I, for one, feel the need."

The cocktails, however, were not a success, though Francis mixed them with a lavish hand and Gibbs drank his thirstily, and Anthony pointed out the choicest books in the shelves that lined Francis's living room. "Mine," said Anthony, "is the front room. But I've nothing of interest except a very rusty old sword and a faded and grumpish portrait of an ancestor." He looked at Deborah. "Want to see it?"

Deborah followed him through the small hall into the front room which in her own apartment was the drawing room.

"After all," said Anthony, "you might like to know something of your—er—family. There he is above the mantel. A bit faded, as I said. And there's the sword above him."

Deborah looked and heard Chloe laughing rather harshly in the next room, and Anthony said in a low tone:

"Deborah—I don't want to frighten you. But there's something I want to say. If you—if you just weren't alone up there it would be so much better. You see, whoever murdered Mary Monroe must know that you were at the piano. Well—suppose the murderer thought that you saw him. Suppose—oh, don't look like that, Deborah! I hate to say this. I wouldn't have said it at all, ever—but Brocksley was killed because he knew something."

"You mean," said Deborah incredulously, "that the murderer may attack me!"

"The murderer can't possibly be sure that you didn't see him kill Mary," said Anthony gently.

There was a silence, then Deborah whispered: "Oh," sharply.

And Chloe was saying: ". . . of course, I'm scared. I'm terrified. These dark old halls—you feel as if something might reach out from the shadows and—and—I'll take another cocktail, Francis." Francis said: "I made 'em plenty strong," and there was the tinkle of ice in the shaker, and Gibbs said: "Nonsense, Chloe. Nobody wants to murder you. There's a purpose to these things. Somebody's after something."

"That," said Chloe, "or just murdering for the fun of it. Either is bad enough. That's plenty, Francis."

"All the same," said Francis, "I for one am going to take no chances. It's queer how few clues have been left. Reading and hearing about murders, you always feel that there can't be a murder without some elaborate preparation for it. And these seem to be—oh, spontaneous. Swift. No plans."

Gibbs laughed in a rather ugly way. He'd probably, thought Deborah, managed to gulp down several cocktails and never drank with grace. He said: "Spontaneous, huh? Well, it's too spontaneous for me. All I hope is, there's no more of it."

There was again the thin sound of liquid being poured into a glass. Then Francis said soberly: "It seems to me the police ought to look for motives. And if they can't find motives, then there's only one conclusion. And that is, of course, a homicidal maniac——"

"And what a pleasant little thought that is," said Chloe throatily.

"Who would have motives?" said Gibbs, still in an ugly way.

"Well," said Francis, "look at it like this. Among the residents are—how many people? You two, and Tony and me. Deborah Cavert. Makes five. Dolly Brocksley and Tighe and Pigeon. Eight."

"And Juanito."

"Nine. And your cook. Ten."

Gibbs laughed. "Tulip! She didn't murder anybody."

"Exactly. That's the way we all feel about ourselves —our own household. The point is, does anyone else realize that we didn't do murder? Who of all those ten people seems to have potentialities as a murderer?"

"Tighe," said Chloe.

"Pigeon," said Gibbs.

Francis said: "Have another cocktail, Gibbs," and Chloe seemed to remonstrate, and Francis said: "Well— all I hope is, there's no more of it. Brocksley, of course, must have known something. And he was a strong man physically."

There was something odd in his tone—something that Deborah heard and something that Gibbs must have heard, for Gibbs said in a voice that gave Deborah a swift vision of his thick black eyebrows drawn angrily together: "What do you mean by that, Francis?"

"Obviously," said Francis, "it would have been very difficult—I mean the sheer physical strength involved."

There was, quite suddenly, something unsaid hovering in the air; something ugly and strange and inescapable.

Then Chloe spoke quickly: just where, did they suppose, Brocksley had been murdered—in the hall, in the Brocksley flat . . . "What do you suppose he would be doing on the second floor?" she said and added: "But the motive's clear enough in his case: he knew too much."

Deborah turned to Anthony again.

"It's begun," she said, half whispering. "Everyone suspecting everyone else. Wondering if this is the hand —this the source of danger." She paused, and Anthony's eyes were dark and pitying, and she said, "Thank you for warning me. I hadn't realized that I—knew too much, too."

"I only want you to be careful," said Anthony. "Don't take any chances. Don't go to the door until you know who's outside. Don't go into the halls alone. Don't——" His low voice changed, and he said: "I hate to frighten you. And I hate your being alone——"

"Deborah." It was Chloe calling. "I'm going. Thanks for the cocktails, Francis. They've given me courage to pass that place upstairs in the hall. I'll never see it again without feeling——"

"Oh, shut up, Chloe," snapped Gibbs.

The groups in the hall had diminished during the little interval. Blitz under Deborah's arm wriggled and growled most undiplomatically at a policeman, and Gibbs went back to finish what was left in the shaker, which annoyed Chloe.

"I feel as if I'd been dragged through a knothole backward," she said. "Come on, Gibbs. I've got to go to sleep, and I'm afraid to go into the flat without you."

"Nerves, Chloe?" said Gibbs. "Didn't know you had any."

"I've got plenty," said Chloe. "What's happened to the elevator?" She pressed her vigorous thumb on the bell again. Gibbs growled: "Stairway's still working," and the policeman approached.

"It's all right," he said. "They've finished." He shook the grilled iron door, thrust his head against the bars, and shouted huskily to someone above: "Let the cage down, boys." There was the clash of a closing door. The policeman said: "It'll be down in a minute."

"What were they doing with the elevator?" asked Gibbs.

"Oh, fingerprints," said the policeman with false airiness. "Lots of fingerprints. And blood."

"*Blood!*" It was a sharp whisper from Chloe. The policeman glanced at her appraisingly.

"Sure. Blood. On the floor."

There was a crisp silence. Then Chloe said: "M-much?"

"I dunno," said the policeman cheerily. "Enough, I guess."

The cage droned into sight, the door opened and gave exit to two unbelievably thin and alert young men with hats on the backs of their heads, who looked at Deborah, looked at Chloe, looked at Gibbs and Anthony and Francis and the policeman, all in one embracing glance, and vanished into the Brocksley flat in practically the same instant, and the policeman said:

"Don't be worried about it. I guess it's all cleaned up now, anyway."

"O—oh," said Chloe with a kind of gulp and entered. Gibbs followed, and Deborah, clutching Blitz, who growled and sniffed, and Anthony.

"I'll just see that Deborah's apartment is—all right," he said and pressed the button for the second floor. Francis stepped backward and turned to speak to the policeman, and both vanished as the small cage droned upward.

In the dim light Deborah was aware that Chloe was looking uneasily downward at the floor.

"I don't see anything," she said, moving a step or two to one side, and looking again. "Not a thing. Do you suppose that policeman was telling the truth?"

"Don't know why he'd lie," said Gibbs crossly. "Stop dancing about like that. It's probably under my feet. I trust you all realize that everyone of us has made fingerprints innumerable in this wretched little box."

They did realize it. No one spoke, and the elevator stopped with a lurch. Deborah's eyes went involuntarily to the patch on the carpet where there had been that supine, black huddle. There was nothing, now, of course, except a policeman sitting in a small chair which was tilted back against the wall. Chloe looked at him, gasped, and said:

"Why did you take *that* chair? Wouldn't you prefer an easy chair?"

There was a perceptible edge to her voice. The chair was, as Deborah knew, a Chinese Chippendale, acquired mysteriously from an old cousin of Chloe's and, though somewhat marred and battered by spirited young Riddles, was still one of Chloe's prized possessions.

The policeman said comfortably: "Oh, this is all right, thank you." He looked at Deborah: "That your apartment?" he said with a toss of his thumb toward the Cavert door.

"Yes," said Deborah, holding Blitz's mouth against a violent desire to express himself.

"H'm," said the policeman. "Well, I tried to get a chair there, but your mother wouldn't give it to me." He lowered the two front legs of the chair. It creaked frailly, and Chloe gasped again, and Deborah said:

"*Who?*"

"Ain't it your mother? The old lady in there."

"Annie's got back," said Chloe. "Well, thank heaven for that. Good-night, Deb." She looked at the policeman and smiled ominously: "I'm afraid that chair's not awfully comfortable. Can't I get you another?"

He squirmed back against the wall, and the chair moaned.

"Suits me," he said blandly. "This is a swell chair,

ma'am. That is, it don't look like much, but it sure sets elegant."

"Oh," said Chloe with dreadful sweetness. "Isn't that nice!—Come on, Gibbs!"

She disappeared with as near a flounce as Chloe, being built on sinuous lines, could achieve. Gibbs followed, the chair creaked again, and Anthony said, looking relieved:

"It's Annie, all right. Well, I'm glad of that. I'll come in with you and make sure."

But it wasn't Annie.

Blitz wriggled out of Deborah's arms and barked and made a small dash toward the drawing room, where he stopped short, wagging his tail moderately, with a nice suggestion of polite recognition rather than ecstatic welcome.

And Juliet Cavert, slender, crisp, dignified—with a neat band of flesh-colored ribbon around her throat, wearing a prim dark suit with a real lace collar and a spotless frill around each beautiful hand, her gray hair smooth, and little blue wreaths of smoke from a slim cigarette, which she held in an ivory holder, floating calmly about her face—sat there, waiting for them.

"*Juliet!*"

"Yes, Deborah, I've been waiting for you. Where have you been?"

"*Juliet——*"

Juliet Cavert's beautiful black eyebrows lifted.

"Well, Deborah. Do collect yourself, my dear."

The cool crisp voice was like a sliver of ice. Deborah slipped dazedly out of her coat. She was vaguely aware that Anthony caught it for her and placed it across a chair and that Blitz looked at Juliet and retired quietly under the divan.

"But I thought you were in Florida," said Deborah.

"I was in Florida. As you see, I have returned. Your father is about the same. Perhaps a little better. I feel quite safe in leaving him for the time being. Now then, what's all this? Where have you been? Why is—— "

One hand motioned delicately toward Anthony.

Deborah had a slightly hysterical impulse to say: "Oh, that's my husband. You must meet!"

She restrained it and presented Anthony briefly. Anthony bowed and murmured. Juliet lifted her eyeglass for a long chill look before she chose to say: "How do you do?" It was one of her less agreeable accomplishments. Deborah said:

"Then you got my telegram?"

"Telegram?"

"Yes, of course. Telling you not to let Father see the papers."

"Oh, yes," said Juliet.

Anthony interrupted. He looked very distant and very chilly himself and had no compunction whatever about interrupting Juliet. He said:

"But you must be mistaken, Miss Cavert. Deborah has forgotten that the telegram was not delivered."

Juliet looked at him. Her eyes did not waver, and a look about Anthony's mouth kept Deborah from rushing in with explanations. Presently Juliet said vaguely: "One has so many notes—messages . . ."

"When did you arrive?" asked Anthony. There was again the grim look in his face that Deborah was beginning to know, but there was under it something like a queer sort of anger, too.

Juliet lifted her chin.

"I arrived tonight," she said. "Although I cannot understand what possible interest the time of my arrival is to you. It's very kind of you, I'm sure, to take an interest. Now, Mr—er—White——"

That, of course, was inept; Juliet hadn't often to resort to so clumsy a trick. Anthony was proof against it, however. He interrupted her sharply again and said definitely:

"My name is Wyatt, Miss Cavert. I was under the impression that it was not altogether unfamiliar to you."

Juliet looked white.

"Mr. Wyatt," she said, "do forgive me. I was about to say, if you'll excuse us now—my niece and I have much to talk of—this dreadful affair."

She had risen. Anthony said:

"Certainly, Miss Cavert. I live just downstairs, you know." Odd, thought Deborah, how like a threat that sounded. She stood, too, rather numbly. And Anthony again astonished her. For he said: "I'll just say good-night to Deborah," walked over to her, and before Deborah realized his intention kissed her soundly.

"Ahg—" said Juliet and achieved, "Really——"

"Good-night, Miss Cavert," said Anthony pleasantly. "Come to the door with me, Deborah."

Juliet said nothing.

Deborah dazedly obeyed. At the door Anthony looked down at her and grinned briefly and somewhat defiantly.

"Couldn't help it," he said in a low voice. "Please don't mind." He became sober again. "Look here, Deborah, don't take any chances. And call me if you—need me." He took her hands and looked for a clear, intent instant down into her eyes. Then he was gone, and the door was closed, and Deborah turned wearily and perplexedly back to face Juliet—who would in all probability, thought Deborah fleetingly, take some facing.

"Who's this young man?" said Juliet at once. "How do you know him? What's he doing here?"

"His name's Wyatt," said Deborah.

"Dear child, I know that. What's he doing here?"

Blitz poked a cautious head from under the divan, reconnoitered, and wriggled quietly out and toward the hall, where he disappeared. Deborah sighed.

"He's been very kind," said Deborah.

"Kind?" said Juliet, lifting her eyebrows. "I should have thought that 'fond' might describe it better."

Deborah realized that she was very tired and that Juliet's little flurry over Anthony was actually of no importance whatever. She said wearily:

"When did you know of the—murder?"

Juliet looked at Deborah, glanced about for an ashtray and found it.

"In the papers," she said then. "This is a terrible thing, Deborah. I—I felt I had to come to you."

Deborah tried to do sums in her head, not very successfully.

"You must have come at once," she said. "As soon as you knew of the murder."

"Directly," replied Juliet.

Deborah hesitated.

"You read, of course, all about Miss Monroe?"

"Oh, yes. Dreadful affair." Juliet sat down, put out one slender hand, and turned off the light on the table beside her. "My eyes are tired," she said. "What about this murder of Brocksley, Deborah? Do you know anything? Have you heard anything?"

"Only what Chloe told me." Deborah repeated that briefly.

"Then," said Juliet slowly, "so far as you know

they've not been able to capture the murderer? I mean, he is still at large? There are a hundred hiding places in this old house. Have they searched everywhere?"

"I don't know. I suppose so. Did they question you, Juliet?" asked Deborah suddenly.

Juliet's slender shoulders lifted.

"Very briefly," she said. She took a deliberate breath, fastened her eyes upon Deborah steadily, and said: "I drove up in a taxi. I was getting out at the entrance, or rather just below, for the curb near the entrance was crowded with cars, when a policeman appeared and inquired the—-er—purpose of my coming. I was obliged to explain that I lived here. That I had just arrived from Florida. He said," interpolated Juliet dryly, "that it was a hell of a time to come home. When I heard what had happened I must say I agreed with him. I had a few words with a person they called lieutenant and retired." She stopped, took another breath, rose, and said: "I'm going to sleep. I am frightfully tired and distressed. This is a very painful thing. Tomorrow . . ." Her voice trailed vaguely away. At the doorway she paused: "We'll talk of things tomorrow," she said. "Please see that the door is bolted."

"Juliet," said Deborah, "did you know Mary Monroe?"

Juliet *was* tired. She was quite gray with fatigue.

After a moment she said: "I knew Mary Monroe slightly, Deborah. She was more or less in the public eye some years ago, you know. A great many people knew her. While we are speaking of this, Deborah, I might say that—while I have never been one to interfere with your affairs, still I do think that your acquaintance with Anthony Wyatt might better be kept on a—shall I say more formal level? I've no doubt he's a very pleasant young man. But I believe he was extremely well acquainted with Miss Monroe."

"If you mean to imply that there was anything in his friendship with Miss Monroe which would in any sense prevent my own acquaintance with him, I think you must be more direct in what you say, Juliet."

Juliet put up her eyeglasses and lifted her beautiful, curved black eyebrows.

"My child," she said slowly, "I believe you are defending him. Dear me."

It was exactly the kind of dry, coolly pointed sentence that had always been difficult for Deborah to combat. In the face of concerns of real gravity and importance, it became trivial. Yet, of course, Juliet was not at all a trivial person. Deborah said:

"Yes, I am defending him.—Let's leave this, Aunt Juliet. You are very tired."

Juliet's face became still and her mouth rather tight.

"Very well," she said. "I hope we both rest well."

She turned unperturbedly away. Passing a chair in the hall, she bent to take up the sleek broadtail coat that lay there. And standing in the doorway, watching Juliet's slender retreating figure and that satiny coat trailing over her arm, Deborah was conscious of the strangest sensation of actual physical dizziness. For quite suddenly she realized that the inevitable gardenia was not on Juliet's coat. The broad collar bore no trace of its usual defiant white flower.

Juliet's door closed, there was the sound of running water in her bathroom. Still Deborah did not move.

The gardenia in the policeman's hand. The gardenia with the creamy center and the brown edges. The gardenia from the vacant flat overhead, that, they said, could not have been there long.

With Juliet the gardenia was a symbol—a declaration —a flag. She would have gone without food, probably, to provide herself with the thing which to her, unaccountably perhaps but with almost passionate vehemence, symbolized the world she had known, the world to whose edges she clung, the world to whose inner circles she was determined to return.

Its absence, Deborah told herself, meant only that this one time, under stress of circumstances, Juliet had no gardenia. It would have been impossible to secure one on the train. That was it.

But she could not get the memory of the brown-edged flower, looking so strangely delicate and incongruous in the policeman's broad hand, out of her mind.

Juliet and the gardenia. Juliet and the telegram that was not delivered. Why wasn't it delivered? If Juliet had not left Florida at the time it was sent—and she hadn't, according to her own story—why wasn't it delivered? Somehow Deborah's first hypothesis—that is, that the report of its nondelivery was a part of some vaguely understood police enterprise—seemed, now, unlikely. Juliet had not received the telegram. And Juliet had been on the verge of pretending that she had received it. *Had* pretended it until Anthony caught her up so directly.

Queer how immediately and certainly an antagonism had developed between Anthony and Juliet. It was almost as if they had already known and disliked each other. Yet they hadn't.

Juliet and the gardenia. Juliet and the telegram.

Deborah was cold and tired; the stillness and the night were oppressive. Just outside the door a man had been done to death—swiftly, terribly, silently. And the thick old walls brooded and watched, and the very air was heavy and still. The house was too big, the corridors too dark, the policeman only mortal.

Alfred Brocksley had been murdered, horribly, because he knew something.

And she, Deborah Cavert, had actually felt the breath of a bullet past her cheek. And was in danger because of that.

She forced herself to move and see that the door was locked and bolted. The policeman was, of course, still outside. She went to the front windows. Eden Street lay quiet again and tranquil, its street lights calmly radiant, its shadows unmoving. Two cars only remained, and they were discreet and dark. She wondered if the police had gone and what they had done before they went. Across the street suddenly three figures came into view; three men walking along with measured footsteps; they were silent, dark blurs. When they reached a point half a block beyond, they turned right about face and walked as measuredly back again. Deborah shivered a little and let the curtain fall into place.

On the hall table lay Juliet's black pinseal bag and her gloves. Absently Deborah picked them up; Juliet was very orderly. She would want them. Deborah smoothed the gloves—smoothed them and stopped all at once as if her fingers had frozen.

The gloves were fabric, a soft shade of beige. And across each palm ran a saffron stain like a bar.

It was a stain that Deborah recognized, for it was the red, dry stain of rust.

She stood there terrified, fascinated.

There was no use telling herself that Juliet had grasped some railing in descending from the train; a railing would have been caked with soot.

Rust.

Presently she put the gloves down again upon the bag.

She went back to the living room, took up her own coat, whistled, or tried to whistle, for Blitz. He heard the dry, queer sound she made and came trotting anxiously to meet her. Again she left lights burning along the hall.

Blitz curled up on a chaise longue in Deborah's bedroom, but kept his ears cocked uneasily.

The red geranium fell from her coat, and Deborah picked it up and looked at it for a long time before she put it carefully into a glass of water. Long into the night she was conscious of that spicy fragrance, and when at last she slept, she kept dreaming. Dreaming that Juliet's gloves were all covered with rust and that there was rust on her hands, too; dreaming that she, Deborah, was driving, driving, driving along a swift-spreading lane of light and that someone was at her side—someone mysterious whose identity was not quite certain. Once she awakened suddenly and completely and thought, not sleepily but with the oddest clarity, "But I've been married. I was married last night," and went back to dreaming again.

Juliet woke her.

It was ten o'clock, she said crisply, and here were the morning papers, and where in the world was Annie?

Blinking, yawning, Deborah explained Annie, took the papers, and roused.

"What's happened?" she said. "Have they found the murderer?"

"It's all there," said Juliet.

Juliet had not rested well. That, or she was ill. The morning light was as cruel and ugly as the lights the night before had been kind, for there were lines about

Juliet's eyes and mouth that Deborah had never seen before. There was an odd sagging place under her clear, firm chin. There were dark pouches under her eyes, and her skin had lost its last, cherished vestige of youthfulness and looked dry and old and a bit flabby. It was not Juliet, really—yet, of course, it was. But a certain elasticity and spring had gone completely.

Deborah looked away from the older woman. Juliet was tired. The train trip, the worry. That was all.

She took the papers.

There were headlines—Gambling Den Uncovered. Well, at least the murders at 18 East Eden were not in the headlines.

Deborah's eyes plunged on swiftly—she cried out something unintelligible and remembered later that Juliet said: "Oh, yes—there was a gambling establishment."

The essentials were actually in the headlines. For they said: Gambling Den Uncovered. Second Murder in North Side Apartment. Blonde Woman Sought by Police. Penthouse Rendezvous of Wealthy. Police Discover Small Select Gambling Establishment. May Be Motive for Murders.

Juliet said rather harshly:

"There's no use reading it all just now, Deborah. It seems that Brocksley's murder has precipitated things. The police——" Juliet paused and moistened lips that, for the first time in Deborah's knowledge, had been touched with a lipstick. "The police have discovered that Mary Monroe maintained a gambling establishment. In the back rooms of her house on the roof. It was, according to the papers, extremely exclusive. But a great deal of money was made and lost."

"Money," said Deborah without any expression at

all. Motives. Motives for murders. And Anthony . . .
So that was why he had owed Mary Monroe money. A
matter of business, he had called it.

"Certainly. Do pull yourself together, Deborah."

"How did they . . ."

Juliet shrugged.

"Juanito seems to have known of it all along. After
Mary Monroe was murdered, the—roulette wheels, all
that sort of thing—seem to have been hidden somehow
in the vacant apartment. The apartment," said Juliet
stiffly, "just over our heads. The police broke in last
night."

Deborah stared at Juliet's changed, ravaged face.

"The blonde woman they talk of," she said huskily,
motioning blindly toward the headlines—"is there—do
you know anything about that?"

Juliet did not reply at once. She did not look at Deborah, but instead at the small red geranium.

Finally she said: "No, Deborah. Do you?"

It was unexpectedly sharp and cruel. Deborah's hand
went involuntarily to her own soft gold hair, and Juliet
followed the gesture and said quickly and with a suddenly haggard face:

"You look cold, Deborah. Here, put this eiderdown
around you—I'm going to get some breakfast."

CHAPTER XIV

THAT was Saturday, December 9th.

It was a still day, with heavy brooding clouds and, now and then, a threat of snow in the air.

By the time Deborah emerged from her own room, Juliet's bag and the gloves had disappeared. And there was in all the newspaper accounts no mention of a creamy white gardenia whose petals were turning brown.

There was, however, a great deal else, and Deborah read and reread and finally, out of it all, marshaled a fairly orderly and definite résumé of the situation.

In the first place there was an implied although never definitely stated conviction that the two murders were linked.

And in the second place the discovery that Mary Monroe actually ran and maintained a gambling establishment in the house on the roof provided certainly any number of possible motives for what had been up till then an entirely purposeless crime. The police were, of course, trying to obtain a list of her clients. And the house on the roof was perfectly situated and suited to the needs of the quiet, small, and extremely cautious establishment she had maintained.

The fire escape, Deborah supposed, was a simple and quick exit. Even, perhaps, entrance; after all, Mary Monroe had seemed to prefer it. Probably there were not many people who patronized the place—and those who did come paid heavily for the dubious privilege. It must have been conducted with the utmost quiet and decorum; otherwise it could not possibly have existed for several years without the residents of the apartment house knowing of its existence, to say nothing of the police.

Or did the apartment house residents know nothing of it? Brocksley must have known; he must have known and, perhaps, derived some income from keeping that knowledge secret.

Tighe, too, directly below the roof, could not have failed to know of the existence of the enterprise—Tighe and the silent, moveless little man who knew so much and said so little. Yet it must have been Pigeon who had given the police whatever evidence they had regarding the mysterious blonde woman.

Pigeon.

Deborah wondered if enough attention had been paid to Pigeon. It was very easy to accept him merely as a background; he was so silent and unobtrusive, so entirely the servant of an important man. Wasn't it possible that, instead of being merely an observer as he appeared to be, he was somehow strongly and directly connected with whatever dark and ugly program was going on which included murder? But then that was possible with any of them, she thought reluctantly, and returned to the long columns of print.

For the most part the statements of the tenants of the apartment house were not particularly revealing.

"Mrs. Gibbs Riddle's story." "Gibbs Riddle (well-known portrait painter) who lives just above the Brocksley flat." Nothing that Deborah didn't know there. Francis's story: halfway down it she saw Anthony's name and went back to read more thoroughly.

It was headed: "Did Sound of Radio Prevent Rescue?"

"'My radio was going,' said Mr. Francis Maly, who shares a bachelor apartment with Mr. Anthony Wyatt, directly opposite the Brocksley apartment. 'It may have prevented our hearing the victim's cry for help. Mr. Wyatt left about five or ten minutes after seven. I'm not sure about the exact time, for the janitor rang at the back door just as Mr. Wyatt was leaving. I let him in, and we worked over a leaky tap in the kitchen until we were notified of the murder. There was no sound at all from the main hall. Mr. Wyatt was telephoning during part of the period of time during which Brocksley might have been murdered and much nearer the door than I. But he heard nothing.'

"Juanito Murphy, janitor for the building, claims to have passed through the lower hall at exactly two minutes after seven. 'I looked at my watch,' said Mr. Murphy, 'because I usually stoke the fires at seven, and I saw I was late. I entered the hall from the back entrance' (a small door behind the elevator shaft which leads along a passage bisecting the apartment house) 'crossed it and went through the vestibule into the street. There was no one in sight. The hall was empty.' Questioned regarding his errand, Mr. Murphy admitted that he was eager to see the evening papers and had gone to the street with the intention of securing one. He returned by way of the street and back entrance of the apartment house and thus did not pass through the hall again. He had an impression, he said later, that there was a bag of some kind standing near the door to the vestibule. He could not, however, describe the bag and seemed to retain a very vague memory of it. 'It was just a black sort of square bag,' said Mr. Murphy.

Questioned as to whether it was a traveling bag, a brief-case, or a portfolio, he could offer no further identification, and so far as could be discovered no resident of the apartment house could be found who knew anything of such an article. He knew of no stranger in or about the apartment house."

Anthony's story differed in no essential from what she had heard except that he had stated quite definitely and certainly without compunction that he had talked to "Miss Deborah Cavert in the flat above for at least ten minutes, having telephoned her at seven." Ten minutes! It had been nearer three or four at the most; he was determined, then, to provide her with some sort of alibi.

At the present stage of affairs, that, of course, had little significance. Later, if the time during which Brocksley was murdered became narrowed down still further, it would go far to establish Deborah's innocence. With thoughtful eyes she looked at the printed statement. She and Anthony knew that the murder had to occur between the time when Dolly went to the Riddle apartment and the time when Deborah, so shortly after seven, had opened the door and found Brocksley dead in the hall. That would be, assuming Dolly's testimony to be accurate and true, between five minutes till seven and perhaps seven or eight minutes after seven. A narrow enough margin.

She picked up another paper; read another account of the "gambling den."

This was a paper which had taken up its cudgels against the existing administration and began with a somewhat startling inquiry: "Can any gambling den exist without police protection?"

Deborah, knowing what she knew of the house on the

roof, was inclined to think that, in all events, this one had, and skipped a rather lengthy exposition of the topic.

There was, in this account, a detailed description of the roulette tables, taken apart and folded with amazing neatness and readiness, the detachable, rolled, felt covers, the curved Black Jack table, the two roulette wheels, and a thing called Chuck-a-Luck which looked in the accompanying photograph very much like a bird cage. "The equipment," said the account, "was modest. There was nothing ostentatious about the whole establishment. There was no bar. There were no elaborate devices for protection against hijackers or the police. To some this might indicate a complete assurance of safety. In spite of the extremely quiet and simple note which characterized the establishment, probably more real money crossed the tables than in any other establishment in the Middle West."

This account, too, had something to say of Mary Monroe's staff:

"It goes without saying that there must have been, even for so simple an establishment, a staff of croupiers and dealers. It is said that Miss Monroe herself was an expert Black Jack dealer. Yet it would be impossible for her to maintain the establishment without assistants. So far as can be learned, there is no clue to the identity of these assistants. Certainly the one-time diva lived entirely alone in three small rooms at the front of the house."

Assistants, of course. Croupiers. Deborah wondered fleetingly if Brocksley could possibly have been one of them.

She looked at a photograph of Brocksley; he posed in long hose against a balustrade and smiled fatuously. In life, his vanity had been tiresome; in death it was, some-how, pathetic.

A name stood out in the column beside the photo-graph:

"Mr. August Tighe occupies the third-floor apart-ment directly below the famous opera singer's pent-house . . ."

Chloe had said something of Tighe. And she had said that Alfred Brocksley would get his fat throat cut. And he had.

She remembered, suddenly, that there'd been blood in the elevator. And that neither Chloe nor Gibbs nor Anthony had spoken of its possible meaning; it might be extremely significant. There were, she decided slowly, three hypotheses.

The most reasonable one was that the murderer had escaped by way of the elevator, and blood from his clothes had got onto the floor of the cage; in that case stained clothing—stained, at least, to that extent—could not be easily hidden or prevented from coming to the eyes of the police.

The second hypothesis was that Brocksley had been murdered somewhere else and brought to the second floor. That implied, then, that the residents of the second floor were innocent of the crime and conversely that the murderer was connected with either the first or third floors and thus was throwing suspicion toward the second floor.

But there was an equally reasonable third hypothesis and that was, of course, that the stain of blood on the elevator had been deliberately placed there in the hope of inducing the second theory—which would mean that —well, that Gibbs Riddle, or Chloe, or even Dolly would be under strong suspicion.

Chloe—Gibbs Riddle—Dolly Brocksley. Francis
Maly and Anthony. And above, Tighe and Pigeon—of
them all, Tighe and Pigeon were the only two who
Deborah felt were capable of murder. And she knew
that if, inconceivably, Tighe came to call at the moment and talked to her in his suave and gracious way
she would be immediately convinced that so pleasant
a person could not possibly have done the things that
had been done.

However, the police had, now, many directions to
look for clues, and the clues were those which ought
certainly to direct the course of inquiry from the
tenants of the apartment house.

Of course, it was true that the roulette wheels and the
various accouterments which had belonged in those
mysterious back rooms of the house on the roof had
turned up in the vacant apartment overhead.

And there was only one time when they could possibly
have been moved, and that was during the night following the murder of Mary Monroe. The night during
which Deborah had waited for the police who didn't
come. And had heard vaguely sounds from overhead.
Those sounds, then, had been real, and they were the
sounds of feet and of those photographed objects being
moved. Being moved at midnight—down a fire escape
and into a vacant flat over her head and hidden.

Someone then had been determined to keep from the
police the knowledge of what had existed in the house
on the roof. So determined that that midnight expedi-
tion had, with its dangers and its difficulty, been a
necessity.

And Anthony had not notified the police of the
murder.

Anthony. Anthony, who had owed money to Mary Monroe. Anthony to whom she was married.

If Anthony had notified the police at once of the murder, there would not have been time to remove the evidence of gambling.

The rest of that cold still morning was to Deborah merely an endless repetition of the whole table of facts and surmises, until she knew its every possible combination.

The morning of Saturday, December 9th. The day of Deborah's first direct encounter with Lieutenant Waggon. And of the extraordinary thing Tulip was to precipitate.

Anthony did not telephone. Juliet sat over her desk, with her slender back turned to Deborah uncommunicatively and a pen in her hand, but did not write letters. There were two police cars outside, and several times Deborah heard voices in the hall, but she saw nothing then of the police.

She was restless, terribly taut and apprehensive, and Juliet seemed to share her feeling, for once when the elevator door clanged her head jerked upward nervously, and once when the telephone rang sharply she turned swiftly toward it, as if strung on a wire, and snatched at the receiver.

Her face and her voice changed, though, after the first greeting, and she said: "No, ma'am. Miss Cavert is not at home. Who shall I say called?—Thank you."

"Isabel Ferry," she said crisply to Deborah. "I don't feel quite up to seeing her." She looked at Deborah and said suddenly: "Why don't you do something, Deborah? Take Blitz out for a walk. Do run along; you make me nervous, fidgeting about like that."

Blitz bounced gleefully, and Deborah got into tweeds and obeyed.

In the hall a policeman was still on guard—a different policeman, and he sat in a shabby old armchair from Gibbs's studio, and the Chinese Chippendale was nowhere to be seen. He looked at her but did not try to stop her. The door to the Riddle apartment was open, and there were voices from inside, and Deborah caught a glimpse of another policeman standing just inside the entrance.

On the first floor, too, was a policeman who said good-morning pleasantly enough but followed Deborah out to the steps. He said nothing nor made any perceptible gesture. Yet Deborah was aware that a man in an overcoat and felt hat turned up rather suddenly and seemed impelled by a desire to walk exactly fifty feet behind her the whole time. He did get entangled a bit crossing Michigan Boulevard owing to an unexpected change of the traffic lights, but emerged very shortly after, though a bit breathlessly.

The gray vista of lake and sky was inexpressibly soothing. The air was cold and moist on her cheek. She stayed out, walking briskly along the Lake, as long as she dared. It was when she returned that she discovered again that the inconceivable does happen.

For Tighe had come to call. Or rather he was just leaving, and he was at the door bidding Juliet the most gracious of farewells when Deborah stepped out of the elevator. It struck Deborah, however, that his manner was somewhat lost upon Juliet, who was looking very queer. He saw Deborah, beamed, bowed, and said:

"My dear Miss Deborah. Good-morning. Good-morning. I'm so very glad to see that this very unpleasant affair has not—er—troubled you."

His words were flamboyant. His manner was superb. Deborah felt herself soothed and subtly flattered and knew she was greeting him with the greatest friendliness. Juliet said crisply: "Good-morning, Mr. Tighe. So nice of you to come to inquire. We do appreciate it, Deborah and I. Good-day."

There was a definite note of finality in her voice. Tighe bowed again, his pendulous pale lips smiled so warmly at Deborah that it stirred a responsive smile on her own mouth, and then he had lunged into the elevator and was gone.

"I'm going out," said Juliet shortly. "Were you followed when you were out with the dog?"

"Every moment," said Deborah. "But most respectfully. You won't be long, will you?"

"Not long. Call me a taxi, will you, Deborah?"

And she hadn't more than gone, wearing again her broadtail coat and no gardenia, when Lieutenant Waggon arrived.

He was heralded by a certain pomp and ceremony in the person of a very broad-shouldered sergeant, and Deborah felt sure that he had known that Juliet had gone out.

He followed Deborah into the living room, sat down slowly, and looked deliberately about him. It was a slow blue glance that took in the beautiful thin old rugs, the mahogany table that had belonged to the Caverts since revolutionary days, the portrait over the mantelpiece—a Cavert grandfather, by a somewhat inferior artist but prized nevertheless by Juliet—the books lining the walls in the adjoining room—and, Deborah thought likely, the mimosa on the piano (now becoming a trifle dry), the number and brands of the cigarette ends which she'd forgotten from the previous day and left in the ashtray, and the dark spot on the pale green damask divan where Blitz had once gnawed a bone and which had resisted the efforts of cleaners ever since.

Then he looked at her and smiled gently, and Deborah's heart which had been pounding in her throat became quieter.

"Your aunt's got home," he said, as if commenting idly upon some piece of neighborhood news. "How'd she leave your father?"

How much did he know about them? Deborah replied something polite, and Lieutenant Waggon's motherly look became more pronounced.

"Good thing she's got back," he said. "You oughtn't to be alone here. Wouldn't want to see my daughter staying alone in a place where there'd been a murder."

Deborah swallowed somewhat convulsively and missed the calm blue look Lieutenant Waggon gave the sergeant over her shoulder. He drifted quietly away, and it was only later that Deborah realized that he was gone.

"But then," said Lieutenant Waggon, "I expect you know some of the people in the apartment house pretty well, don't you? Living here four years."

"I've been away a great deal," said Deborah, at once alarmed and cautious.

He noted the caution. His expression became almost benign.

"Don't you be worried, Miss Deborah," he said. "And don't you answer anything you don't want to answer. There's some things you might be able to tell me and I'd like to know about. But anything you don't want to answer, just don't do it. Fact is, I'm pretty hard up for evidence. You might not know a thing, and yet again you might know something I need quite a lot. You might not even know that you knew it. But I don't aim to worry you."

What was he doing? Warning her against himself as he appeared to do? Or winning her unwilling confidence? She steeled herself against the mild look in the calm blue eyes opposite and said:

"What can I tell you?"

He had followed her thoughts as if she had spoken them. He shook his head rather sadly.

"You're afraid of me, Miss Deborah," he said. "I don't suppose I can convince you that there's no call to be afraid of me. This is the way things are: I'm sort of up against it with this murder. Too many clues and not enough. That is, too many people who knew Mary Monroe. Too many people who might, owing to her business, have wanted to kill her. But nobody that actually did want to kill her—nobody that we can find, I mean. There's clues—and again there's no clue strong enough to be of much help. Seems to me that you folks here in the apartment house ought to know something of her. Seems to me"—something very cold and icy was all at once fixed in the blue gaze—"seems to me somebody in this apartment house has *got* to know something about it."

"You mean," Deborah heard herself saying, "Brocksley?"

He nodded.

"Brocksley. That's a murder that occurred because I couldn't find the murderer of Mary Monroe soon enough. The two murders are part and parcel of the same piece. And there's the same trouble with the murder of Alfred Brocksley that there is with the first murder. And that is, no clues. Everybody's got an alibi.

Nobody could have got into the apartment house without being seen by the men on the job. Yet we can't discover who did it. And we can't find the knife that did it. Oh, of course there's plenty of knives in the house. One or two straight-edge razors in the Tighe flat. A carving set in the Riddles' sideboard that would slice a hair. An ornamental sword in the flat below this one that's sharper than any ornamental sword ought to be. By the way, this young fellow downstairs—Wyatt's his name—says he was talking over the telephone with you last night at about the time the murder occurred. That right?"

"Yes."

"Says he called you up just before seven o'clock and talked to you for ten minutes and asked you to go for a ride and then he came straight up to this flat."

"Yes—that is, I don't know exactly how long we talked."

"Aunt hadn't got back at that time?"

"No."

"Then you were alone here?"

"Yes. Annie—that's our only servant—is quarantined."

He nodded, and she realized that he knew also about Annie.

"I see your telephone is in the hall. Near the door. Didn't you hear anything from the hall outside while you were talking to Wyatt?"

"Once, just as he called, I thought I heard the elevator. But I didn't pay any attention to it."

"Didn't open the door and look out?"

"It wasn't anyone to see me," said Deborah. "But it's only an impression that I heard the elevator."

Had her evasion betrayed her? There was no reading

the bland blue gaze that had, now, its unearthly quality
of omniscience.

"So Wyatt came up the back way. Why?"

"Simpler," said Deborah. "His car was over on Vine
Street."

"And you saw nothing of my men when you left?"

"Nothing."

"How well did you know Mary Monroe?"

He had, she supposed, intended to surprise her. Actually it was as kind a question as he could have asked.

"Not well at all," said Deborah. "I had heard her
sing, of course. Many times. But I didn't know even
that there was a gambling place on the roof."

"Didn't go up there to lose a few dollars, then?"

"Never."

"Did you like her?"

Deborah saw the little trap in time.

"Oh—I didn't know her well enough to like or dislike her. She seems to have been well enough liked."

"But you never went up there to gamble?"

"No. Never."

He looked at her again with that all-discerning gaze.
Then he went to other topics. How long had she known
the Riddles? What did she know of them? Was Juanito
a good janitor? How did Dolly Brocksley and her husband get along? Did they quarrel? Oh, she didn't know.
Well, then, what about these two men in the apartment
directly below: Wyatt and Francis Maly, what did she
know of them?

There was a faint stir behind her, and Deborah jerked
around in time to see the sergeant reëntering the room
and looking remarkably smug. He'd been gone, then, all
that time. What had he been doing?

Lieutenant Waggon cleared his throat, and she turned

quickly back toward him. He was leaning forward. He said quietly:

"Why did you go to see Mary Monroe?"

Deborah's heart stopped beating. He knew. But he couldn't know. At least he couldn't be sure until she herself had admitted it. And if it were another trap—if he actually didn't know . . . She steadied herself and in emergency borrowed his own weapon of deceiving candor and said:

"I don't understand you, Lieutenant Waggon. It sounds as if you are suggesting some—oh, admission. Confession." She looked at him soberly and said: "I didn't kill Mary Monroe."

He looked at his watch, looked at the officer in the background, looked at Deborah and rose.

"My child," he said with disconcerting motherliness, "I'm not smart enough to depend upon wringing confessions out of people. I still have to get sound material clues. But somehow—in the end—we do get them. Fingerprints, maybe. Witnesses. One way or another. We'll find the woman that's mixed up in this sooner or later," he added as if in idle afterthought and picked up his cap.

"W—woman," said Deborah and pulled herself together. "Yes, of course—the papers said you were hunting some woman."

"Um'm," said Lieutenant Waggon, looking out the window. "She was seen leaving. Guess she was the woman that had tea with Mary Monroe. And wiped off all her fingerprints. Or—maybe—thought she got 'em all. Well, thank you very much, Miss Deborah."

The door closed behind them—the sergeant still smug, Lieutenant Waggon still bland and motherly and inscrutable.

But he couldn't be sure. He simply couldn't be sure, no matter how strongly he suspected. For if he were sure that it was Deborah who'd been seen leaving the house on the roof, he would not have needed to ask questions; he would not, even, have delayed her arrest to do so. But what had he meant by his not very well veiled reference to fingerprints and the woman who "thought she got 'em all"? Had she missed any? What had she touched that she'd forgotten? She strove to recall the details of those hurried, terrified moments during which she and Anthony had gone from telephone, to teacups, to piano . . . to the bracelet on Mary Monroe's dead wrist.

And then there was the police sergeant's remarkable smugness. What had he managed to accomplish during that catfooted retirement that gave him so satisfied a look? She went swiftly through the apartment. But there were few signs of disturbance. Someone had looked through the cutlery in the dining-room buffet and in the kitchen. A lock on one of Juliet's traveling bags had been scratched but not opened, she thought, for it resisted her own fingers, and there was nothing else. Nothing, that is, until she went to her own dressing table with a faint notion of restoring herself after a crisis that had left her shaken and white and found that every tube of lipstick she possessed had inexplicably disappeared.

Lipstick. But why lipstick? Barring a possible and overwhelming yearning for beauty on the part of the police sergeant, there was no answer, and it was just then that Chloe arrived.

She was looking rather dark around the eyes, but her lipstick was heavy and defiant, and she wore her favorite green silk gown with the full slit sleeves and the twisted belt, and her usual air of faintly arrogant insouciance.

She sat down in a deep armchair and stretched out her long pretty legs, thus displaying a length of chiffon hose, one or two incipient runners, and very high-heeled slippers. She sighed, ran one white hand through her tousle of black hair, twisted her body luxuriously, yawned, and said:

"I heard Waggon leave. Thought I'd see how you were getting on. How did the interview go?"

"All right. I don't know."

"You seem very cool about it. He nearly scared me to death a couple of times." She paused and looked, for an instant, less assured. "I don't like him," she said.

"How did you know he was here?—Cigarette?"

Chloe accepted the cigarette, mumbled, lighting it, "Tulip," puffed a time or two, and leaned back in the chair again to look at Deborah through wreaths of smoke.

"Tulip told me," she said more intelligibly. "She doesn't miss much. I hear, too, that Juliet is home. Well, I'm glad. Not that she and I have ever felt any particular yearning for each other's company. Still I hated to think of you alone here with all—this—going on."

"How's Dolly?" asked Deborah.

Chloe lifted one curved shoulder.

"All right, I guess. They've still got a police matron with her. They'd arrest her if they could shake my testimony. But they can't. Dolly was with me when the murder had to occur. And that's that." Chloe's sleek black eyebrows drew slightly together, and the small green flame lit itself in her eyes. "What I'd like to know is what this blonde woman they keep talking of had to do with it. Dolly's blonde. But she didn't kill Brocksley. And I don't believe for a moment that she killed Mary Monroe."

"They've got some evidence, I suppose, that involves some woman."

"Well, naturally. But what is it? Juanito may have told them something. They finally took him to the police station last night. Kept him there half the night. And he certainly spilled plenty; I think he's responsible for the story in the papers this morning. Did you know there was a gambling place upstairs, Deborah?"

"No," said Deborah violently. "No."

Chloe flicked a quick green glance at her.

"Well, you needn't bite me because I asked," she said. "After all, it seems to have been a very nice establishment." She laughed shortly, a kind of throaty, whispering chuckle.

"Did many people in the apartment house know of it?" asked Deborah.

Chloe's look of amusement vanished.

"I don't know," she said. "Juanito, of course, knew. I'm inclined to think Brocksley knew, too, being renting agent. And I suppose Dolly knew. Otherwise—it's hard to say. It was really rather smart of Mary Monroe to manage as she did. A perfect situation; no one would have dreamed of the place being there. And it seems she was very careful about her—guests. It wasn't actually a club, but it was, in a sense, far more exclusive than most clubs." Chloe smoked and shrugged her lovely shoulders and said: "I'm too poor to gamble."

"Chloe's nervous, too," thought Deborah. "There's something about her that isn't quite easy and flippant and natural, though she's trying to be."

Chloe put out her cigarette and leaned toward Deborah. She said: "Deborah—the night Mary Monroe was murdered, at about the time she must have been killed —you came to my flat. Remember?"

Something closed in Deborah's throat. She met Chloe's shining green eyes steadily, however, and nodded.

"Yes, of course."

"Well—I don't want to know anything about—why you were there—why you were frightened." Chloe's eyes plunged deeply into Deborah's. "But I do want this: You saw me. You saw Tulip. *And you heard voices in the bedrooms.*" Her green eyes shone compellingly into Deborah's. "*Didn't you, Deborah?*" she said.

"Yes," said Deborah. "Yes, of course. You said it was the children——"

"Never mind what I said." Chloe rose abruptly. "That's what you heard. I can count on you, Deb. And if that black wench, Tulip, goes back on me I'll——" The fire in her eyes licked out like a hungry little flame, and her lithe hands twisted quite as if she had Tulip's black neck in their clutch. The gesture had, in fact, a tinge of something so horridly real that Deborah made a startled little motion, and Chloe caught it and concluded with sudden and deceptive mildness: "I'll make her regret it."

"Well, yes, it looked as if you had some such notion," said Deborah somewhat crisply, and Chloe laughed, although the lambent flame in her eyes lingered.

And it was just then that Anthony telephoned and wanted to know anxiously though rather guardedly if things were all right. With Chloe there, Deborah found herself replying constrainedly.

Anthony caught it at once.

"Is Juliet there with you?" he said.

"No," said Deborah. "Chloe."

"Oh, but I'm just going," said Chloe and went, her

green silk whispering along the rugs, and her beautiful feet swift and graceful.

And Anthony had news.

"I've got to see you," he said urgently. "Is it all right?"

He came up at once. He looked very tired and worried.

"I didn't dare tell you over the telephone," he said. "Someone might be listening. But they've got Pigeon at the police station. God knows what he'll tell before they get through with him."

CHAPTER XV

AND after all there was nothing that they could do. Especially in view of the things Lieutenant Waggon had said, and failed to say, in his interview with Deborah.

"I didn't know he was here," said Anthony. "Well, there's one thing certain. He may suspect you, but he's not sure. So the thing resolves itself to this: either Pigeon definitely tells that you were there, or he doesn't tell. If he tells—well, it's a good thing we made that trip to Crown Point last night; we've still got the jump on Lieutenant Waggon. If he doesn't tell, we are exactly where we were. And we'll just have to wait. But, Deborah, if Waggon comes to see you again, don't say anything. If he presses you to damaging admissions tell him, as if you were speaking frankly and openly, that you don't understand what he means, but that—oh, look helpless and flutter a little and say you are frightened——"

"I was terrified."

"All right, look it. Act it. Pretend to be just a little dumb and say you think you ought to see your lawyer. That you don't know anything about the murder, but that you are all of a dither at actually being questioned by police—it's terrible and you've got to see your lawyer. You might," said Anthony a little diffidently, "cry a little. But not much."

Deborah considered. It sounded rather weak, but

after all her position was not exactly strong. And
Lieutenant Waggon's questions had a neat way of sliding past one's guard.

"Very well," she said. "I'll try."

Anthony was frowning worriedly.

"I don't like it about your lipstick," he said. "And
what he said about fingerprints. Think, Deborah—is
there anything you forgot? Anything at all that you had
touched? Or anything that you could have got lipstick
on—cup, spoon, anything?"

She shook her head. And suddenly remembered a
green glass lamp rocking perilously above a drawer that
stuck, and her own hand going out to steady it.

*"The lamp—I'd forgotten. It's fingerprints they've got,
Tony. My fingerprints!"*

He listened and, she thought, tried not to look
alarmed.

"It's bad," he said. "But he is still not certain. And
don't forget that if it comes to the worst we still hold
an ace that he doesn't know about." He frowned. "At
least," he added, "that I hope he doesn't know about.
I suppose you read the papers this morning——"

"Oh, yes."

"Surprised?" He was looking at her narrowly. It
struck Deborah that he really wanted to know.

"Why, yes. I didn't know that was a gambling place
up there."

"I knew. But I didn't tell you because—well, I just
didn't."

Not, thought Deborah, a good reason. She said
slowly: "I suppose that was why you owed Mary
Monroe money?"

His little air of evasion disappeared, and he looked at
her directly, though with a touch of embarrassment.

"Yes, it was. But I'm not really a gambler. I mean, it always seems, well, just silly; gambling, I mean. For me, anyway, a sheer waste of money. But I did go up there a few times for the entertainment—would lose a few dollars and leave. And one time it happened, as it does happen, that I lost more than I had in cash. Not much—a two-weeks salary check was enough to cover it. Trivial compared to real gambling debts. But I wasn't exactly proud of it."

Again it was convincing.

"There must have been quite an organization," said Deborah thoughtfully. "She certainly couldn't run the thing alone. There must have been assistants."

"Oh, of course," said Anthony agreeably.

"Isn't it probable that the murders are linked up with that?"

"Motives, you mean," said Anthony. His dark eyes were enigmatic again. "I shouldn't wonder. Anyway, it's on the lap of the gods now that the police have got hold of it."

"But if you went there," persisted Deborah, "didn't you see the—oh, croupiers—dealers—whatever they call them?"

"I didn't go much," said Anthony. He rose and began to walk impatiently up and down, his hands thrust in his pockets. "I wish I knew what Pigeon is telling right now. See here," he said, "have things been going along all right? No attempts to enter the apartment? Nothing at all out of the way?"

Deborah's heart gave a little plunge, and she did not realize till Anthony had gone how deftly he had sheered away from her questions. "No," she said. "Lieutenant Waggon was here. Tighe, for a moment this morn-ing——"

"*Tighe?*"

"Yes. I don't know why he came—just a social call, I suppose. He was very affable. And Chloe came in for a few moments. That's all."

"I suppose you realize that Tighe and Chloe are both, after all, residents of the place."

"But——" said Deborah and stopped, and Anthony said: "I know how you feel. I know how it makes me feel. The thought that somewhere here there's a—murderer. It—well, it's not a nice thought. But don't forget, Deborah, that Mary Monroe's dead. And Brocksley—poor old Brocksley with all his airs and poses."

Alfred Lord Tennyson Brocksley—posing, strutting, throwing out his chest—and in the end meeting reality. Meeting his final curtain with no rounds of applause and no bows.

Mary Monroe had had, at least, an audience. A witness. And Deborah was that witness.

Deborah said abruptly:

"Have you any other news besides this about Pigeon?"

"No," said Anthony. "I went down to the lab for a little while this morning but couldn't work. Formula went all wrong overnight. Funny—this case is rather like a chemical problem. You start building up molecules, adding one property after another, hoping all the time to get the exact combination you want. And then finally you think you've just about got it and want to add something to make it soluble, maybe—to—to clarify it," said Anthony, getting a little involved in his simile, "and then—bang!—it's all off—everything destroyed or changed so it doesn't work, and you have to start all over again.—Francis and I talked the thing ragged and still know nothing. The police were after

Gibbs this morning, too. I don't know—looked as if they had something on him."

Gibbs—that was what Chloe had meant. An alibi for Gibbs. But he had no alibi for the time when Mary Monroe was killed. He had been walking, Chloe had said. And in one of his black rages. And now Chloe in the smoothest way in the world had suggested a trade with Deborah: Chloe's silence for Deborah's.

"What's the matter?" said Anthony, and she told him.

"I see," he said when she'd finished. "So Chloe's fixing things for Gibbs. And it really was the voices of the children that you heard and not Gibbs at all. Well—we get in deeper and deeper." He rose and went to the window and looked down to the street. "'Oh, what a tangled web——' eh, Deborah?"

Deborah, looking at the dark silhouette he made, standing there before the window with his hands in his pockets and his smooth dark head bent, said nothing, and Anthony added suddenly: "It's queer about those two."

"Queer?"

"Yes. They fight so much, you know. Chloe and Gibbs, I mean. All but come to blows—in fact, I'm not sure they don't! And yet they are just plain crazy about each other. Need each other, I mean. As they need food. Water. Air. It's—primitive. They live for each other," said Anthony in a thoughtful voice. "I think they'd kill for each other."

Deborah's breath caught, but she said crisply: "I must say they conceal their affection very ably."

Anthony whirled around toward her. His voice and expression changed.

"You sound exactly like your aunt," he said disapprovingly. "I do hope you'll control any such tendency, Deborah. At least as long as you are my wife."

He had meant to say it lightly. But the last two words did not come out easily, and Deborah looked up suddenly and met his eyes and as quickly looked away.

"You don't like my aunt, do you?"

Anthony did not reply at once, and when he did speak it was with too casual an air:

"We didn't seem to strike any greatly sympathetic cord, last night. You probably noticed it."

"Yes," said Deborah, refusing to smile. "Why is it?"

Anthony offered her a cigarette, lighted one himself, strolled toward the piano, looked at the mimosa disparagingly and observed that it was about time it was sent to its grave, and finally said:

"What did she think of our—er—your new boy friend?" and grinned.

"Not very much," said Deborah soberly.

"I expect my final embrace was a little disastrous," said Anthony. "It was altogether due to your aunt Juliet, Deborah. She practically drove me to it."

"It wasn't, then, my personal charm?" said Deborah irresistibly and immediately regretted it.

She needn't have, however, for Anthony merely looked at her rather coolly, said: "Oh, I shouldn't say that, Deborah," and added: "She must have returned to Chicago as soon as she heard of Mary Monroe's murder."

"Yes."

"Trip by train takes two nights and nearly two days. Mary Monroe was murdered Wednesday night. You sent Juliet a telegram about seven o'clock that night which was not delivered. Therefore, if she was notified of the murder through the newspapers she couldn't

possibly have known of it until about Thursday noon
—the murder was not discovered until Thursday
morning, and the Associated Press dispatches couldn't
have reached the papers before Thursday noon. Yet,
Juliet arrives here Friday evening." Anthony blew a
little cloud of gray smoke toward the drying mimosa
and shook his head: "Can't be done."

It couldn't, of course. And Deborah had been avoid-
ing it—it and the thought of a gardenia and two red
stains across a pair of gloves. She said weakly: "Perhaps
she flew."

Anthony shrugged. "Perhaps. Did you ask her?"

"What do you mean?"

He looked at her quickly and intently, looked at his
cigarette, then shrugged again, and crossed suddenly to
stand just above her.

"See here, Deborah," he said. "I want you to know
this. I believe you. I'm going to keep on believing you.
But I want you to promise me that when you get ready
to talk—you'll—you'll tell me——"

Confusedly Deborah rose and found her hands in
Anthony's, and the door opened and Juliet Cavert
walked into the hall and into the living room. Her eyes
went to Anthony at once, and she put back her short
veil and observed:

"Oh—Mr. Wyatt——" Her look said: *You here
again!* She placed a small package, tied heavily and
sealed, upon the table, threw back her coat, and added:
"There are a great many police outside. I trust there
has been no further—unpleasant occurrence."

"*Unpleasant*——" Anthony looked a bit startled,
became comprehending, dropped Deborah's hands, and
was at the window. Deborah hurriedly joined him.

There were certainly two police cars below and several

figures, blue-uniformed and much foreshortened, were entering the apartment house. There was about them an air of briskness and enterprise which was not exactly soothing.

"It's Pigeon," said Anthony, leaning to look at a group just vanishing into the entrance below. "I can see his cap." His eyes met Deborah's, and he said: "I'll see if I can discover anything."

The door closed behind him, and Juliet slipped wearily out of her coat.

"I was stopped by a policeman—Lieutenant Waggon. He questioned me at length and in an extremely familiar manner. Quite as if he were an acquaintance of many years. But," said Juliet, looking exhausted, "I, of course, could tell him nothing about these dreadful murders. Fortunately it was on my return home. I had already got to the bank before it closed."

"Bank?"

"Yes." Juliet removed her hat, touched her smooth hair and, looking desperately tired and gray, said: "I got my jewels out of safe deposit. There they are on the table."

"Your jewels! But Juliet—why in the world did you do that?"

Juliet fingered the package.

"Oh," she said quietly, "I only wanted to look at them. See about one or two settings. This seems to be a good time."

Deborah opened her mouth to protest and checked herself. After all, if Juliet wanted to look at her jewels, why not? The police were below and had brought Pigeon back to the apartment house. Why? What would Anthony find?

And no matter how much she longed to evade it, there

was something she must ask Juliet. She was still standing, and her hands clutched themselves together behind her back, and she said, trying to keep her voice
steady and without overtones of meaning:

"Juliet, when did you first hear of Mary Monroe's
murder?"

Juliet did not look at her and did not reply. The
silence grew and prolonged itself, and there was a murmur of men's voices from the hall outside, and the clang
of the elevator door, and Blitz trotted along the hall and
barked sharply and listened. The little dog's bark seemed
to rouse Juliet, but still she did not reply to Deborah's
question. She said instead:

"I am extremely tired, Deborah. Let's not talk of
Mary Monroe now. It is a very dreadful thing. The
whole apartment house seems—seems charged with it."
Her voice broke and became deeper, and there were
countless fine lines in her face. Blitz barked again, and
she said, "Hush, Blitz. It's nothing."

And after that Deborah somehow could not repeat
her inquiry. Not just then. Not until Juliet looked less
broken and strange.

Juliet picked up the sealed package, weighed it in her
hand, and said rather bitterly: "It's much lighter than
it used to be," and turned abruptly away.

It was shortly after that that Tulip arrived, announcing her presence by a prolonged ring of the bell at the
kitchen door. Deborah, answering the summons,
paused with her hand on the bolt and cried: "Who is
it?" guardedly, before she opened the door.

Tulip plunged into the room, eyes rolling over her
shoulder.

"Lock the door, Miss Deb. Lock the door," she said.

"Ain't no telling what's around these days. Last night there was something up there on the fire escape. Middle of the night. Creeping 'way up there. Maybe a man. Maybe—something else. Lock the door, Miss Deb."

She panted and concealed something bulky under her white apron. And her coming ushered in another of those queer facets of life that surrounded the murder of Mary Monroe. Odd, terrifying windows into the secret places of other lives.

For Tulip had brought a request from Chloe and a package. The package was an odd, irregular bunch of something, soft and not very heavy, wrapped in a newspaper dated the morning of December 6th and tied with a cord. And the request was that Deborah hide the package.

"Just," said Tulip, her eyes rolling nervously from the package to Deborah and back again—"just until the police is gone. She said I wasn't to say more, Miss Deb. She said she'd slit my black throat if I tell you what it is. But I don't reckon she meant that—think so, Miss Deb?"

"No; certainly not," said Deborah too forcefully and took the package. It smelled of turpentine, and Tulip said:

"I guess Miz Riddle didn't mean it. But she do look kinda mean sometimes."

Deborah thought it possible. She said:

"You know what this thing is?"

She was not prepared for the look that peered suddenly from the Negro woman's eyes. It was a look of strange jungle fear of the unknown, of terror, of death. And at the same time there was a queer, innate understanding that life is death and death is life—something

that Deborah of the remote white race could never comprehend as Tulip comprehended. And because she understood, she was afraid.

Her skin became tinged with purple and glowed. Her
nostrils opened a little, and her supple mouth drew back
from strong wide teeth. The white cap and apron and
sleek black dress that on Tulip had always looked
jaunty and a little flip seemed now ridiculously artificial.

She looked at the package, said: "No'm" uncon-
vincingly and vanished, a sleek swift figure sliding
toward the door, which closed stealthily but firmly behind her.

And Deborah somewhat hopelessly regarded the
package.

She had weakened to the extent of an exploring poke
or two with a cautious forefinger when Juliet came into
the kitchen, and Juliet had no scruples. She dragged the
story out of Deborah in short order, looked at the package, and pulled open the drawer of the table decisively.

"Don't be ridiculous," she said to Deborah's protest. "I don't at all like Chloe's doing such a thing. We
have a perfect right to look at it, and I shall do so."

She picked up a carving knife and cut the strings with
one deft sweep.

"Now then," she said. The paper rustled. Rustled
and pulled apart, and Juliet's hand suddenly faltered
and she gave a thin sharp scream. It was the only time
in all Deborah's life that she could remember having
heard Juliet scream.

CHAPTER XVI

THEN Deborah looked and very nearly screamed herself.

For a tall, large-bosomed woman with black hair and a maroon velvet gown looked out at her from a torn and shredded canvas. And the face and the velvet gown and the strong white hands had been hacked and slashed with a knife until the picture hung in mad irregular pieces, which yet clung together with a queer, almost animate vitality.

Deborah looked and could not tear her eyes from the thing. Again Mary Monroe looked at her and talked of the house on the roof—the house that held a secret in those back rooms—of wind at the door—of keys—of music. Mary Monroe sang, and the air was hot and held the scent of tuberose. Mary Monroe stopped singing because she was staring at the door with those terrible black eyes. And then Mary Monroe was a heavy lump of a thing in maroon velvet—empty and drained of life.

Blitz sensed something and whimpered and looked at the two women with perplexed, troubled eyes. His tail beat anxiously on the floor, and the small sound stirred Deborah from a kind of paroxysm of remembered horror. She looked at Juliet and cried sharply:

"*Don't—let me——*" and caught at Juliet. But Juliet was not going to faint. She turned stiffly to Deborah and said in a strange voice:

"Wrap it up. Is there kerosene in the house?"

"What are you going to do?"

"I'm going to burn it. In the fireplace. No one will know. It's got to be burned."

"You can't—you can't——"

Juliet did not seem to hear her. She was wrapping the thing loosely in paper, hiding it feverishly.

Her eyes glittered, and she talked jerkily and as if she were not conscious of Deborah's presence.

"Kerosene," Deborah heard her say. "But I don't need kerosene. There's a scent of turpentine. Turpentine burns."

And again: "There'll be a smell in the house. But it won't matter—it won't matter—nothing matters . . ." And once she said something clearly and reasonably, and Deborah was to remember it, because it was the only real explanation, cryptic though it was at the time, that Juliet ever gave for what she did. She said: "I cannot permit a tangible connection with—with Mary Monroe." It was difficult for her to speak that name, and she fell again, feverishly, to wrapping the folds of paper around folds of red smeared canvas that resisted her fingers.

There was something horribly nightmarish about the scene. Deborah was never to forget it. The trip to the front of the house, Juliet carrying the terribly slashed portrait. The fireplace. The matches being struck. Juliet's body scrunched awkwardly down above the hearth. Her incredibly steady white hands.

And then the sudden leaping of the flames as they caught. The thing moved as the paper flamed up and fell away, and as the heat grew the canvas began to writhe and twist and Deborah could endure it no more and fled.

It was hours later when she emerged.

Hours during which she had traveled again every

variation of the dark maze into which they—she and Anthony and Chloe—and Juliet—had been plunged. Once she arose and found the bag she had carried the night before and took from it a small gold circle which she turned in her fingers and tried again tentatively on her hand and looked at slowly and thoughtfully before she removed it. She put it carefully away.

Afterward Deborah was to realize that one of the most subtly cruel aspects of the affair at 18 East Eden was the necessity to wait. To wait in a sheer frenzy of controlled anxiety until things happened. Until the police did this or that, until this development took place, until that line of inquiry was exhausted. To wait, which was worse, for the newspapers or for what stray bits of news those equally concerned were able to gather, before one could know just what had happened. To wait while every moment and every word threatened.

And now Gibbs Riddle was in the thing and Chloe was fighting like a tigress to protect him. Evidently Mary Monroe had been sitting for Gibbs. Evidently something had occurred which roused him to a horrible, vicious burst of fury. As evidently it was to have been a remarkable portrait. Black eyes above maroon velvet; that was how Chloe had known the maroon velvet was Mary Monroe's favorite gown. She had been wearing it for the portrait.

An acrid smell of something burning crept in under the door, and Deborah flung herself across her bed and buried her face in the eiderdown.

Gradually the room darkened.

Juliet was sitting calmly over a book when Deborah finally emerged. And she had swept and cleaned the hearth, and there was only a faint lingering trace of that smell of burning.

That evening was chiefly memorable in that nothing
happened. Nothing, that is, except Anthony's cryptic
telephone message, the arrival of the night's papers, and
Deborah's talk with Chloe shortly after dinner.

Anthony's telephone call was unsatisfactory. It was
short, blurred in transit, and not too clear in content.
He wanted to know, mainly, if Deborah was all right,
said not very lucidly that he was across town and didn't
say why, and added a request not to worry, which is
perhaps the least soothing message capable of human
utterance.

Not a word about Pigeon. Not a word about the
police. Not a word about what he was trying to do.

The papers were about equally noncommittal. If the
police had been able to discover the identities of Mary
Monroe's patrons they were preserving a discreet
silence; there had been, at least for public consumption,
no startling developments during the day, and so far as
Deborah could discover things remained in a kind of
status quo which, considering the nature of the events
themselves and the steady approach of long, dreary
night hours during which practically anything might
happen, was not, to say the least, conducive to cheerful-
ness.

She watched Juliet fold the papers carefully and
smoke with delicate primness her one after-dinner
cigarette; she had gone to the window a hundred times,
discovering only that the police cars had again gone and
still she knew nothing of what had been done—that
the guards remained about the house—and that Tighe
had gone somewhere dressed formally in white tie and
tails and a gleaming silk hat which made him look, from
her window, more than ever like a huge, lunging spider.
Pigeon was not to be seen as usual accompanying him,

silent as a shadow, gray and deft and unbelievably quick. It was a remissness which increased Deborah's uneasiness. Certainly the sight of Pigeon was not exactly a treat for the eyes. But a Pigeon not fulfilling his duties as bodyguard meant either a Pigeon in the hands of the police or a Pigeon at large, free to roam the dim old halls of the apartment house. Of the two, Deborah actually preferred the former.

"For heaven's sake," said Juliet sharply. "Do stay away from the windows. You are positively wearing a path. Like a creature in a zoo."

Which was exactly as Deborah felt—trapped, hemmed in on all sides, weary, terrified, uncomprehending, seeking a way out. It was then that she went to see Chloe.

Juliet did not look at her when she announced her intention. She looked instead at the fireplace and said: "You might tell Chloe that we felt that there was only one safe disposal of the—extraordinary thing she sent to us."

The hall was lighter, and Juanito was at that very moment putting in new and brighter electric bulbs and whistling softly as he worked. The police, then, had not detained him. No one else was about, and Deborah on an impulse spoke to him:

"What did you tell the police, Juanito?"

He was not averse to talking. He looked at her with smoldering black eyes and had a grievance.

"I told 'em the truth," he said sulkily. "The whole truth. If they don't believe me, what else can I do?"

"You mean about the—the gambling place upstairs?"

He shrugged and screwed a bulb carefully into place. Light leaped from it upon his face, and he said: "I told 'em there was one and that Mary Monroe ran it. That's all I know. That and about the keys."

"Keys?"

"Keys, nothing but keys. Keys to the apartment house. Keys to the vacant flat. Keys to the house on the roof. Anybody knows keys are the easiest thing in the world to lose."

"You mean—you lost keys? Keys to the apartment house?"

"No. There are no lost keys to the apartment house. To the flats in it—perhaps. I lost one bunch of keys. And Brocksley had keys. All they talk of is keys, keys, keys. Anybody can make keys fit any lock, if they just use a little patience. But will they listen? No."

He moved to the sconce on the opposite walls and selected a bulb from the corrugated pasteboard box he carried. Deborah followed him.

"You mean," she said gropingly, "that nobody but the tenants had keys to the front door? But that Brocksley had keys to all the apartments? And that you lost another bunch of keys to the apartments?"

He shrugged and said nothing, and Deborah was conscious of something like horror.

"Do you mean to say that there are two sets of keys roving about somewhere? That whoever has them can enter any of the apartments——"

His unusual approachability was vanishing rapidly. He gave her a sullen look and said:

"I have keys, certainly. Here, in my pocket. And Brocksley had to have keys, being the renting agent. I don't know who has his keys now. Maybe police— maybe not. That's everything I know, but the police don't believe me. They questioned me for hours. Who comes to the apartment house? Who came to see Mary Monroe? How long did they stay? How often did they come? What do you know about this tenant and that tenant? Has anyone thrown away rubber gloves? What kind of cigarettes does Number 4 smoke? What goes out in the wastebaskets of Number 3——"

"*But that's our apartment——*"

"What packages arrive at Number 6? What does the cook in Number 4 have to say? And then they keep at me: Did you kill Mary Monroe? Did you kill Alfred Brocksley? Did you gamble? Did you move the roulette wheels?" His dark smoldering eyes were all Spanish, and his red hair and freckles became the mystery rather than his name. He said, looking at Deborah: "*Me* kill! Me, Juanito—a dove of peacefulness"—and reached toward his hip pocket with a furtive sliding motion that sent Deborah's heart fluttering to her throat. His black eyes were unfathomable and hot, and his red hair weirdly out of place, and he held Deborah transfixed while he drew slowly from his pocket a very large and crumpled red handkerchief. He touched his forehead with it and restored it to its pocket and still stared at Deborah.

"The police! I *hate* the police!" observed the dove of peacefulness and picked up his box. "Do you need any new bulbs, Miss Cavert?"

"N-no," said Deborah and knocked somewhat hurriedly upon the door to the Riddle apartment. Juanito, waiting for the elevator, had begun to whistle softly through his teeth again.

Deborah unconsciously followed the whistled tune and, suddenly aware of it, whirled again to stare at Juanito.

He did not look at her, and words accompanied the phrase in her mind. She cried, "*Juanito!*" and he jerked toward her.

"Juanito—what is that you are whistling? Where did you hear it?"

He looked blank—or was it only that his black eyes were altogether impenetrable? He said: "I don't know. It was just a tune. I must have heard somebody singing it."

"Who?"

He didn't know, either, when or where he had heard the fragment of music.

"Seems to me I heard somebody singing it. Don't remember who it was," he said, opening the elevator door. "Guess it must be some new tune. Is it, Miss Cavert?"

"No," said Deborah. "It's called 'Elégie.'"

"Oh," said Juanito and vanished.

And she was quite suddenly alone in the paneled old hall with its high ceilings and empty elevator shaft and stairway and small door. Brocksley had died just there —not ten feet away from where she stood—and at about this time.

She knocked again at the Riddle door—and the sound was loud and hollow and disturbing in that silent place, as if there were ears besides her own to hear it. But, of course, there was no one. No one, that is, except Chloe on the other side of the door, who said: "Who is it?" and waited for Deborah's answer before she opened it.

A strange, desperate Chloe with eyes like fiery green jewels. Inside, Gibbs, white and drawn, was pacing the floor.

"Come in, Deb," said Chloe. "Did you get the package?"

"Juliet looked at it," said Deborah. "She burned it."

There was a queer, short silence. Then Gibbs said with a kind of groan: "You may as well tell her, Chloe," and flung himself out of the room. Chloe watched him leave.

"It's terribly simple," she said to Deborah. "But still, I think Gibbs is more worried about it than he needs to be. I don't—I don't understand why he is so frantic. Nerves, I suppose. They can't really hang anything on him with what they've got. You see—well, it's like this, Deborah: The night Mary Monroe was murdered he—he was out for a walk. As I told you. But it's no good to keep silent about it now, for Juanito saw him go and told the police. He went out the front entrance but, of course, he could have gone up the fire escape, shot Mary Monroe, returned, and swung up the fire escape again. A man could get it down easily with a rope and as easily swing it up again. And—well, you see, the whole trouble is he had a terrible quarrel with Mary Monroe that very morning. And Juanito heard them."

She rose and paced the floor in her turn with long graceful strides; she was wearing a yellow satin tea gown with flowing sleeves and a somewhat bedraggled train which swirled and jerked like the tail of a nervous animal when she walked, and looked, despite her white-faced anxiety and sundry spots on the yellow satin, extremely sleek and handsome.

"That's the trouble. Juanito heard them. And they were both rather violent. You know Gibbs, Deborah, when he's really roused—or perhaps you don't. He's really pretty—lurid. And there's nothing Mary Monroe loved more than a fine large scene with plenty of scope for dramatics." Chloe turned in her pacing and kicked her train savagely and said: "They stopped short of

physical combat, but that was all. Gibbs came in here
trembling with rage and took that portrait, the finest
thing he's ever done, and slashed it to pieces with a
carving knife. Tulip yelped and hid. Now she thinks
the place is haunted. Sees people wandering in the halls
and creeping up the fire escape. Well, I tried to stop
Gibbs, but I couldn't. You saw the portrait. He brooded
around all day. I thought he'd quieted down, so I went
out to tea. When I got back—well, you know about that.
Kids all yelling. Gibbs disappeared. And—Mary
Monroe—murdered——"

Chloe's hands went up to her own throat as if she
felt stifled.

But she continued:

"Well, now the police know that. And they know,
too, that Brocksley had some kind of evidence—Dolly
told them that. But she didn't tell them what the evidence was and swears she doesn't know. So now they
are after Gibbs—keeping after him——"

"But Gibbs has an alibi for the time of Brocksley's
murder. And they seem to believe that the same person
did both murders——"

Chloe stopped pacing and gave Deborah a hunted
green look.

"He hasn't an alibi. He was here in the apartment,
and so was Dolly, and we all three sat right here in this
room. But, Deborah"—her red tongue licked out
around her lips—"Deborah—a few minutes after Dolly
came in he—he went into his studio. We've had these
partitions put into the apartment; it isn't like the rest
of the apartments in the building. Dolly and I couldn't
possibly see the hall and the outside door. Tulip says
he didn't go out the back way, of course. And he *was in*
the studio. But—you see we can't prove it."

And that was the substance of Chloe's story.

She did say before Deborah left that Dolly was still held in her own flat and not yet permitted to see anyone. And she had heard some news.

It had come by the queer grapevine telegraph whose scraps of news they were beginning to snatch so avidly. To doubt—yet to believe.

Someone had been told by someone who had overheard someone telling someone else.

In this case it was Tulip who had got it from Juanito, whose ear probably had been pressed to some door.

"It's Anthony," said Chloe. "They say the bullet that killed Mary Monroe has been traced to his revolver. They say that he is to be arrested." She brooded. "It's our only hope," she said and looked at Deborah.

Deborah was white to the lips and knew it.

"Have they already arrested him?"

A flare of hope leaped into Chloe's eyes, and she tried decently to hide it.

"I don't think so," she said. "If they had they wounn't be hounding Gibbs."

That was true, of course.

And after all, thought Deborah soberly as she was returning to the Cavert apartment, it was altogether possible that Gibbs had killed Mary Monroe. She remembered something Juliet had said long ago: ". . . if he just doesn't kill a client in one of his blind rages."

This time, however, on hearing the story, Juliet said nothing at all.

It was late in a silent, sleepless night before Deborah realized that she hadn't asked what the quarrel was about. But it didn't matter. *Was* it Anthony's revolver? Where was Anthony? "It's our only hope," Chloe had said.

A sleepless night. Eventually, however, she must have slept, for she waked suddenly and widely, blinking her way through a confused dream of voices. Voices somewhere, subdued, stealthy. Somewhere a door closing cautiously.

She listened, wide awake now and terribly intent.

There were no more voices.

And if a door had closed there was no evidence at all of anyone having closed it. The place was dark and quiet, and Blitz at her feet had not moved.

CHAPTER XVII

SHE groped into the dark and found the table light. The room was cold, with the curtains stirring at the open window, but there was no other motion. Because it was so cold, Deborah reached for the brown tweed coat that lay across a chair and pulled it around her shoulders.

And it was because she was cold and still in the clutch of that singularly real dream and sat huddled under blankets, with the light still on and Blitz curled up forbiddenly on the foot of the bed and the brown tweed coat pulled around her shoulders, that she found the thing she found in its pocket. She had twisted around to look at the clock, and the coat was disarranged, and somehow a small silver object fell from its pocket and lay there on the edge of the blanket, and it was a silver lighter and the initials A. W. were clear upon its surface.

And instantly Deborah's mind flashed back to a moment when she had stood facing Mary Monroe with the stubborn drawer of a mahogany table in her hands and an incredible litter of small objects, among them a silver lighter, tumbling from it to lie in a heterogeneous heap upon the floor. She could remember nothing further of it, but probably she had slipped the thing into her pocket—absently—distracted by Mary Monroe—and because of the turmoil of events into which she had been immediately plunged had never thought of it again.

That was all she knew of it.

That and that in all probability it belonged to

Anthony. But it was owing to the lighter and to the clear detachment of after-midnight hours that certain facts began irresistibly to array themselves in Deborah's mind.

Anthony had explained his presence in the house on the roof. It was an explanation that was simple, and that fitted the case convincingly. It sounded true.

And Anthony had had a revolver in his hand and had said that he had picked it up at the door of Mary Monroe's house and had later lost it. It, too, had sounded true. But put like that, in so many words, it was less convincing. And now, if Chloe's news were true, that revolver belonged to Anthony. No, not necessarily that revolver, amended Deborah hastily, but the revolver from which had sped the incredibly swift bullet that had put an end to the glowing, vigorous life that was Mary Monroe.

Anthony's revolver. But that didn't mean that Anthony had killed Mary Monroe with it. It might mean that the police would arrest him—it might mean that they would charge him with murder—but it was only circumstantial evidence. Circumstantial evidence. But that was terribly convincing to juries. Always had been.

But any number of people might have had access to Anthony's revolver. Francis, first.

Francis.

Deborah sat upright suddenly, clutching the coat tightly around her. After all, why not Francis? He had ready access, presumably, to Anthony's revolver. He could as conceivably have had a motive for murdering Mary Monroe as could anyone else in the house. Besides, thought Deborah with a touch of malice, he would be rather admirably cast as the villain of the piece; his pleasant, civilized suavity, his observant, handsome eyes, his somewhat spectacular beauty, his graceful detached air, were all almost irresistibly suspicious. He could have killed Mary Monroe; he could have secured Anthony's revolver, dropped it on the roof, and fled down the fire escape and then returned the same way to recover it after Anthony himself had lost the thing; he could have returned the revolver; he could have deceived Anthony; he could easily be a real and consummate actor or a skillful liar. The antagonism she had felt in him and had attributed to his own suspicion of her and, in a small degree, to some faint jealousy of her own relation to Anthony which excluded Francis, and which he must have recognized, might be owing to something else entirely. He, too, could have secured one of the two sets of keys that, according to Juanito, were mysteriously at large. And certainly there was an intangible feeling in the house that locks and keys were of strangely little value as protection.

And he was quick, graceful, and subtle. True, his own suspicion of Deborah had seemed altogether too real and threatening for her own peace of mind. And it was true, too, that there was something direct and terribly brutal about both crimes; something feral that went ill with civilization. Francis, thought Deborah somewhat fantastically, might have been, given the inclination and moral obliquity, a poisoner. And he would have planned the thing subtly and cautiously where Gibbs, for instance, would have given way to a sudden fit of rage and would have been violent and incautious.

But neither man could have murdered Brocksley. Francis's alibi was Anthony, as he was Anthony's alibi. And if the police were inclined to doubt Gibbs's alibi, it was because they did not know Chloe's quickness of ear and observation. It was true that, owing to the arrangement of the two front rooms in the Riddle apartment, Gibbs could have passed from the second room (his studio) through the little hall and out the door without being actually seen by Dolly or Chloe. But to believe that he did so was to reckon without Chloe's powers of comprehension, which were actually as subtly keen and acute as those of any red Indian. True again that Chloe might have been lying, but Deborah believed her.

Francis or Gibbs. Or Juanito.

But Juanito had no earthly reason to murder Mary Monroe. And he had been questioned exhaustively by the police; but, then, she was inclined to think that everyone in the house had been questioned and had been, in Lieutenant Waggon's mind, individual and separate objects of suspicion. Juanito, however, was merely a rather silent and sulky fixture about the apartment house. A fixture who grumbled when the dogs tracked the vestibule steps, who came with strange wrenches and bolts when there was trouble about the bathroom plumbing or sounds in the radiators; who accepted five dollars at Christmas time with neither gratitude nor demur and preferred the lunch hour for using the vacuum cleaner in the halls and on the stairway, particularly, Juliet always said, if one had lunch guests. He had admitted passing through the hall at about the time when, in the elevator or on the second floor, Brocksley must have been dying. That, thought Deborah, fleetingly, must have given the murderer (assuming of necessity his presence somewhere near) a very nasty moment or two. But there was no faint reason to suspect Juanito; no clue at all leading to him. He was perhaps a reluctant and sullen witness to certain facts of everyday living in the apartment house, but that was all. And besides, if he had been inclined to murder anybody, Deborah was inclined to suspect that he would have done so primitively, savagely, with one of his own wrenches. No, it couldn't be Juanito.

Deborah's hand tightened on the silver lighter in her hand.

And it couldn't be Anthony.

She paused again to consider the purely physical circumstances surrounding the death of Alfred Brocksley. At seven Anthony had called her over the telephone. At a few minutes before seven Dolly Brocksley had left her husband in their first-floor apartment and had gone up to the second floor. Deborah remembered the faint drone of elevator which she had heard as the telephone rang. Was it Dolly? Or had Dolly come earlier and had Deborah, sunk in thought, failed to hear, that time, the sound of the small elevator?

What then? Anthony had talked to her for only a few moments; a long five or six minutes afterwards she had opened the door and found Brocksley there in the hall. And during that interval Anthony had taken time to telephone the Brownstone and order dinner.

How had Brocksley got there? At seven—perhaps a moment or two before—he had been alive. At about eight or nine minutes after seven, at the most, he was dead. During that short interval he had left his own apartment and must have been killed either in the elevator (although the blood stains there had proved, really, nothing) or in the second-floor hall. He was a heavy man, and while it would have been possible to drag the body for a few feet, it was not possible that it had been moved any distance.

How long did it take to kill a man?

It had taken only a second to kill Mary Monroe—an unbelievably little and fleeting wisp of time.

And both murders were, as Anthony had said, swift and direct and, somehow, savage.

She frowned at the lighter and put it away in the drawer of the bedside table. A little gold ring was there, too, and she looked at it thoughtfully.

No, it wasn't Anthony. And she would warn him— tell him about the revolver—the very instant he telephoned or came.

And it was just then that she heard an odd, dull sound.

A sound that was repeated.

Alarums and excursions, thought Deborah, and listened.

Again the sound was repeated, and then it came in a series of small thuds. And it came from the apartment immediately below and sounded exactly as if someone were pounding on a thick rug with—well, with what? A blunt instrument, thought Deborah, and realized she was frightened and was taking refuge in flippancy.

What was Anthony doing?

When had he returned from his mysterious errand across town—and *what was going on in the flat below?*

What could anybody be doing—pounding like that in the middle of the night? A swift recollection of the cold brutality in the manner of Alfred Brocksley's murder swept across Deborah sickeningly.

Blitz stirred and growled and listened, and Deborah was thrusting her toes into sandals and clutching her dressing gown and coat somehow around her for warmth.

She had to do something. Call Juliet? But that would

avail nothing. Call the police? Yes, by all means. But the telephone would be too slow, if—if there were actually danger in that dull repeated sound.

There was a sudden silence. And in the silence the feeling of menace and secret and evil knowledge that had somehow crept in and made its being in the thick old walls became all at once tangible and dreadfully oppressive until Deborah could endure it no longer.

Just outside, in the hall, with his solid blue back to the wall and his revolver ready, there ought to be a policeman.

But there was not.

The chair against the wall was empty. The hall was empty. The elevator shaft and stairway were empty.

The lights Juanito had placed in the sconces along the walls made the whole place garish and bright and showed the mars in the lower panels of the door leading to the Riddle flat.

There was not a sound to be heard.

Indeed, it was only owing to that blank, heavy silence that Deborah heard what she did hear. And that was the gentle little click of a closing door. But this time it was real—whatever the other thing had been. And it was, it had to be, the small door behind the stairway and elevator shaft.

Never afterward could Deborah account for the immediate sense of danger that gripped her. It was sheer animal instinct, for there was no way for her to know or guess what hand had closed that small door.

Blitz, unheeded, pushed at Deborah's ankles and growled. And Deborah stared into that brilliant silent hall and quite simply did not dare to descend to the hall below and Anthony's flat. Something stronger than herself drew her shudderingly inside her own door. "After all," she heard herself saying aloud, "the telephone is best." Her throat was numb and queer, and Blitz looked at her with perplexedly cocked ears.

She turned toward the telephone, and as she did so it rang.

It was Francis Maly, and he said: "Where is Anthony?"

"Anthony!"

"Yes, of course. Where is he? Don't you know?"

"No—no."

Someone else was with Francis. She could hear him murmuring in an aside. Then he said:

"Look here, may I come up? Oh, I know it's late. But it's important. It's about Tony."

"Isn't he there?" said Deborah in a small voice.

"I don't know where he is," said Francis impatiently, and the telephone clicked and Deborah put down her own telephone and sneezed.

Her feet were like ice; she managed to get into stockings before Francis knocked. She opened the door again somewhat timorously. Francis stood there, looking very tall in a scarlet dressing gown and incredibly handsome with his white hair smooth even at that turbulent moment and his dark blue eyes shining. But his brown face looked less brown, and there was a policeman beside him. They exchanged understanding looks, and as if there had been some prearrangement, the policeman remained outside when Francis entered.

"Don't be frightened," he said. "Where's Tony gone to?"

"I—I don't know," stammered Deborah.

He searched her face as if doubting her denial. Finally he said abruptly:

"Look here, Deborah, I think we ought to have a talk. Do you mind?"

It wouldn't really matter, thought Deborah, observing Francis's determined attitude, whether she minded or not.

"Very well," she said. "Won't you sit down?"

He followed her into the library opposite and sat down near her, pulling the chair around so that he could look directly into her face.

But it was really Deborah who began.

"What has happened downstairs? What was that pounding?"

"Oh, that," he said. "Did you hear it? I awoke to find myself barricaded in my room. I couldn't get out. You don't happen to know anything about it, I suppose?"

"*I!* I know nothing of it except I heard something——"

"The heel of my shoe," said Francis. "Against the floor. A policeman finally heard me, dug up a key—I suppose the police have keys to the whole place—and entered the apartment. The door to my room had been locked on the outside and a chair wedged under the knob. And the whole place had been thoroughly ransacked, simply turned upside down, papers everywhere. And Anthony is gone."

"Who was it?"

"Who searched the apartment, you mean? Do you think I'd be sitting here if I knew! I heard absolutely nothing. Don't know what finally roused me. Two policemen were on guard in the vestibule. Neither of them saw anything. Then I discovered that Anthony is still gone. I haven't seen him since he had a talk with Pigeon this afternoon."

Deborah's hands met and clutched themselves together. So Anthony had seen and talked to Pigeon. What had he learned? Francis said:

"I suppose you know what Pigeon told him?"

"No," said Deborah. "I only know that Anthony telephoned just after dinner. He said not to worry." She moistened her lips. "Perhaps it was the police who searched your apartment and locked you in?"

"They don't search like that," said Francis succinctly. "Things are flung about as if a dog had been worrying them." He paused and said unexpectedly: "Just what is Anthony to you?"

"Anthony!"

"Certainly. Anthony. And you needn't look at me as if I have no right to ask. Anthony was my friend long before you knew him. I have a right to ask you what you are doing with him. Why you are—using him."

"*No!*"

"Well, then, what do you call it? See here, I don't care because you are a woman, because you've a certain amount of beauty, because you do seem to need help. *Why* do you need help? That's what I want to know. And why must you pick on Anthony to help you? And why—*why were you not surprised when I told you Mary Monroe was murdered?*"

So that was it. That was what that accusing look in his eyes had meant. He went on rapidly: "I could swear you knew of it. And that you didn't want anyone to know that you knew of it. Oh, you needn't pretend wide-eyed innocence. I know, I tell you."

He stopped and looked at her and said: "Deborah Cavert, I don't know how or why you are connected with the murder of Mary Monroe. Or the murder of Alfred Brocksley. But I would have to be blind and deaf and dumb if I didn't know there was something. And that, somehow, you've got Anthony on your side. I've seen something of the world. It's girls like you, soft and helpless and pretty, who can do the most contemptibly selfish things. If you are saving yourself at Anthony's expense, I'll make you sorry." He paused again and gave her a long, searching look. His brown face still looked a little pale, and quite suddenly the faintly mocking expression which he so often wore vanished entirely. He said gravely: "And if you are not—I'll come over to your side, too."

So he knew. Not everything, but enough. And Anthony was gone.

Francis very slowly, looking at her soberly, put out his hand, and Deborah placed her own in it.

"Pax," said Francis. He tried to say it lightly, but his pleasant manner failed him. And in the grave little silence between them she was suddenly aware of a confusion and tremor of movement and sound somewhere in the house.

Movement and sound. Francis heard it, too, and stiffened, and there were heavy feet pounding across a hall and down stairs.

Francis dropped her hand and flung himself to the door. It opened and someone was screaming. A horrible, high-pitched scream that rose to the very roof and stopped suddenly, sickeningly, at its height.

And downstairs policemen were pounding on the door of the Brocksley apartment.

CHAPTER XVIII

It was Dolly Brocksley. And she had been strangled—strangled, or very near it, while policemen were pounding on that door, finding keys, breaking it finally, to find the policewoman unconscious on the kitchen floor with her hair in curlers and a great bloody bruise on her chin, the back door standing wide open, and Dolly black in the face and senseless on her bed, with the bedclothes in mad disarray and dreadful ugly marks on Dolly's thin little throat.

But she was not dead.

Although they worked—the emergency squad from the police station and hurriedly summoned doctors—half the night to save that little flutter of life. Worked while Francis and Deborah and Juliet sat in the shabby Brocksley drawing room and waited, trying not to look at the opera scores stacked upon the battered piano, which, so many, many times they had heard tinkling away zestfully while Brocksley's voice had roared out ambitious, concientious scales.

Chloe was there, too, her black hair wildly tousled and her face white but the only practical one among them, for she took charge of the policewoman and, by dint of some mysterious combination of cold water, smelling salts, and sheer nerve force, had her conscious and talking in very short order. But she could explain nothing. She had heard some kind of commotion, she said, in the apartment across the hall; somebody pounding. It had roused her, and she was about to call the

police when they apparently heard it, also, and entered
the apartment. She had listened at the door—"being,"
she said parenthetically, putting her hand to her hair,
"undressed." But it was only some prowler, and Mr.
Maly and one of the policemen, "Getch, it was," went
upstairs and she had gone back to bed. But she was
nervous and couldn't sleep and finally thought she heard
a noise in the kitchen. She went out cautiously. But
not, it seemed, cautiously enough.

For the blow had come the instant she opened the
swinging door from the butler's pantry.

"And that's all I know," she said. "Except that I
think I ought to get a day off tomorrow."

And no one, even when Lieutenant Waggon, unbelievably wide awake and calm, arrived and took things
in hand, knew more.

Gibbs, who had roused and followed Chloe downstairs, looked white and angry but swore stoutly, if
sulkily, that he knew nothing of the thing. And Tighe
and Pigeon apparently were both sound asleep when
roused, some time later, by the police.

"Both of 'em asleep," Deborah heard one policeman
say to another. "Tighe in yellow silk pajamas. Pigeon
in a nightshirt. And if you ever want to see something
to give you a nightmare, take a look at that lousy little
devil in a nightshirt. All skinny and shiny, with his
eyes looking at you queer like a snake's."

Deborah mutely and the policeman vocally conceded
that it would be no agreeable sight. And then someone
said that Dolly was breathing and able to talk but didn't
know who had attacked her, and Lieutenant Waggon
sent them all back to their own apartments and went to
Dolly.

It was by that time four o'clock in the morning. They

scattered languidly under the eyes of the augmented groups of policemen. There were about the whole affair only two definite and acknowledged facts. One was that, though the door at the back of the apartment was wide open, none of the guards about the apartment house had seen anyone enter. "Of course," one of the guards said, "somebody might've crawled down the fire escape. Or the back stairs, keeping close to the shadow of the wall." But nobody had approached it from the street. Or alley.

And the other was that whoever had entered the apartment had meant to kill Dolly. Had thought, in all probability, that she was dead when, alarmed by the pounding on the door by the policemen whom her scream had brought, he had fled.

Francis went upstairs with Juliet and Deborah and searched the apartment under Juliet's weary, chilly gaze. There was, of course, no one there.

And when he had gone, Juliet refused to talk.

"Let's get some sleep," she said abruptly. "Tomorrow's another day. Or if it isn't," she added with rather grisly appropriateness, "it won't matter. Good-night, Deborah." And she closed her door firmly.

And it was not until morning—the strange, gray morning that did finally arrive and find Deborah still wide-eyed and terribly tired—that she told Deborah her news.

Some time during the night her jewels had been stolen.

"And I'm awfully sorry, Deborah, to be obliged to tell you that the little string of pearls your mother left you was with them." She looked at Deborah with eyes that overnight had sunken into gray pockets. "I'll try to make it up to you some way, my dear."

That, as Deborah recalled it later, was actually the beginning of that day. Sunday, December tenth. Another still, gray day, with nerves on edge and a queer, uneasy tightness in the very air.

An inauspicious beginning.

For Juliet was right as usual. The jewels had disappeared, seal and wrapping and all. She had put them under the pillow in her own room. And in the morning they were gone. And that was all she knew. But she did not want to report the matter to the police. Not yet. "Not," said Juliet, "until this dreadful affair is cleared up. Think of the papers, Deborah. The police. They would be sure to connect it somehow with the murders. It would be very dreadful for us."

And Deborah wearily, and because Juliet was always right, agreed. Later, said Juliet, they would notify the insurance company. But not today when the office would be closed. And again Deborah agreed. After all, it didn't much matter—not with Anthony still gone.

Sunday. With Anthony still missing, Juliet increasingly nervous and irritable as the day wore on, the morning papers noncommittal (knowing nothing, apparently, of the brutal attack upon Dolly, and obliged to retell the events that had already been told), and a general air of gloom and depression that became more and more pronounced. Even Blitz was uneasy and inclined to bark sharply at small sounds, and Deborah had a cold in her head and was sleepy and pale except around her small nose, and she listened, until her very ears were tired, for the telephone to ring. And once when it did ring and Juliet reached it first, Deborah nearly suffocated with suspense before it proved to be only Annie, who had seen the papers and was quite beside herself. Juliet hung up with a bang.

"She seems to think," she snapped, "that if we shake our heads they'll drop off. Thank God for scarlet fever." She looked out the window at the gray, heavy sky. "And I'm not so sure she's far off, really," she added somberly.

And when the noon came and still there was no word of Anthony, Deborah went into her own room and closed the door and sat there looking at the red geranium, still brave and gay and crimson, and sneezing, and finally putting her face in the pillow and crying a little.

And she thought how strange it was that one small word or two had changed the whole course of her life— or at least might well change it. If she had said no when Mary Monroe invited her to tea—if she had not paused there in the vestibule to disentangle Blitz's leash. If she had been five minutes earlier or five minutes later.

She did not know, then, that no power on earth could have prevented her own entanglement with the murders at 18 East Eden.

Chloe came in about one, invited them somewhat absently to lunch, and went away after Juliet stiffly, though with a longing look in her eye, had regretted that she had letters to write. Tulip was known to be an extremely good cook.

Neither Juliet nor Chloe referred to the portrait nor to the faint odor of burnt canvas and turpentine that still lingered in the flat. At the door Chloe paused. She looked ill, dark around the eyes and pale as if she, too, had not slept, and there was something odd and unfamiliar about her that Deborah did not comprehend until she said:

"A policeman came in this morning and demanded all my lipstick. Every stick of it! Did they take yours, too?"

"Yesterday."

"Why?"

"I don't know."

"Have you heard anything of Anthony?"

"No."

"Oh," said Chloe and went away, her green silk skirt whispering along at her lovely heels. Some faraway words struggled through Deborah's memory and made themselves heard: "Bind on thy sandals, O thou most fleet—Over the splendor and speed of thy feet"— but that didn't fit Chloe exactly. Deborah turned away and was aware that another and more urgent memory was struggling to become articulate. Something connected with lipstick. A lipstick and some trivial fact that was small and had been unimportant and that now tried to make itself remembered, as if it had become quite suddenly important. It tantalized her and was elusive, and she finally gave it up.

It was some time later that, going out for the noon extras which a boy was crying in the street (and which she was destined not to see), she met Tighe. The policeman was not in his accustomed place in the hall that morning, and Deborah, ringing for the elevator, heard it start from the third floor. It came slowly into sight, and suddenly she realized that someone was in it. A dark bulky shadow, not too clear behind the grilled door and in the dim light in the cage.

There was a queer, tight feeling in Deborah's throat. Then the bulky figure moved and became definite as the door opened and Tighe was saying: "Good-morning, Miss Deborah," and sliding something that gleamed into his pocket.

He looked at her, and one fat yellow hand went up to remove his hat, and she saw that he was smiling suavely with queer gray lips and that his forehead and fat chins looked moist and shiny. "He's frightened," thought Deborah confusedly. "Frightened, and his heart isn't what it was."

He said a bit jerkily, as if he'd been running a race:

"Going down, Miss Deborah? You rang, didn't you?" He continued to hold the door open for her, and Deborah stepped inside the cage. After all, why shouldn't he be frightened?—a man who hires a body-guard doesn't do so for the fun of it. That was certainly a revolver he slipped into his pocket when he saw that the person who had rung was only Deborah. On the spot; that's what they called it when a man was cornered by his enemies, and there couldn't have been a better place—or worse place, rather—than in that small, slow elevator.

Tighe was still puffing but had a better color.

"How's your aunt this morning?" he said pleasantly. "I do hope she has recovered from the shock of that unfortunate business about her jewels."

"*Jewels?*" said Deborah doubting her ears.

"Yes, of course. The jewels that were stolen. The——" He stopped abruptly. "Oh," he said, "I'm sorry. Perhaps you didn't know. Or rather I must be mistaken."

"Oh, no," said Deborah. "The jewels were stolen. Just last night. But how did you know? How——"

He interrupted her, smiling but with a tinge of discomposure in his bearing.

"Pigeon told me that there had been a theft in the apartment house last night," he said. "I'm sure I don't know how he knew. He's a wily little devil—knows everything that happens. Really amusing chap."

Deborah was in no frame of mind to be diverted.

"No one knew about the theft of the jewels," she said.

Tighe's yellow eyes flickered and moved, and Deborah went on: "The police don't know. The insurance company hasn't been told of it. There's only one way for Pigeon to know, and that is if he took them himself." She stopped abruptly. The yellow eyes opposite her seemed to move and close a little, but Tighe laughed.

"My dear child," he said pleasantly. "What alarming candor in one so young! Forgivable, of course, with youth and charm. But later———" His great shoulders moved in an adroit little gesture of distaste, and the elevator stopped with a jerk. "I don't know where he gathered his knowledge, Miss Deborah. And I'll admit that Pigeon has his faults. But I assure you that he—well, frankly, I think he is too much—er—alarmed regarding his own personal safety recently to do much prowling about the apartment house at night. Stealing jewels doesn't, moreover, exactly coincide with his undoubted genius in—other lines of endeavor. Oh, hello, Maly."

Francis stood in the open doorway of his apartment.

"Morning, Tighe," said Francis. "Good-morning, Deborah. Any news of Tony?"

"No," replied Deborah, and Tighe, bowing and smiling, with only a tinge of haste, withdrew, nevertheless, rather promptly. Francis watched Tighe open the vestibule door and waddle down the steps to the street door. And Deborah said: "Have you?"

"Only a little, but it's reassuring. I ought to have let you know. He's all right, I think."

"Where is he?"

He glanced around the silent hall. The door to the Brocksley flat was closed and silent. There was no motion from the stairway. The door from the vestibule to the street had closed with a dull jar under Tighe's departing hand, and there was no one in the vestibule.

"Won't you come in? This hall—isn't too pleasant lately. I don't know where the police are, do you?"

"They can't be far away," said Deborah and entered the door which Francis pushed wider for her.

"Will you walk into my parlor?" he said smiling down at her. "Indeed, it really is my parlor. Here's a chair."

"What did you hear from Tony?" asked Deborah, accepting a deep leather armchair which smelled faintly of tobacco and glancing about her. Books in shelves which extended across what was, in the Cavert apartment, a doorway, a litter of magazines, a laden desk and open typewriter. The morning papers everywhere. The rotogravure section had secured and reproduced in colors a photograph of one of Gibbs's paintings, and it lay at Deborah's feet so that her brown suède toe touched the pictured face.

"Tony's all right," said Francis soberly. "At least I got word from the police that he's doing something or other on his own hook and that a plain-clothes man is trailing him and at last report he was perfectly all right. Tony would be wild if he knew he was being followed. But he hasn't telephoned, and I can't tell him. And, of course, I do feel much relieved to know that there's someone with him, whether he knows or would like it or not. I was pretty worried last night."

It was a weight lifted quite literally from Deborah's heart. She smiled rather mistily at Francis. And then because something in his face made her feel a little shy and embarrassed, she said:

"He's all right, then. I was worried, too.—I had never seen this portrait before, had you?"

"That one in the rotogravure? No. I believe it's one of Gibbs' very early canvases. Before he developed his present somewhat photographic technique. He's changed a lot, of course, as he's grown older. He may be great, though, yet. After all, people like portraits to be photographic." He looked at his watch and reached toward the dials beside him. "Mind if I turn on the radio? It's about time for a news broadcast, and they may say something new about our affair. It's very stimulating to be in the news. Stimulating but rather shattering to the nerves, too."

Photographic, thought Deborah. Gibbs was altogether too photographic. Well, there was one of his portraits that, now, would never go down to posterity.

She sneezed, and Francis said: "I'll close the window," and a voice came from her elbow, startling her and announcing that when the musical note sounded it would be exactly one minute and three seconds after three o'clock, and Francis laughed:

"Don't be alarmed," he said. "It's only the speaker. Ah—here's Tony, at last. Good God, Tony, where've you been? *And what's wrong?*"

Anthony stood in the doorway and looked at them.

"Tony!" cried Deborah and echoed Francis's inquiry. "*Tony, what's wrong?*"

He sagged wearily against the door casing. He was unshaven, and his face was drawn and white. For a moment he said nothing at all, just looked from Deborah to Francis and back again. Then he seemed to make an effort to pull himself together, straightened his shoulders, jerked off his hat with a weary gesture and tossed it into a chair, and said:

"Nothing. I'm all right."

There was something queer and uncertain about his voice. Deborah thought wildly: "He's been drinking." And Francis looked as if he thought the same thing, for he went to Tony and took his arm and said: "Here, you look all in, Tony. You'd better lie down. Shan't I make you some coffee?"

"I'm all right," said Anthony still in that odd, uncertain voice. He let Francis take his topcoat and passed a hand that was unsteady across his ruffled dark hair. His eyes, even, looked heavy and as if their vision were blurred. His shirt collar was wrinkled, and something sagged one of his coat pockets downward. He seemed to be vaguely aware of his dishevelment, for he smoothed his hair again and put a hand to the coat pocket and pulled out a revolver.

"What in the world, Tony——" began Francis, and Anthony said, without any inflection at all: "I picked it up at a pawnshop last night. Don't suppose it's any good."

"But what for, Tony?" cried Francis. "For God's sake point the thing some other way."

Anthony laughed shortly.

"Thought we needed a revolver or two. Somebody took mine—police, I guess. Besides—there was a fellow following me."

"Tony," said Francis, "you'd better take a cold shower. Have a whisky——"

"That was a detective following you, Anthony," said Deborah. The revolver; she must warn Anthony of what Chloe had told her. But he was looking fixedly at the revolver in his hand, and she said: "I'd better go," and a voice from the radio said clearly and compellingly so that they were obliged to listen:

". . . the latest news about the Mary Monroe murders which, owing to the popularity of the late diva and the strange and bizarre circumstances of the crime, have turned the eyes of all Chicago upon the old apartment

building at 18 East Eden Street. We are reliably informed that an arrest and murder charge will be made
before night. A new and interesting slant regarding the
gambling den, where it is said hundreds of thousands of
dollars passed over the green felt tables, has been exposed by the discovery that the owner of the apartment
building, who has remained suggestively in the background up till now, is actually a man of considerable
influence in politics. A headline says that the police are
taking every precaution to prevent a third murder.
This and other latest developments of these sensational
crimes will be found in the afternoon extra which is
now on sale on the . . ."

"Turn that off," said Anthony. "Don't go, Deborah.
I want to talk to you."

Francis snapped off the radio and said promptly:
"I'm just going out to post some letters. You'll excuse
me——"

And Anthony said, "Come into my own sitting room,
Deborah—I need a drink."

She watched while he went to a cupboard and poured
himself a small glass of brandy, belatedly offered her
some which she refused, and sank wearily into a chair
opposite, and she realized that he wasn't drunk at all.

For he said: "Don't mind me. I suppose I look like
something out of an ashcan. But I'm not drunk. And
I'm not sick. I—it's just that I was up all night. And
I've come upon a sort of—queer thing."

He looked at her and then looked away. His eyes were
brighter from the brandy, but a gray shadow lay over his
face. "You see, Deborah, somebody was murdered once
in the house on the roof. And died—only he didn't die.
And I think he came back to murder Mary Monroe."

CHAPTER XIX

"Who?" whispered Deborah after a long moment.

"I don't know. Listen. Here's the thing from the beginning. See what you make of it."

She interrupted:

"Where have you been? What started you——"

"I've been for the most part hanging around the vicinity of St. Justin's Hospital. Waiting to see superintendents—doctors—nurses—ambulance drivers. And most unwelcome with all of them. You see, I had nothing at all to go on. Only a few words. But I'll begin at the beginning. When I left you yesterday I went to try to discover what, if any, evidence Pigeon had given the police which might involve you. Well, he didn't say anything; that is, nothing about you. He did say that at exactly five minutes to seven, the night Mary Monroe was murdered, he looked out of their kitchen window and saw a woman with blonde hair coming down the fire escape from Mary Monroe's house. It was dark, but the light from the window fell upon a portion of the fire escape, and he just caught a glimpse of blonde hair. But it was long hair, wrapped in sort of braids around the woman's head. So that lets you out, Deborah—at least just there."

"Did you talk to Pigeon?"

"Tried to. He wouldn't talk. I know that they questioned him until a man of ordinary stamina would have broken down. But Pigeon is not ordinary. And if he knows anything else he's determined not to tell it. I

don't know why he has let up on you or what he intends
to do; probably just at the moment his main desire is to
avoid getting too tightly in the clutches of the police. I
think he's scared; and not only scared of the police,
either. I don't know why, but I do know that he had
something to do with the murder—and if my theory is
right he actually knows who killed her. Or at least—he
knows the whole story and the motive; whether he'll
tell or not is a different matter. You see, Dolly Brocksley
knows what Brocksley knew. He told her. And she told
me."

"*Told you!*"

"Yes. Scared, I suppose. Or——"

"Wait, Tony. Did you know someone tried to murder
her last night?"

"What!"

Swiftly Deborah told him.

"And they don't know who it was?"

"There was no clue. She just barely escaped with her
life."

He rose and began to pace up and down the floor.
His eyes looked dark and angry in his white face.

"Little Dolly. So he tried to get her, too. Well, it was
too late. She'd already told what she knew. And it's
little enough, God knows."

He flung himself into a chair again, and Deborah had
the instinctive wisdom to wait, and sat there, a slender
crimson figure with wide gray eyes. "She sent for me,"
he said abruptly. "Dolly, I mean. Insisted upon seeing
me, and the policewoman finally came for me. But after
I got there Dolly didn't want to talk. I suppose she was
afraid of the policewoman, afraid of Pigeon, who's involved, terribly afraid of the murderer—whoever it
is—and yet had to tell somebody. I don't know why she

chose me. Anyway, the policewoman was just outside the door where she could hear everything. So Dolly wrote what she knew—or what she wanted to tell me. And here it is." He found in a pocket a folded scrap of paper and gave it to Deborah.

Dolly's handwriting was large and sprawling. The note was evidently written hurriedly and nervously.

"Have to tell someone," she had written, "who won't tell the police. Maybe you will know what to do. Promise me not to tell police."

"She was terrified," said Anthony. "She showed me that and looked at me, and I nodded."

Below, Dolly had continued:

"Brocksley told me what he had heard. It was part of a telephone talk. A few days before the murder. He heard Pigeon say this: 'Go to Mary Monroe. She will tell you that I've told you the truth. . . . No, I wasn't in her house when it happened, but they told me. I had to clean up the blood. . . . And I went to St. Justin's every day to inquire. I was there the night you died.'"

"*The night you died!*" cried Deborah.

Anthony looked at her wearily.

"Yes, I know. Sounds just nonsense. But it—well, it's true. Only I don't know who it is."

"What did you do?"

"Went to St. Justin's, of course. There were just three things evident from that telephone conversation— or rather the part of it that Brocksley somehow overheard. One was that Pigeon was sending someone to see Mary Monroe—according to his own words, in order to corroborate something he, Pigeon, had told the person to whom he was talking. Second, that something had happened in, probably, Mary Monroe's house, some time ago which involved cleaning up blood and later trips on Pigeon's part to St. Justin's to inquire. And third, that—well, that someone had died. Yet here was Pigeon talking over the telephone apparently connected with the person involved and saying 'the night you died.'"

Deborah opened her mouth and closed it again, and Anthony said:

"And while Pigeon has his talents, I don't think he can connect so directly with the sulphuric regions. Or any other not of this world. No, the voice coming over the telephone was alive and physical enough. Well, as we know, Brocksley threatened both Tighe and Pigeon with his knowledge; or at least as we suspect—he may have threatened only to tell of the gambling place."

"Tighe——"

Anthony said wearily: "It's an open secret that Tighe was Mary's partner. And Pigeon was croupier. And Juanito helped out occasionally as general handy man, when there was need. Remember, the patrons were few. And very rich."

"Why didn't you tell me that before?"

He looked at her without speaking for a long moment or two. Then he said quietly: "I didn't want to, Deborah. I thought the less you knew of the thing the better."

There was something unspoken; some reason not offered. He went on at once:

"Well, of course, I went straight to St. Justin's. It was the first clue we'd had which seemed to me might involve a real motive. Contrary to everything that's been suggested as a motive, there've been mighty few real ones. Mary Monroe was, actually, very well liked and very honest. But I had only this fact to go on: presumably somebody had been wounded in her house, had gone to St. Justin's, where he'd been ill for some time—for Pigeon called 'every day to inquire.' There would be only the fact of a wounded person, brought in from probably near this address. Not much, and it's a huge hospital. They wouldn't let me see records, of course, and it wouldn't have helped much if they had, for I had no notion whom I was inquiring about. Didn't know, even, when the thing had happened. However, I tried to see this one and that; if he was wounded and there was the blood that Pigeon cleaned up, it might have been a surgical case, so I hunted down heads of surgical departments—all very busy and not wanting to be bothered; nurses, even the anesthetist who'd been there for four years, and lives in Gary and was at home for the week-end. She didn't know anything; or couldn't remember anything; though I took her out to dinner and plied her with food and drink. All this took time. And, of course, I had no right to be making inquiry, though I tried to give the impression that I was an insurance man. Hospital records are open only to insurance men and the police. Well, anyway, she did finally suggest that I try to see the ambulance drivers. So back I came to the city. And I spent the rest of the night, Deborah, hanging around the ambulance entrance of St. Justin's and talking to everybody I could get hold of. Tony, the Pinkerton detective. I began to see it was a needle in the haystack—my inquiry, I mean. For how could they possibly remember one case, with only a possible gunshot or knife wound to go on, and an equally possible neighborhood where he was found? And, perhaps, the ambulance didn't go for him; it was as likely that he'd been simply dumped at the entrance of the hospital. That does happen, you know," said Anthony.

"Well—it's a long story. I hunted out the night porters who'd been on duty; finally went back to the ambulance drivers. And about dawn today, when the day shift came on, one of them remembered something that had happened and been talked of at the time, for it was rather a feather in the cap of the young interne who'd gone out with the ambulance. It was only this, but the address was near enough: One night some time ago, there was a call from the Brahms Street police station. They hurried out, and the policeman on the beat had come upon a man in an alley who'd been shot. At least, the ambulance driver thought it was a man, though he couldn't be sure when I asked him. He just supposed, naturally, that it was a man. Anyway, the thing that made him remember it was this: The man died. Literally died. His heart stopped beating. That was after they'd got him to the hospital and were working on him. Well, they thought he was gone. So the interne decided to experiment with a very strong combination of heart stimulants; I don't know what all he gave him; adrenalin, I suppose. Anyway, the man's heart began to beat again."

"But that happens——"

"Yes, I know. It happens often. But somehow——" Anthony rose, shoved his fists in his pockets, and began to stride restlessly up and down the room again, pausing to stare at the telephone without seeing it. "Somehow, I didn't like it. It was almost as if he had made himself come back for some purpose. A purpose so strong that it conquered death. Oh, I know that isn't sensible; he was simply snatched back from the brink by medical science."

He turned and looked at Deborah and said quickly:

"This is all speculation, of course. Don't forget it has still to be proved. But just suppose for a moment that it *is* the situation. That this man—'case,' the ambulance driver kept calling it, but it seems as if it must have been a man—suppose that this man was actually murdered in Mary Monroe's house and then came back to life again. That is, recovered. He would have probably a doubly strong motive for revenge, for the thing presupposes some quarrel—a deadly quarrel —during which he himself was wounded. And now at Pigeon's behest he has come back to resume it. And he kills Mary Monroe."

"According to Dolly's note, he was to go to see Mary Monroe only in order to verify something Pigeon had told him."

"Yes, I know. But suppose—suppose something happened. I don't know what. But something that made him want to revenge himself upon Mary Monroe."

"*Who?*" cried Deborah.

"I don't know. I inquired for the interne who saved the case, and he's gone from the hospital. Couldn't find a trace of him. I tried again to see the records, but they are locked up over Sunday. Anyway the records wouldn't help much in the way of identification."

"There would be a description of the man, wouldn't there?"

"If we could find that one case. After all, things do happen in a great city; cases brought in, taken care of, sent away and forgotten. I'll try, of course."

"It involves Pigeon more than anyone else. Why not just give it to the police and let them question him?"

Anthony looked at her incredulously.

"The only reason Pigeon has kept you out of it so far, Deb, is because he doesn't want it known that he was actually in the house on the roof that night. Oh, yes, it was Pigeon in the back room. I'm sure of it. But if he says he saw you up there, the police will immediately say to him, 'What were *you* doing in the house on the roof when Mary Monroe was murdered?' No, Pigeon only wants to keep out of the whole thing. And if once the police had any evidence like this, he'd tell everything in self-defense. We are safe so long as he is safe. It's all wrong, of course, but there it is and we can't help it. Our hands are tied."

"But the police ought to know."

Anthony gave her a look of mingled exasperation and weary impatience and pointedly said nothing.

Deborah looked again at the scrawled little note. "What shall we do?"

"I don't know. I'll go back to St. Justin's first thing in the morning. I'll have to think about it, Deborah. I've got to keep you out of it."

Deborah cried at a sudden thought: "Your revolver, Anthony! They've traced the bullet that killed Mary Monroe to your revolver."

"*What do you mean? Who told you?*"

She told him rapidly.

"So that's what happened to it," he said when she'd finished. "The police took it. But they—— Why, that's nonsense, Deborah! They couldn't trace the bullet to my revolver."

"When did you last see it?"

"I don't know. Let me think. The night of the murder, I guess. You see, that revolver that I picked up on the roof and then lost in the darkness—a prize bit of clumsiness, I'll admit, but I can't help it now; just at that moment I had . . . things to do—anyway, it was the same model as mine."

"Anthony!"

"Yes. That much is true. But that didn't mean it was my revolver. And the possibility was so far from my thoughts that I didn't look at the number. Anyway, I wouldn't have remembered the number of my own. I seldom even look at the thing."

"When did you last see it?" persisted Deborah.

"The night of the murder. I got to thinking, among other things, of the revolver and how it had been of the same model as mine—not, however, a very interesting point, for it's a well-liked and popular model—a small .32. And I went to my desk over there and looked, and it was there. I didn't pick it up. It was where I always keep it."

"Could anyone have taken it?"

"Francis, I suppose. Possibly Juanito, but I doubt it. And Francis—well, gosh, Deborah. It wasn't Francis. He never went near Mary Monroe's. Besides, he—I know him too well."

"Juanito says he lost a ring of keys—keys to all the apartments in the building. He says he lost them some time ago. And he says, too, that Brocksley had some keys and that he doesn't know what happened to them."

Anthony was staring at her oddly.

"See here, Deborah—do you realize that someone who is strongly interested in this thing—or at least who ought to be—has never, so far as we know, even inquired about it? Has never peeped? We don't even know who it is, because all our dealings have been with Brocksley. That's the landlord. The owner. Always present in spirit and never on the spot."

"Who is the landlord?"

Anthony shrugged. "I don't know. You heard what the news broadcast said. He's always quoted by Brocksley or Juanito. That's all I know."

"His lack of bodily presence doesn't mean he's the murderer," said Deborah rather sharply. "I just made a point about the keys, Anthony—if two bunches of keys are missing, why, there are two people who could enter your apartment—anybody's apartment—and who could have taken your revolver and replaced it without your knowing it the night of the murder. I feel sure that's why the murderer came back up the fire escape again—to recover the revolver, I mean."

"And sat down and played 'Elégie' on the piano?" inquired Anthony. "No, Francis was here all the time. He would have known if anyone had entered the apartment."

"Well, there you are again; it could have been Francis himself and no one the wiser. Although, too, if he were in the back of the house someone could have entered it and taken and later replaced your revolver."

"Pigeon," said Anthony, "could enter the same room with you and walk right under your nose and you'd never know it. But I don't think now that it was Pigeon who was the murderer. He may be scared now of being held as an accessory before the fact, for he certainly sent someone to see Mary Monroe. And he must be afraid of the murderer serving him as he did Brocksley and for the same reason. I'm inclined to think, after what Dolly told me, that Pigeon so far has saved his skin merely because he is smart enough to watch out—protect himself. He has more evidence than Brocksley had. But Brocksley wasn't smart."

"When did the police take your revolver?"

"I don't know. They've been around a lot. I missed it yesterday when I had seen Dolly and had decided to slip off by myself to see what I could find."

"I wonder what the detective who followed you made of it all?"

Anthony grinned.

"I don't know. But I do wish I had known it was a detective. Made me sort of jittery. I'd think he was there and then think he wasn't. Had more than once a sneaking notion that it was the murderer himself. Particularly after I'd talked to the ambulance driver. It was a gray, ghostly morning, you know. And I kept thinking of what he'd told me. Still keep thinking of it," said Anthony, suddenly grave again. "Can't get it out of my head. Somebody, once murdered himself, coming back for revenge. I don't like it. See here, Deborah, can't you go away——"

"You know I can't."

He looked at her slowly. The brandy and the talk had in some degree restored him, for he looked less white and tired. He said abruptly: "Odd how—how different things seem after you've talked to somebody who's clear and firm like you, Deborah."

Clear and firm. When she felt so desperately the need to lean, herself, upon him! But there was suddenly a deep, warm pleasure in that mutual dependence, brief and scarcely recognizable though it was. And she met Anthony's look, and the quiet moment prolonged itself. Prolonged itself until the door from the main hall opened and Francis entered, whistling and announcing his presence tactfully.

"I'll go," said Deborah. "You need to rest."

"And shave," said Anthony, touching his chin. "I must look like hell. Any excitement on the street, Francis?"

"Police car outside. Didn't see anything."

Deborah took her coat. Anthony said: "Don't worry. Chloe's information was probably all wrong."

At the doorway Francis glanced at Anthony, hesitated, and said: "I'll take her upstairs, Anthony."

The elevator was at some other floor, and they walked up the stairs quietly; there was a queer, uneasy feeling along her knees when Francis quite deliberately stepped ahead of her at the abrupt turn. However, they saw no one, although there was a burst of piano playing behind the door to the Riddle apartment.

"Gibbs," said Francis. It stopped with a clash of keys as abruptly as it had begun. "He's nervous. High-strung."

He left her at the door of her own apartment.

The apartment was quiet, and Blitz did not as usual bounce to the door to meet her.

Juliet had taken him with her, probably; out to post her letters or for a walk. Deborah turned into the drawing room.

Lieutenant Waggon sat there, quietly reading the Sunday papers.

CHAPTER XX

HE LOOKED up, smiled, and rose.

"How do you do?" he said pleasantly. "I was waiting for you."

Deborah stood as if frozen, looking at him. He said:

"I was waiting to know why you were in Mary Monroe's house. There's no use denying it, you know. I know that you were there.—Perhaps you'd better sit down."

She couldn't have moved if her life depended upon it. She couldn't have taken her eyes from those calm blue eyes opposite—so icily blue, so dreadfully calm and certain.

"Oh, very well. As you like." He said: "Why did you wipe off the teacup you touched? Why did you wipe the spoon and the saucer? Why did you put your hand on the lamp?" He hesitated. He was fumbling into his pocket, bringing out something wrapped in tissue paper and unrolling it. Something small. "Why did you put this cigarette to your mouth and then throw it away?" Cigarette. "What cigarette?" thought Deborah.

"It's an Egyptian brand—want to see it? Perhaps then you'll tell me why you touched it to your mouth, then without lighting it flung it down toward the hearth. What happened just then, to keep you from smoking it?"

Egyptian. The cigarette Mary Monroe had given her. The cigarette she had put to her mouth before she discovered that its flavor was disagreeable to her and had then tossed toward the fireplace and forgotten. Had turned toward the table and tried to open a drawer,

which, Mary Monroe had said, would hold other cigarettes.

"Oh——" said Deborah in a queer high-pitched
voice.

He pounced upon it.

"It's your lipstick," he said. "A shade that goes with
a blonde. And now we've proved it is the kind you use
and that no other woman in the house uses that particular kind. Besides—there were your fingerprints on
the lamp. It was easy enough to get a sample of them
for comparison without your knowledge. We've got
everybody in the house fingerprinted by now, although
I doubt if they know it. So you were there. And why did
you wipe off the teacup? Why?"

What had Anthony told her to say? What had he told
her to do? Nothing that was of any use now.

"*Why?*"

He was towering above her. Long and lean and
omniscient. He knew.

"*Why?*"

"Because——"

"*Because?*"

"She was shot," said Deborah at the end of her
strength and took a great gulp of air.

"Who shot her?"

"I—I don't know," said Deborah. "I don't know."

How much did he know? How much had she confessed? He turned away from her, walked to the window
and back again, and said:

"Who told you to wipe off the teacup?"

(Anthony. No, no, not Anthony. She must not think
of him. She must keep all recognition of that name, even,
from her thoughts, for Lieutenant Waggon could tell
what she was thinking. And there was Anthony's too

apt and simple explanation for his presence; Anthony's failure to report the murder; *Anthony's revolver*.)

She shrank backward, shaking her head, staring at the advancing face, pinioned by the certainty in it.

"Tell me. Quick. Who told you to wipe off the tea-cup? Who warned you of fingerprints? Who was with you in the house on the roof?"

"I can't—I can't—I can't——" It must be her own voice, but it didn't sound like that of anyone she knew.

He looked at her thoughtfully. His expression changed, became mild again and less terrifying.

"I won't hurt you," he said. "See here, I've got a daughter just about your age. I wouldn't want to drag you into a murder case if you really are innocent of it. Police are human, you know. Why not just tell me the whole thing and let me help you?"

"No. No." She did not realize that she was admitting knowledge, until she had spoken. But it didn't matter, for he already knew.

He looked at her again thoughtfully. Then he said: "You'd better sit down. Now then, just answer my questions. Don't lie. You don't look like the lying kind. But you evaded me pretty skillfully last time I talked to you. Sit down."

She obeyed finally, her eyes fastened upon him.

"Now then, you saw her shot?"

"Yes."

"Who did it?"

"I don't know."

"Don't know or won't tell?"

"I don't know," wailed Deborah.

"Suppose," he said gently, "you tell me the whole thing." Probably some flicker of alarm leaped into her eyes, for he said quickly: "Or rather just tell me what happened up to the murder."

Up to the murder. Well, there was nothing that would entangle anyone but Deborah.

So, faltering and swift by turns, frightened and relieved, her eyes never shifting, she told it. Told it briefly, as it happened. She had met Mary Monroe; the singer had invited her to tea; she had gone; they had talked; Mary Monroe had offered to sing. And singing, she was shot from the doorway.

"What did you do then?"

"Tried to telephone the police. The wire was cut."

"That was last Wednesday night?"

"Yes. About dusk—no, later. About six o'clock."

"And the murder wasn't reported till next morning. Couldn't you have let us know during that period of time, even if that wire was cut? I'm afraid," said Lieutenant Waggon gently, "that you'll have to tell me more. Just when, for instance—just when Anthony Wyatt came into the thing."

Deborah's lips moved, and no sound came out of them.

Lieutenant Waggon said very mildly, very gently:

"Miss Cavert, we already know that Anthony Wyatt is involved. And how deeply. I don't know which of you killed Mary Monroe. But—I'm going to know. One way or another. If you are in love with this man Wyatt, there's no use in your trying to protect him. For I'll get at the truth sooner or later. So why not just tell me the whole thing?"

"No——" whispered Deborah.

He looked at her again, shrugged in a mildly deprecating manner, and went to the telephone.

"Hello," he said. "O'Brien, please. . . . Oh, Sergeant, it's Lieutenant Waggon speaking. Arrest Anthony Wyatt. . . . Yes, go right ahead, it's all right. . . . Sure, tell the newspapers. This arrest will hold all right. . . . The revolver. Other evidence to come . . ." He put his hand over the mouthpiece and spoke to Deborah: "Anything to say now?"

"No—no——"

They couldn't prove he was there without her evidence. They couldn't prove it.

Lieutenant Waggon spoke into the telephone again: "May be another arrest shortly. . . . Yeah, the woman. . . . Oh, and O'Brien—I'm up in the Cavert apartment. You might bring Wyatt up here before you take him to the station. . . . The charge? Oh, yes, murder."

He put down the receiver.

He strolled into the drawing room, glanced quietly at Deborah, and went to a window. The silence deepened. Didn't he intend to speak? Did he intend simply to wait?

She must not speak, herself. She must not let that assured silence drive her to speech. So long as she said nothing Anthony was safe . . . so long as she said nothing . . . She repeated that phrase inwardly over and over again and locked her teeth together, as if that would help, and watched Lieutenant Waggon.

The duel of silence continued until Lieutenant Waggon himself broke it. He said, as if idly, contemplating the street below and speaking in a seemingly absent-minded and soliloquizing manner: "There's always state's evidence. I can't promise anything. But still witnesses for the state usually get off pretty lightly. Accessories, sometimes. Especially if they can show they've been coerced. Threatened."

"I wasn't threatened," said Deborah in a choked voice.

He did not turn and gave no evidence at all of sharpened attention.

"Yes, sir," he went on contemplatively. "If my daughter was sitting there being questioned, I'd say, 'You just tell the truth. And don't worry about anybody else. They can usually take care of themselves all right.' Of course," he said thoughtfully, "I'm mighty careful about the kind of men she knows. I've seen a lot of women made fools of, one way and another. Nice women, too. Just can't help believing any sort of story. The nicer the women are, seems to me, the more they'll believe. One of you two," said Lieutenant Waggon, with no change in his voice, "killed Mary Monroe. Was it you?"

"No."

"Then it was Anthony Wyatt."

"*No.*"

He turned to face her again then.

"If you don't know who killed her, how do you know it wasn't Wyatt?" he said.

O'Brien must have been very near. Or that terrible struggle of silence had lasted actually as long as it had seemed to Deborah. For he came just then. He and another policeman and Anthony. Anthony still unshaven, still white and tired; Anthony staying very close beside O'Brien—as if something held them together. Deborah couldn't have spoken then, and Anthony saw her look and said with an attempt at a smile: "Don't mind, Deborah. I don't."

Lieutenant Waggon said: "So you killed Mary Monroe?"

Anthony flung his head upward.

"Don't deny it," said Lieutenant Waggon. "There's a witness." He did not indicate Deborah by gesture or word. There was no need.

Anthony's eyes did not waver from Lieutenant Waggon, but Deborah cried sharply:

"*No—no—I said nothing. Don't believe him, Tony— don't——*"

"*Take her out!*"

The policeman was beside Deborah. She cried: "I won't go! I won't go!"

"*Carry her.* Get her out of here."

Deborah pulled away from the policeman, and Anthony said: "Wait, Lieutenant. I'll give evidence. I'll tell you everything I know about it."

"Well——"

"I was there on the roof. I came on business to see Mary Monroe. And if the revolver that killed her was mine, I didn't know it. I didn't kill her."

"Was she dead when you got there?" said Lieutenant Waggon very quietly.

For a long moment Anthony did not reply.

Anthony Wyatt—or Deborah Cavert. If he admitted that Mary Monroe was dead when he arrived—then Deborah Cavert had murdered her. If not——

Anthony said: "Look here, Lieutenant, you want a case, don't you?"

"I've got a case," said Lieutenant Waggon.

"No," said Anthony. "You haven't. You have no evidence that you can present to a jury. Only the revolver, and anybody could have used it."

"I've got evidence that you and Deborah Cavert were there at the time of the murder."

"I said evidence you can present to a jury. Evidence that can go into court records. You see, Lieutenant, your witness of my presence is my wife. Deborah Wyatt."

Lieutenant Waggon's face did not alter in any line except that he was very still. O'Brien turned suddenly as if to speak and stopped at the look on the Lieutenant's face.

"How long have you been married? A day or two? Don't bother to lie. I can find out if you're telling the truth."

"Oh, he's telling the truth," said O'Brien suddenly. "The girl's got a wedding ring. I saw it when I was searching——"

Lieutenant Waggon gave him one clear calm look, and he wilted and stopped confusedly.

"Why didn't you tell me?"

"I didn't think it meant anything—might've been her mother's. Might've been—oh, just a joke or something. Might've been——"

"You," said Lieutenant Waggon in a markedly fond manner, "might've been dropped on the head as a child, but it wasn't hard enough."

He turned to Anthony.

"You're under arrest, charged with the willful murder of Mary Monroe. You married that girl to save your neck. You married her to keep evidence out of court. You——"

"I married her," said Anthony, "because I love her."

"Oh," said Lieutenant Waggon, "I see. And so you don't announce the marriage, and no one knows of it. And you live downstairs and she lives up here."

Anthony looked very white and did not touch Deborah with his eyes. He said: "Go away, Deborah. I'll tell the police the whole story."

"You're damn right you'll tell it all," said Lieutenant

Waggon. "But you'll tell it all at the police station. Conditions there are a little more—suitable."

Anthony said: "I'll tell you everything I know. But I want to say that I do have evidence involving Pigeon. He knows——"

"Arrested murderers always have evidence like that. We'll hear your evidence later," said Lieutenant Waggon, making a mistake. "Was that what you were doing yesterday? Trying to make us believe you were after evidence? If you didn't kill Mary Monroe and this girl didn't kill her, who did?"

"I don't know," said Anthony desperately. "But there's a motive."

"Take him along, O'Brien. I'll follow."

O'Brien moved, and Anthony said sharply: "Wait. Look here, Lieutenant Waggon—they say you don't make mistakes. I'll admit we kept evidence from you, and that we did it to save ourselves. But I'll tell you now that if you don't put Pigeon where you'll be able to get your hands on him when you want him, you'll make a mistake you'll never get over."

"*O'Brien!*"

"Come along, here," said O'Brien hurriedly.

At the door at last Anthony looked at Deborah, and she went to him swiftly, and he put his free hand on her shoulder and looked down into her eyes.

"I'll be all right," he said. "Don't look like that, Deborah. I didn't kill her, so how can they prove that I did?"

(But they *could* prove—they could prove anything they wanted to prove, they could prove——) She said only "Anthony" in a sort of sob.

"I say, it'll be all right," said Anthony. "Now remember what I said, Deborah, and don't take any chances. And don't worry——"

"O'Brien," said Lieutenant Waggon again.

And quite suddenly a door had closed and Anthony and O'Brien were gone.

And Lieutenant Waggon looked thoughtfully at Deborah and said to the remaining policeman in a casual way: "Better round up Pigeon. Take him over to the station."

"Yes, sir."

The door opened and closed again. Deborah looked across at Lieutenant Waggon. He looked at her, sat down slowly, crossed his knees, and continued to look at her without any expression at all. Finally he said:

"You may as well tell me the whole thing. It can't hurt you now. And it might help."

Deborah flushed.

"We didn't dare tell——"

"Well, you can now. Go ahead. Start where you were trying to telephone the police. And see here—tell everything. Don't miss anything. Even if it seems trivial, unimportant. Tell it anyway."

So Deborah automatically, thinking of Anthony's white face, conscious of the silence of the place, so heavy that her own voice falling into it did not seem to disturb it, conscious of many things—told her story. She faltered a little when she came to Anthony.

"So then he said he'd help me. And we wiped the fingerprints off the teacup and the spoon and the music——"

"Music?"

"The song she was singing. I was accompanying her. It was 'Elégie'——"

"What's that? Sing it."

Sing it. "I can't—I——"

"Just to give me a notion as to what the tune is?"

She went to the piano; her fingers were cold and fumbling on the keys. But into the silence she did project a weirdly faulty melody that tinkled eerily and was ragged and jumbled when she reached the phrase, "the laughing days have gone." Just there that tall red figure had toppled.

Lieutenant Waggon said dreamily: "Who in the apartment house plays the piano besides you?"

"Why, I don't know exactly. I suppose Brocksley did. Gibbs Riddle. Aunt Juliet a little. Perhaps Dolly Brocksley."

"Dolly Brocksley——" A knock at the door interrupted him. It was the policeman, and he said breathlessly: *"Pigeon's gone!"*

"What's that!"

The policeman looked somehow wild and disheveled, though he was actually very neat.

"Pigeon's got away. Nobody knows where he's gone. Tighe don't know. Nobody knows——"

He stopped abruptly under the look in Lieutenant Waggon's face and took a quick step backward. There was an instant of icy stillness, then Lieutenant Waggon said: "Get out."

The policeman vanished. Lieutenant Waggon stopped at the door and looked at Deborah. "Stay here."

There was the rapidly diminishing sound of footsteps beyond the door. And Deborah stared at those wide, dark old panels and gradually, slowly, fought her way to the understanding of what had happened, of its implications, of its needs.

Needs. There was now something she must do. Something she could no longer avoid doing. But she would not think beyond the primary fact of its accomplishment.

Juliet would soon be returning. Deborah went straight to the locked bag in Juliet's room, the bag which had resisted the efforts of the policemen but which, still, had not fallen under any real suspicion. It resisted her own efforts to unlock it.

The mere locking of a bag. Trivial. The work of an instant. Yet it was not accident that Juliet had locked that bag, for she would not have dared to leave it open. Not at least until she had burned the thing it contained, and she did not dare do that, either. Not when the betraying odor would creep through the halls and passages and lofty old rooms.

So Deborah went to the house on the roof.

It was by no means an easy thing to do.

In the first place there were almost certainly policemen guarding it. Guarding it in the hope that someone in the apartment house would do the very thing she proposed to do. A murderer returns to the scene of his kill. Was it, like most axioms, based on a truth? Well, she was not the murderer, but she must return to the house on the roof. And she must, somehow, avoid the police.

It was true that, with the arrest of Anthony, the police guarding the house might have been withdrawn. It was possible, also, that they had joined in the pursuit of Pigeon. It was almost certain that with the arrest the closeness of their guard would be relaxed. But she could not be sure, and she went, after a thoughtful moment, to her telephone. It was chance, too, whether or not the telephone wires had been tapped and whether the presumable listener had not yet been removed, following Anthony's arrest as the murderer. But it was a chance worth taking.

She called the number of the Riddle apartment, and Chloe's throaty voice replied.

"Chloe—I don't know what to do——"

"What about?"

"Pigeon. You see, I——" Deborah hesitated, gulped, and lied in her teeth. "I think he just went into the drugstore on the corner."

"Well, what about that?"

"The police are searching for him. Do you think I ought to let them know?"

Chloe replied something that was half impatient and half indulgent and wholly disrespectful to the police and to Deborah's sense of duty and hung up. But the little ruse succeeded. Not two minutes later Deborah watched from the kitchen window as two uniformed figures emerged from the fire escape, crossed the court and disappeared, running, toward the street. Probably, then, the coast was clear. It did not occur to Deborah that if that exit was visible from her own window it was also visible from four other windows.

Two policemen. One to guard the house, one still on duty at the telephone, both of them smarting under Lieutenant Waggon's rebuke and eager to retrieve themselves by capturing Pigeon.

Yes, the coast was clear.

Hurriedly she snatched her coat; the day was raw and cold. She pulled the soft fur coat around her and looked at it and thought of many things and wondered how she could have been so blind. So terribly blind. So culpably childish. So blandly accepting without question what Juliet gave her.

The hall was quiet and empty; the Riddle door was closed, and no sound came from beyond it. The elevator shaft was empty, and the black lane of the stairway stretched emptily upward.

The house was utterly silent. There was no sound of voices, no footsteps, no small mild drone of the elevator. It was as if there were no one but Deborah in all those far-flung, rambling layers of rooms and winding, long passages. Juliet was out; Anthony by now was at the police station, waiting for Lieutenant Waggon. And Lieutenant Waggon and the police had gone to search for Pigeon. Pigeon who was silent and wily and, inconceivably, frightened; Pigeon who knew something of the secret of the house on the roof; Pigeon who knew how to elude police guards and to vanish with his dangerous knowledge.

Lights were on in the hall and emphasized its emptiness and its silence. In that silence, if there were furtive footsteps one could hear them. Deborah took a long breath and closed the door behind her and went to the stairway. She was halfway up and approaching the turn when she realized she was walking on tiptoe, holding her breath, wishing her taffeta petticoat wouldn't rustle faintly but betrayingly at every motion. The turn of the stairs was empty, too. And there was no one in the hall above. And still silence.

She reached the small door behind the elevator and stairway. It opened with a screech of a hinge that sounded loud and sharp but aroused no responsive sound anywhere. The passage was dimly lit, but nothing moved along it. Nothing, that is, except Deborah, and there was only the little hiss and rustle of her skirt echoing against the walls on either side to give evidence of her passage.

All around her and below her the old house waited
with its knowledge, with its secrets and its hushed
stillness.

Anthony had warned her; had told her not to do
exactly what she was doing. Anthony had talked of
motives; of a man who had been murdered. But there
was something she must do, something that Anthony
did not know, something that his arrest made imperative.

Again she did not think beyond the accomplishment
of her errand. And she reached and opened the door
leading upon the fire escape. She opened it cautiously
and noiselessly.

Dusk had fallen. The court below was gray and
dreary. The fire escape stretched upward into a darken-
ing, lowering sky, and the parapet of the roof made a
black, wide strip.

There was no sight or sound of human presence in all
that dreary blankness. She let the door close behind her
and remembered the spring lock. Well, she would go
down the fire escape when she returned.

The railing was cold and damp, and Deborah had
never liked height. She forced herself to look only at
the damp and rather slippery steps and not past them,
through spaces. And she reached the roof and emerged
at the opening of the parapet wall.

Flat, black, dirty. Chimneys, incinerators, venti-
lators. The house itself, dark and dingy and passive.
Nothing moved. There was no sign of life. No sound anywhere. No sound except, away below, the murmur of a
passing automobile which only emphasized her own
remoteness. Quite suddenly she realized that if she had
removed the threat of the police she had also removed
their protection.

She took a step upon the board sidewalk, and it clattered so suddenly and loudly that she stepped from it to the roof and walked there.

Darkened windows; no light in the house. No policemen anywhere. And the door yielded under her hand. Yielded and opened and disclosed again Mary Monroe's crowded little drawing room, dark, now, with shapes looming here and there and the piano in the corner catching a ghostly highlight and the air musty and stale and cold.

She stood there, wishing her heart would not race so furiously and permitting her eyes to grow adjusted to the twilight. The fireplace—the telephone—cut off now, probably. Or perhaps not. What did they do when there was murder in a place? How long before they cut off the telephone, and who paid the bill? . . . There was the chair in which she had sat and talked to Mary Monroe. There was the table with the stubborn little drawer. Someone had picked up all those small articles which had littered the floor. She could suddenly see Lieutenant Waggon's long, patient face bent over them, his blue eyes traveling thoughtfully from one object to another, assorting, analyzing, drawing conclusions from each.

There was the green glass lamp where they'd found her fingerprints. There was, again, the piano; and the green velvet curtains against which Mary Monroe had unconsciously posed were pulled back now so that they made two long strips of blackness through which a chill gray streak of remaining daylight fell upon the piano.

She could distinguish objects fairly well now, and she did not wish to turn on the light. She crossed the room quickly and entered the bedroom. There was not much danger of the police returning, for the errand she had herself set them was one they would not soon give up.

She searched the room quickly and thoroughly there in the dusk which robbed things of color but still gave sufficient light. For the Elsa wig was not there. And she had known that it would not be there.

There would have been no reason for the police to take it. And if it had remained in that room after the murder, there would have been some mention of so romantic an object in all those resultant columns of description.

It was not there. Deborah sat down slowly on the foot of the chaise longue.

Juliet. She had escaped, then, wearing the Elsa wig with its braids wrapped coronet fashion around her head. Carrying her hat, trusting to luck and darkness to aid her disguise. Staining the beige gloves, which had left no fingerprints, with bands of red rust. A disguise there at her hand. And one that so far had deceived the only person who saw her flight, and that was Pigeon.

How long had she been gambling—gambling to pay the household bills, gambling to pay Deborah's dressmaking bills and school bills? Gambling, mingling as one of that small inscrutable circle; tight-lipped, primly gowned, watching the turn of the wheel and the fall of a card without a change of expression on her well-bred face. Losing, winning, losing again and saying nothing. When had the losing begun to overbalance the winning? When had she got so terribly in debt as she must now be?

Deborah's dream of subdued voices and a door closing had not, then, been a dream; it had been Juliet giving up a small sealed package. Her jewels had not been stolen, of course; it had been entirely voluntary on Juliet's part. That was why she couldn't let the insurance company know; could not put in a claim. Had the jewels covered that debt, or were they merely a payment to the remaining partner, Tighe, now that Mary Monroe had been killed? What had happened that rendered the last desperate expedient that was Mary Monroe's murder ineffectual?

There were questions still to be answered, perplexities still to be unraveled. But the Elsa wig answered one question all too fully.

There was Anthony—arrested and charged with the murder of Mary Monroe.

There was Juliet—gambling to pay Deborah's bills, to keep that small family together, to meet a hundred needs that were actually extravagances. To keep John Cavert alive and pay for specialists and care.

She thought confusedly of Anthony's evidence and Pigeon's flight. Was it possible that Juliet was the "case" brought so mysteriously to St. Justin's? No. Deborah would have known something of it; and besides, nothing but desperation would have set Juliet on so dark and hideous a path. It would not have been revenge. Well, there were many things to be reconciled; some perhaps which would never be suitably explained and docketed.

Anthony, of course, had known all the time. Anthony had thought that she, Deborah, had acted for Juliet. And he had known that eventually the police would discover and attribute that motive, reasonably and credibly, to Deborah. It would be a powerful motive; irresistible. That was why he had felt she would have no chance of escape from the thing into which she walked so blindly.

Anthony. Juliet . . . Juliet. Anthony.

On one hand a woman she loved; a woman who had stood in a mother's place and had stood there loyally and faithfully. Even that last, fatal, terribly mistaken act had been actually for Deborah. To protect her.

And on the other hand was Anthony. Anthony whose name she shared. Anthony who had known about Juliet; who had given her his name in order to protect her from, madly, the results of Juliet's own affection.

Anthony, charged with murder.

Juliet, whose gray and haggard face concealed so ravaging a secret.

And now Deborah Cavert, who had seen that murder, sat there on the cushion-heaped chaise longue in the bedroom where Mary Monroe had sat and combed the Elsa wig for the last time, and tried to decide what she must do. What she could do.

How many times had the mirror over the shadowy dressing table reflected black untidy hair and a painted face and quick black eyes? There was a faint pervading odor of tuberose from somewhere, and the room was so dark now that the bed was only an engulfing shadow and the chair before the window a black lump.

Deborah realized with a start that she was chilled and cramped and much time had passed and that she could not further endure that ghostly scent of tuberose. She lifted her head rather dazedly and stood.

And it was just then that, eerily and clearly through the silence and gloom, there came the sound of a piano key being touched very lightly in the next room—one note. Several notes.

It went on, faintly, one note at a time which hovered oddly in the air like a clear, strange echo.

And gradually a melody was strung together, and it formed the opening bars of the "Elégie." ... "Oh, sweet spring of other times; green seasons; you have gone forever——"

Quite suddenly it left off. Just stopped existing there in the deep twilight. There was no further sound at all from the room beyond.

The door between the rooms was half open as Deborah had left it, and a strip of shadow identified that opening. Somehow Deborah reached it.

The drawing room was shadowy and still, and chairs and tables made black blotches in the deepening twilight. The piano was barely discernible as a pool of darker, heavier shadow. Behind it a path of gray twilight still divided those heavy black strips that were curtains. There was no one to be seen. There was no sound.

But one of the black curtains had altered its shape against the streak of twilight. Had become singularly irregular.

CHAPTER XXI

AFTERWARD, of course, she knew what was happening below. That Lieutenant Waggon had at last heard Anthony and that there were men then seeking certain records—records which yesterday would have proved nothing but which, that night, were to round out with physical identification an incredibly strange and tragic story. A story which did not hold, however, for Lieutenant Waggon the latent horror which it held for Anthony, perhaps because LieutenantWaggon had seen more of life and more of death and more, too, of evil and of the mysterious, murky depths from which murder strikes.

Then she knew only that the black strip which was a curtain no longer hung straight. And because whatever it was that stood there must have seen her own silhouette against the bedroom twilight, must have heard the faint small whisper of her movement, must know she was there, she said in a chill frozen voice: "*Who is it?*"

There was a little silence. Then someone laughed. Laughed and said:

"Oh, it's you, Deborah."

The voice, however, was high and unnatural, and Deborah did not quite recognize it.

But the black blotch altered its shape again and made for an instant the bare suggestion of a familiar outline against the gray twilight, and something whirled in

Deborah's mind like a pinwheel scattering sparks of light.

She said into the darkness: "Why were you playing 'Elégie'?"

There was a silence again. Then another laugh.

"I don't know. The music is there on the piano. Happened to see it."

"Won't you turn on the light?" she said. "It's so dark. I can't see anything."

The shadow hesitated and moved toward the electric-light switch. Moved certainly and with knowledge as that ghost of a tune had been played certainly and with knowledge.

She could hear soft footsteps crossing the room along the opposite wall. And all at once something unheralded, something inexplicable happened to Deborah; something that brought with it a clear, hard flash of understanding.

She said into the darkness:

"You couldn't possibly see the notes of music. It is too dark. Why were you playing that song?"

She could sense rather than see the little jerk, the stifled motion of surprise, the quick, smooth recovery.

"Of course—I suppose I was only thinking of it— Mary Monroe, you know, and how she was singing it when she died."

The footsteps were nearer the electric switch. Deborah said:

"How did you know she was singing it when she died?"

Again there was that feeling of stifled discomposure and smooth recovery.

"I read it in the papers," he said and laughed and turned on the lights. And in that blinding brightness

Deborah stared at Francis Maly and cried: "It was not in the papers!"

He was tall and graceful and pleasant. Only his eyes looked too bright. He looked at her and blinked and smiled and said softly:

"So it was you at the piano. And now you think you have trapped me into admitting something only you and the murderer could know. Don't you realize that it doesn't matter? You are alone up here. You should not have come."

He looked at her consideringly, gently, still smiling, and talked pleasantly.

"I see that you are alone. No one knows we are here. You may scream if you like, and no one will hear you. It was different with Brocksley. That was really a little dangerous for me, not simple as this murder will be. Brocksley,"—he laughed very softly—"I've been longing to tell about that. And my confidences will be quite safe with you."

He was a little nearer her.

"Tony, you see, was on the telephone. He didn't see me leave, and I just carried the little remote-control radio box into the hall with me. I called Brocksley, told him to look at—something on the floor of the elevator. He looked. It took only a second. I sent the elevator to the second floor, and I went to the remote-control box and turned the dial quickly to another station. So Tony would think I was still in the next room—fooling with the radio. An orchestra, it was. Loud. Then I ran quickly up the stairs, dragged him into the hall, ran downstairs again. And came quietly back into the apartment and tuned the radio again. Then I washed my pocketknife and my hands. Juanito, luckily, came along through the lower hall while I was upstairs. Everything was simple. The trouble with most murders is elaboration." He shook his head in a softly deprecating way. "Where there is a plot to baffle detection, there are clues. I made no plans. Therefore I left no clues. Therefore I am successful. As I shall continue to be.—My third murder! Odd what a sense of triumph a thing so really trivial and momentary can give."

He continued, approaching her softly and gradually, like a beautiful cat stalking: "There is no one else here. Anthony is in the hands of the police. No one knows you are here. Which shall it be? My knife? The one that slit Alfred Brocksley's throat? Or a drop from the roof to the street? That might not kill you—perhaps a twist of your little neck first and then the drop. No one will know. An accident. Suicide—and Anthony charged with murder. No, no, my dear, don't look at the telephone. You surely don't think I would permit you to use it." He paused, regarding her thoughtfully. "The knife would be better—yet with Anthony arrested for the crime—no, no, better leave it." He laughed at some sudden thought as if it amused him heartily. "Three murders that will be in this room. Mary Monroe. You. And I. But I was murdered first. Right there where you are standing. I was murdered. And I died." He laughed again. "I died! But I came alive again. I am really a ghost, you know, dear Deborah. A ghost. Come back for revenge." He paused again and looked at her scrutinizingly and said: "Will you come back for revenge, Deborah? After I've killed you in this room? After Anthony has died for what I did? Death isn't much, you know, Deborah. It's just going down between two walls with a light shining from the top; and when you fall so

far between those dark walls that the light is gone—then
that's death. You may come alive again, too; but you
still will have to die first."

His hands were touching her now.

He said: "You are very pretty, my dear. Except that
you are so white. As if you already had no blood in
you."

His face had not changed save for a faint grayness
around his mouth. He was exactly as she had always
known him—pleasant, suave, spectacularly handsome.

His hands were touching her face—touching her
throat almost in a caress. And then Deborah forgot
herself and forgot everything and fought him. She
screamed and fought and screamed and bit the hand
that clamped itself over her mouth. She was conscious
of pain, of lights, of blackness, of needing air—of sounds.

And then of nothing.

There was somewhere out of confusion a faint drifting
scent of tuberose. A very ghost of a scent, coming from
somewhere near Deborah. It brought with it another
ghost—a tall, dark-eyed woman clad in maroon velvet
and singing. Deborah stirred and twisted to escape the
twin phantoms and opened her eyes.

She was lying upon a heap of pillows with her fur
coat tossed over her. And somewhere were voices.

She lay there and let the voices change and mingle.
Men's voices for the most part. Men's voices, and she
was in Mary Monroe's bedroom, and she started upward
and remembered and screamed: "*Francis!*"

Only it wasn't a scream, for it emerged as a small
shaky whisper.

But someone heard it and was all at once at her side,
holding her in his arms very tightly.

"Francis—Francis——" sobbed Deborah, beside herself and clutching at Anthony's arms.

"Hush. Don't talk, Deborah. He's gone. We got here—just in time. Don't cry, darling."

"She'll be all right now," said a voice from somewhere near Deborah's head.

"Thank you, Doctor." That was Juliet, yet it was unlike Juliet, too, for it was unguarded and had depths.

The doctor said: "You'd better put her to bed. I'll drop around in the morning."

Deborah was vaguely conscious that the doctor disappeared and that Juliet said something to Anthony and followed the doctor. And as the door opened, voices in the room beyond became suddenly audible.

". . . you'll never get anything out of Tighe." That was a strange voice. "I don't need to." That was Lieutenant Waggon, clear and assured. The door closed again, and Deborah buried her face against Anthony and sobbed luxuriously.

"Oh, Anthony, Anthony, it was Francis! Francis all the time."

"Yes, I know, Deborah. We knew it tonight. The police returned just in time to save you and capture Francis. I was released and hurried here with Lieutenant Waggon. In the meantime I had told him everything I knew and he had sent men to the hospital and they found the records I had tried to find and failed. And the man who was wounded and found on the street below (where Tighe, we think, had left him) and who was brought to St. Justin's was Francis. Do you want to hear now or——"

"Now," said Deborah.

He looked at her rather uneasily. "All right," he said. "I guess it's better that way. You see, Francis had gambled up here, lost a lot of money, and quarreled with Tighe and Mary. That was three years ago. He claimed the game was crooked and threatened to make a lot of trouble for them, and they were really pretty prosperous. So one night he came up here and Mary went to the piano and played and sang to cover the sound of the quarrel and Tighe shot him. And somehow Francis wasn't looking and really didn't know whether it was Mary or Tighe who shot him. Anyway they took him out and dumped him in the street. We know that part of it."

(Francis had died. Had died and boasted of it to her—and had come back.)

Deborah said: "It was Francis——"

"Pigeon," said Anthony, "was, of course, the real crux and pivot of the thing. At least, that's the way Lieutenant Waggon's got it figured. I told him everything at the station, Deborah. Well—after all, Francis recovered. His hair had turned white during his illness, and he—it had been a tremendous nervous shock. The doctor had a lot to say about that after he'd looked at you. However, Francis picked up life in a normal fashion except that he was obsessed by one idea and one only and that was revenge. He met me at the club—it must have been shortly after he'd got well. I—I liked him," said Anthony, looking very white and grim. "He was a good friend—well, anyway, he suggested our sharing an apartment here. So we did. He behaved always in a perfectly normal fashion; he *was* normal, except that he wanted to find out who had shot him and to do murder himself. An uncivilized and somewhat primitive desire, perhaps, but natural enough. He kept watching and waiting, and time went on. If Tighe saw him and recognized him, no one knows or will ever know. Anyway, Francis' presence wouldn't matter to Tighe so long as he kept quiet; no longer threatened to make trouble for them. But Mary Monroe didn't know of it. Not until the very last. Francis must have told her he was coming to talk to her, and she was afraid. Tighe had told her that he sent Pigeon to St. Justin's to inquire and keep them constantly informed; she knew that it wasn't, after all, murder, for Francis had recovered. (Francis Maly, by the way, wasn't his real name; it was Francis Gage.)"

Anthony paused thoughtfully.

"Well," he said, "that's the way things stood when Pigeon enters the story again. The house on the roof still flourishing, Francis living here, patiently, quietly waiting until the moment for his long brooded-over retaliation came. Perhaps he wavered; perhaps as time went on he would have become less and less determined. But Pigeon suddenly had need of him. You see, Pigeon decided that Tighe ought not be permitted to encumber the earth any longer. We don't know what wrongs he wished to avenge himself for; probably he would have killed Tighe himself had it not been too dangerous for anyone so closely associated with Tighe as Pigeon himself. He knew, of course, about Francis' living here and realized that, if he pulled the right strings, Francis would be a perfect tool. So he told Francis (Francis confessed all this before they—took him away. But it was, after hearing Dolly's evidence, quite obvious)—Pigeon told Francis that it was Tighe who'd shot him. And that Mary Monroe would corroborate his—Pigeon's—story. So he sent Francis up to see Mary Monroe."

"And when he came——"

"When he finally came you were there. And she was singing the 'Elégie.' And it was the song that she had been singing the night Tighe stood in the doorway and shot Francis. The doctor talked about that a lot. Repetition of the same scene. The same combination. After brooding all this time, Francis finally returns to the house on the roof, opens the door, and—hears the same song, sees the same scene, and bang! It's like an explosion. An assault on all his finely strung sensory nerves at once. When he experienced that particular combination before, there was a shot. Murder. It's like a trigger to the revolver for Francis. Greed, in the first place. Suffering and nervous shock. Long brooding, accumulated hatred, revenge. It all boils up at once and"—Anthony's voice was a little harsh and uneven— "and the thing to do is to shoot. Shoot Mary Monroe who stood at the instant as a symbol of all he'd suffered."

He rose abruptly and began to pace the narrow room.

"The doctor had some things to say about that, too. He says that that shot released Francis entirely from the restraint of moral law. Says that up till then he had followed what had been before his illness a normal course; after that shot he wasn't—himself. I suppose, though, that's what often happens: the reason for, so often, murder being followed by murder."

Deborah said: "And he had your revolver?"

"Yes. Had taken it with him. Instinct, I suppose, of danger and of the possible need to avert suspicion from himself. But I don't think, really, he had planned to kill her. I always thought the murder was actually unpremeditated. You see, in the tremendous shock and excitement of the thing he'd experienced, and the thing he'd done, he simply dropped the revolver and ran. He did realize confusedly that there was someone else in the room—he didn't know it was you, Deborah——"

"He did in the end," said Deborah. She could not think yet of those moments. "Go on."

"Well, he did think frantically of cutting the wires to prevent anyone's notifying the police until he'd had time to get away—to think, to arrange some plan of self-protection. He didn't even think of the revolver until—well, it must have been when you were leaving. The—footsteps on the fire escape, you know."

"How do you know?"

"He confessed when he saw that the police had him. We've pieced together what we know of Pigeon."

"Where's Pigeon?"

"God knows," said Anthony. "He's just gone. Vanished. He was scared. Scared of Francis—scared of the police—scared (since Brocksley told Tighe of the telephone conversation) of Tighe. Pigeon is gone; they've got out men searching for him. But I doubt very much if any of us ever see Pigeon again. This is one time he started something he couldn't stop. Got himself into a very tight spot."

"Why did he threaten me?"

"Well, Pigeon didn't know actually, at first, whether it was you or Francis who killed Mary. He was, probably, in the back rooms. Remember that noise I heard? Like beads or buttons dropping? Well, those were counters—little wood-fabric circular and oval pieces— oh, you know what they are. And Pigeon in the dark managed to knock some over onto the hardwood floor. At least I feel sure it was Pigeon, because he knew you were there and because no one else could have so successfully eluded me there in the dark. He threatened you, I suppose, from habit. Then when he found you had nothing to offer for his silence and that he was himself (owing to Brocksley and owing to the things he had stirred up in Francis) in much danger he just shut up completely. All Pigeon wanted to do was to keep away from Francis and escape with a whole skin."

"Why didn't he kill Francis—or Francis kill him?" asked Deborah.

Anthony looked at her and returned to sit beside her, smiling a little and looking less strained and white.

"Aren't you a little cool and matter-of-fact about all this bloodshed?" he said. "I expect he would have killed Francis except, perhaps, for the fact that Francis was, after all, still the instrument which he must have hoped eventually to use against Tighe. He was thus in much more danger from Francis than Francis was from Pigeon, who knew and who had, actually, brought Francis' long, patient waiting to its climax. But either —I suppose—at any moment would have killed the other to save his own skin. The main reason they didn't (aside from Pigeon's lingering wish to keep Francis as a weapon against Tighe) was because they were each on guard against the other."

"But Dolly? Francis was with me when she was attacked."

"It wasn't Francis who attacked Dolly—although probably he would have done so had he known what Brocksley's evidence was and that Dolly knew it. He only knew that Brocksley knew something; he didn't know—he probably never knew—what that was. It was enough to learn that Brocksley knew something and was being persuaded to keep quiet by Tighe and Pigeon. (All Tighe wanted was to keep from getting shot himself, and to keep his business quiet so, as soon as things had settled down a bit, he could resume it. It was Tighe, of course, and Juanito and Pigeon who moved the tables and gambling paraphernalia to the vacant flat.

Leaving Mary Monroe dead on the floor.) It was Pigeon—at least we think it was Pigeon—who attacked Dolly. He didn't know that she had already told me what Brocksley had known. And he knew that she was a danger because if she gave that evidence to the police it meant that Pigeon himself was an accessory before and after the fact, and Pigeon's record had already a not too prepossessing aroma. Dolly was his danger from the police; Francis his immediate, direct danger. He could protect himself against Francis. But Dolly had to be silenced. I think he really meant to kill Dolly; the murder would perhaps not be exactly novel to him, and the danger was little, for Tighe would swear an alibi for him. Queer, when you think of it—Tighe and Pigeon and Francis—all afraid of each other. And Tighe and Pigeon hating and fearing each other and yet being forced to stick together."

"Anthony," said Deborah, "who else was on the roof that night?"

He looked at her. In the little silence Deborah could hear voices again in the room beyond—the room where Mary Monroe had sung and died.

"Who?" said Deborah.

"I think you know," said Anthony. "It was Juliet. And she had lost a great deal of money. And I knew it. I knew, too, that Mary had herself taken Juliet's promise to pay. Her note. And then, you see, after I'd lost Pigeon in the darkness and tripped and dropped the revolver and a few more prize bits of stupidity and clumsiness, I pursued somebody down the fire escape and along the street and into a movie—and lost her, too. But that was Juliet."

"The gardenia," said Deborah. "The mimosa—the newspapers that disappeared."

"Juliet," said Anthony. "She had the keys that Juanito thought he'd lost. Pigeon had Brocksley's. Juliet was in and out of the building—she had gone to the roof that night to talk to Mary Monroe; to try to persuade her to give her time—help. Juliet was desperate, you know, Deb, and needing money. And she saw through the curtains that you were there. So she waited, there on the roof. It was dark. She heard you playing 'Elégie'—she heard the shot, but she didn't see who was at the door because she had hidden behind one of the incinerators. But she was afraid it was you. She waited and heard Francis leave, but could not see who he was. She finally crept up to the door and turned the knob. And then I came, and she hid again and heard me arrive and heard you leave and she came to the doorway and the room was empty. And she recognized the vase and took the mimosa and, by the way, left it in the vacant flat until she returned it later that night to your flat—while you were asleep. Next day she returned, taking the chance of being seen, for she would merely have said, that she had just returned from Florida, as she did finally when discovered by the police just as she came to the door the night we were—the night we were married," said Anthony. "She hoped to get hold of her note to pay Mary. It would have saved her if she could have kept it from Tighe's knowledge until—well, until she could pay it. Or something," said Anthony vaguely, not looking at Deborah. "She went into the vacant flat because it was a convenient place in which to wait till she could search or to avoid meeting anyone—that sort of thing. That's how the gardenia got there. She actually returned to Chicago the afternoon of the day Mary Monroe was killed. Stopped in a little hotel near here."

"Oh," said Deborah. Presently she added: "So that was my motive."

"I didn't think you had killed Mary Monroe, Deborah," said Anthony. "But I was afraid that somehow you'd been a—a tool—oh, hell. No, I didn't think that, Deborah. I didn't think anything. Honest."

"Who locked up Francis last night?" she said. "You?"

"No. That was Pigeon. You see," said Anthony, looking embarrassed, "Tighe did know of Juliet's debt and couldn't find her note. So he set Pigeon to searching for it. That's as near, at least, as we can come to the truth, after what Juliet has told us, and I think it is right. Pigeon had Brocksley's keys; Pigeon could get up and down the fire escape and stairways and around the house like a little eel. And did," said Anthony, looking rather savage. "But he didn't find the note because—well, I got it first. That night. And I've still got it. I'll give it to Juliet. I thought I'd keep it till—well, until I knew what to do with it."

Deborah sighed and looked at Anthony, and Anthony said: "How do you feel?"

"All right."

"Think you can stand? I'll help you." Anthony glanced about him and moved his shoulders restively. "Let's get out of here. I don't like this place."

In the room beyond was Lieutenant Waggon—policemen—a confused changing group. The green glass lamp lay broken on the floor, and a chair was knocked over on its back.

Lieutenant Waggon said something kind which Deborah did not hear because she was trying not to look about the room and trying very hard to walk steadily. She remembered very little, too, of the descent through the darkness down the fire escape—nothing of it, in fact, except Anthony's strong warm hands guiding her.

The little passage, the stairway, the hall where Brocksley had died. The Riddle door was closed, but from behind it came voices in furious happy dispute. Chloe and Gibbs, of course.

Juliet met them at the door, and Blitz leaped joyously upon them. Juliet kissed Deborah once, brought her hot coffee, and put her sternly to bed with cold compresses on her throat. She did permit Anthony to sit beside her, which was a great concession on Juliet's part. "I suppose," thought Deborah, "she knows about the marriage." The marriage which would now be annulled.

Anthony took her hand and said: "When you've rested a bit, Deborah, Lieutenant Waggon wants to see you. Don't be nervous about it. It's all right now. Everything. He just wants to know what"—Anthony looked at Deborah's hand and said, "—what happened to you up there."

"When did you begin to suspect Francis?"

"I didn't suspect him," said Anthony. "I'd never have let you get into such danger. It was only after Lieutenant Waggon had sent men to check up my own story about the man who died at St. Justin's that I began to question Francis' alibi for Brocksley's murder. And I realized that while I was telephoning from my room, though I actually had a view from the telephone of the hall of the flat and of the door leading to the main hall, still I'd my back turned to it. And that he could have changed stations on the radio simply by carrying that small remote-control box out into the hall, as far as the wires to the speaker would reach; the connection looks like a flat rubber strip—is dark and not more than an inch wide, and no one would be apt to notice the thing."

"That was the black briefcase—or box that Juanito saw."

"I suppose so. Why did you go to the house on the roof this afternoon, Deborah? Don't talk if your throat hurts but——"

Juliet came to the door. "It's Lieutenant Waggon. He says he wants to talk to"—she took a long breath "—to Mrs. Wyatt."

Anthony looked at Deborah, "Tell him, in a few minutes," he said and Juliet vanished.

Mrs. Wyatt. Marriage.

She was married to the man who sat there looking at her so oddly. Deborah felt a pink wave rising in her cheeks. She said: "I suppose now the next thing is annulment."

"I suppose so," said Anthony, watching her.

"Was it you told Juliet?" asked Deborah.

"Do you think she'd have let me take care of you if I hadn't told her?" said Anthony. He looked at her again, and Deborah wouldn't meet his eyes. He knelt and put his arms around her and quite deliberately put his head down on her breast. "I like to take care of you," said Anthony.

He probably could hear her heart pounding. To steady it, Deborah said: "There are some other things. One anyway. Who played 'Elégie' on the piano that night in the house on the roof? You said it was like a ghost."

"It wasn't a ghost," said Anthony in a muffled voice. "It was Juliet. She did it to remove your fingerprints from the keys you had touched. She was wearing gloves. —I love you, Deborah."

His dark head moved a little, comfortably. Deborah put one hand over it. Presently her other hand stretched out toward the table and fumbled a bit and withdrew a wedding ring and she wriggled her finger into it before she put the hand in Anthony's which was seeking it.

THE END